"That is all 

She glared at him t̶ also chided herself fo pected any. Another the row of stalls, and ̶ ̶ ̶ ̶ ̶ ̶ ̶ ̶ to another, making Katherine squirm where she stood. "I will not do anything illegal or immoral," she cautioned, licking her lips and hating to hear the almost-agreement poised there.

"Nor would I ask it of you. I will only want a small favor. An introduction, perhaps. Or a dance partner to rescue me from some aging ape-leader with a hideous countenance."

"Oh," Katherine said with some relief. "I could do something like that."

COMING IN APRIL

The Gold Scent Bottle by Dorothy Mack

Max Waring left London after losing his fiancee—to his father. Returning four years later, he meets the lovely Abigail Monroe. Max has something of Miss Monroe's, and to get her property back, Abigail must pose as Max's bride-to-be. But pretending to be in love soon becomes more than just a game....

0-451-20003-9/$4.99

Falling for Chloe by Diane Farr

Sylvester "Gil" Gilliland is a friend—nothing more—to his childhood chum, Chloe. But Gil's mother sees more to their bond. And in a case of mother knows best, what seems a tender trap may free two stubborn hearts.

0-451-20004-7/$4.99

Breach of Promise by Elisabeth Fairchild

The village of Chipping Campden is abuzz with gossip when the local honey merchant, Miss Susan Fairford, leases her old home to a mysterious gentleman who calls himself Philip Stone. Time will tell whether bachelor and beekeeper can overcome their fears in order to discover just how much they have in common.

0-451-20005-5/$4.99

To order call: 1-800-788-6262

The Bartered Bridegroom

Teresa DesJardien

A SIGNET BOOK

SIGNET
Published by New American Library, a division of
Penguin Putnam Inc., 375 Hudson Street,
New York, New York 10014, U.S.A.
Penguin Books Ltd, 27 Wrights Lane,
London W8 5TZ, England
Penguin Books Australia Ltd,
Ringwood, Victoria, Australia
Penguin Books Canada Ltd, 10 Alcorn Avenue,
Toronto, Ontario, Canada M4V 3B2
Penguin Books (N.Z.) Ltd, 182–190 Wairau Road,
Auckland 10, New Zealand

Penguin Books Ltd, Registered Offices:
Harmondsworth, Middlesex, England

First published by Signet, an imprint of New American Library,
a division of Penguin Putnam Inc.

First Printing, March 2000
10 9 8 7 6 5 4 3 2 1

Copyright © Teresa DesJardien, 2000
All rights reserved

 REGISTERED TRADEMARK—MARCA REGISTRADA

To Paula Kimball:
Who paid $10.00 for my very first
completed manuscript.
Thanks for starting this
whole writing-career madness!

Author's Note

Sometimes I make up place names just so I can have the fun of peopling them with anyone I fancy. Therefore, Severn's Well and Meyerley Creek are both fictional. So are the racing meets called Helmman and Tremayne, although Epsom Downs is real and existed at the time of the Regency.

In this story I refer to "the City" with a capital "C." This is referring to the "Square Mile," that portion of London that once resided entirely within Roman walls. The City is arguably still the heart of London and is properly indicated with the capitalization.

Chapter 1

Katherine Oakes opened her eyes slowly and looked up from her position flat on the ground. Four equine legs towered over her, and a man with an astonished expression knelt at her side. It was instantly clear that the man was attempting to come to her rescue—the last thing she wished. No, the last thing was having been dragged to London at all, but having this man discern her secret—that she was a woman in men's clothing—came a close second.

But it was already too late to save the moment—the man kneeling over her prostrate body had opened her coat and lifted her shirt in a misguided effort to allow her to get her breath back, and now was staring in astonishment at her breasts bound by a length of linen.

"Yes, yes, I am a woman," Katherine rasped at the man, even as she snatched her shirt ends from his hands and struggled to sit up. If she hadn't had the wind knocked out of her, the words would have been a snarl. The man stood and took a step back, clearly nonplused by the revelation of her true gender.

There was no sense in denying what he had already seen, Katherine acknowledged grimly to herself. If not denials, then flight was in order. She made as if to stand, but a wave of dizziness struck her. Her head swam, and her side throbbed, but after a few deep breaths, now possible, she felt her head clearing.

"You are Katherine Oakes!" the man said, in much the tone he might have said "You have three heads."

Katherine stuck her chin in the air, pleased when no further dizziness touched her, but the gesture had to look silly with her sitting knocked to the floor inside a horse's stall at the bloodstock market, Tattersall's. "I am Miss Oakes," she agreed, then paused to take another deep breath, glad to have got her wind back. "And I would thank you to keep your voice down, please."

"You do not want anyone to know you are a girl!" the man said, still sounding astonished.

"Of course not." Katherine gave him a dark look as she scrambled to her knees. To her chagrin some gentlemanly impulse overcame the man: He offered her a hand up.

She ignored his hand and stood on her own, only momentarily unsteady on her feet. He took another step back, his expression slowly evolving from astonishment into disapproval. Which was unfortunate, for he was more attractive when he wasn't scowling. Well, truth be told, he was attractive even when he was scowling, for his well-shaped lips had only thinned a little over his slightly squared jaw. His pale blue eyes—that pale blue seen at the zenith of the sky on a crisp spring morning—were surrounded by lashes made gold on the ends by the muted light inside the horse stall. His hair was cut close to his scalp, yet somehow implied it would have a wavy texture were it allowed to grow long; it was a military cut, made to fit under a helmet or perhaps an officer's cap. He was not particularly tall, but he had a breadth of shoulder that made him appear so. Certainly the man held himself like an officer: shoulders back, chest up, expression disapproving.

"You have the advantage of me, sir. You must give me your name," Katherine said. She blushed to hear the demand in her own voice. It was an unfortunate habit of hers that she charged when good sense told her she should retreat; the result of being an only daughter with three brothers.

Apparently the man did not care for her tone either, for when he sketched her a bow, it was shallow and clipped. "Benjamin Whitbury," he said baldly.

"Oh!" Katherine said before she could stop herself. She could not imagine how he knew her name, but she certainly knew his. He was not just Benjamin Whitbury, but *Lord* Benjamin Whitbury, a second son accorded the style of "lord" because he was the son of a marquess. He was first in line to inherit the title of the Marquess of Greyleigh should his older brother perish. More than that, though, Lord Benjamin Whitbury's name was included among all the latest *on-dits*. There was a scandal attached to him—no, several. Something to do with his family members all being mad, and something to do with him having been forced to resign his commission in the . . . Army? Navy? Whatever it had been, she recalled the whispers about him had been made in very shocked tones.

His expression darkened, no doubt in response to her exclamation. "And now you will explain, Miss Oakes," he said, and it was his turn to charge instead of retreat, "why you are dressed as a boy, and why you were knocked breathless on the floor of my new purchase's stall."

Katherine half turned to the horse, the animal now munching from a clutch of hay. "You bought Fallen Angel?"

"I did, if it is any of your concern."

Katherine reached out to run a hand down the horse's neck, swallowing the bitter regret that rose in her throat.

"Miss Oakes, I asked you a question."

Katherine swallowed again, and glanced around. The sides of the horse stall were taller than she was, leaving her little to see beyond the opening Lord Benjamin blocked. She guessed this awkward conversation went unnoted by anyone else, which was all to the good. If anyone came along the row of stalls, she would do her best to flee before they could find out what Lord Benjamin had already discovered of her gender.

"I came to say one last good-bye," she answered him finally.

"Good-bye?" Lord Benjamin echoed.

"I own . . . owned her." Katherine bit her lip as she patted the horse, determined not to cry, certainly not in front of this man who had caught her out.

Lord Benjamin moved a step closer to the horse, the movement making it possible for him to see Katherine's face although she still refused to look up at him. If he felt sorry for her, if he heard the waver in her voice, nothing about his expression implied as much. "That doesn't explain what you were doing on the floor, out of breath."

"She kicked me."

"The horse?"

"Of course the horse. Who else could I mean? The Mayor's wife?"

Lord Benjamin's expression flickered for a moment, although Katherine could not have said if it was with amusement or annoyance. "Did you deserve it?"

Now Katherine did glance up, to scowl at him. "I did not! One of the other lads dropped a bucket just as I turned in to the stall, and Fallen Angel kicked out from being startled." Katherine gingerly felt her side where the animal's hoof had caught her a glancing blow. *No broken ribs,* she thought, but there would already be a multicolored bruise spreading across her left side.

"Then I came along, saw you struggling to breathe, and now find I'm speaking with a woman, not a lad. Why the disguise?" Lord Benjamin crossed his arms, a gesture of impatience. The movement caused the fabric of his coat to stretch over wide shoulders.

Katherine took her gaze from his person, feeling a little shaken, no doubt from the horse's kick. She leaned into Fallen Angel's neck, pressing her forehead there. She could refuse to answer, but the truth was she could not afford to aggravate this man, because she was going to have to beg a favor of him. "My papa forbade me to come here."

"As well he should. Females do not come to Tattersall's. It is not a place for . . . refined ladies."

"I know," Katherine said bitterly. She stood back from the horse, offering one last pat. She threw her gaze up to meet Lord Benjamin's, and she hoped it didn't look as much a defiance as it felt. "The disguise was the only way I could come here without making a fool of myself."

She did not add that making a fool of herself had happened a lot lately, and that her father was already looking upon her with a jaundiced eye. "I just wanted to say good-bye to my horse. I suppose that sounds very foolish to you."

He uncrossed his arms and did not answer her at once. "No, not foolish," he said after a long pause. "You obviously did not wish to sell it," he added, making it a question even though his voice was neutral. Katherine could not tell what expression settled on his face, because he bent down to retrieve a boy's brown cap that lay at her feet. When he rose, he held it up. "Yours, I presume?"

She nodded and started to reach for it, but he placed it on her head for her. He angled his head, assessing her, then shook it. "You do not look anything like a boy, you know, even with your hair combed back like that."

Katherine ducked her head, only to raise it again a moment later. "I can walk like a boy, and I can lower my voice. I am quite practiced at it—" The shock on his face stopped her in midsentence.

"You have done this . . . this masquerade *before*?"

Katherine looked at the horse, then the floor, then the open space beyond Lord Benjamin. If she caught him off guard and shoved him a bit, she could just slip around him and be gone before he could think to hold her here. . . .

His hand closed on the arm of the boy's coat she wore, as if he'd read the thought in her eyes. "I do not know what games you play at, Miss Oakes, but I must insist on escorting you home before this . . . this folly of yours escalates to where it can completely discredit you." He seemed flustered for a moment, unable to find the words. "By all that's holy," he burst out as if he couldn't help himself, "you must have a care for your family's reputation if not your own!"

He could not know his words echoed those of her family— even, in these latter years, her brothers, those scamps who had first thought, years ago, of disguising Katherine in lad's clothing in the first place. Oh no, this was hardly the first time she had dressed like a lad; she had done it many times before, dozens of times.

Her brothers had thought it hysterically amusing at first when, at the age of seven, Katherine had said she wanted to see a horserace.

They had thought it "impish luck" when she had predicted the winner of two out of five races that first day they had taken her in their carriage to view the racers thundering past.

But by the time she was eight, her predictions were no longer a game, and the trips to the races had become regular.

"One out of three!" one schoolmate had declared, agog in wonder upon having wagered exactly as Katherine had said he ought, and having a plump purse to show for it. "The gel can call one out of three winners!"

"Most days. She has her off days, of course," Jeremy had conceded. "Horses get sick, and we all know jockeys sometimes rig the results, or—"

"Why, the best punters in the world pray to call the races so well!" his friend had interrupted. "The gel's a nonpareil! Do you think I might adopt her? Or marry her?"

While Katherine was not fey, her brothers came to solemnly acknowledge she *was* endowed with a God-given eye for horse-flesh and for calculating odds, for spying signs of equine ill health, for judging spirit, or nerves, or a winner's heart. Her talent was a gift, undeniably.

Unfortunately, one day their father finally learned that his daughter was not excessively fond of picnicking, as he'd been led to believe; she and her brothers—while they might take a hamper with them—were not dallying in the woods or by an idyllic stream; one day he saw them himself at a race course. He saw Katherine chatting with lowly grooms, saw her waving at a leering old roué who happened to own a racehorse, and saw her brothers treating the entire affair with a casualness that spoke of long-standing circumstance.

After seizing the two eldest by an ear each, and hauling the entirety of his family back home, Sir Albert had learned to his further horror that his sons had been conveying his youngest child to the last place on earth any attentive father would approve that a daughter go, and doing so for years. Despite protestations that thirteen-year-old Katherine was chaperoned by a brother at all times, Sir Albert declared an absolute end to the race-going journeys.

Katherine's schoolroom tutor, the aged Vicar Harntuttle, was ordered to keep the girl busy at her books. "We've been too lenient with her," Sir Albert declared. "It comes from having no woman in the house since Katherine was a mere babe, when her mother passed."

Katherine was forbidden to accompany her brothers to races or anywhere else not expressly approved by Sir Albert, or to engage in any pursuit "unbecoming for a young lady." It did not matter how much Katherine sobbed over the loss of her best, most favorite pastime. Filled with guilt at his prior ignorance, Sir Albert insisted she was not to set her dainty little slippers near racing soil ever again.

Katherine's brothers had gone back to school filled with terror at their father's wrath . . . and yet—with the resiliency of youth—had returned home once again in the summer, hatching thoughts on how to thwart parental wishes. Clearly, Papa's dictates or no, a God-given talent such as Katherine's must not be wasted—and, besides, their quarterly allowances were, they felt, rather paltry. They made a pact. Katherine's talent must be exercised; they simply needed to be more discreet than they had been before. And they would live by Papa's own edict, to the literal letter. . . .

With all the illogic of the youthful, her brothers asserted among themselves that Papa had declared Katherine's slipper-shod feet were not to set a single step near a racecourse . . . but he'd never said she could not clomp about the courses in boy's boots. He had not wanted his *daughter* seen at the races—and so she never was again, at least not without a disguise that made her appear to be a lad, an assortment of their castoffs that made her look much like every other lad wandering among the bustle of the local races.

Her brothers had taught her to walk like a boy, and to speak in a common vernacular. They had also maintained stoutly—in the face of Vicar Harntuttle's infrequent questioning other-wise—that Katherine ought maintain her short hair. It would have been nice if Katherine's hair had not been quite so singular in its dark, rich auburn tones—but combing it straight back from her forehead helped. Her hair was mostly hidden under a soft cap anyway, a cap always pulled low over her pretty brown eyes. The usual chaos at any race served the masquerade well, for what was one small "lad" who only observed or asked a few questions in light of all the toffs, jockeys, drunks, owners, and eager-eyed wagerers that swarmed everywhere?

For Katherine it was liberating, intoxicating even, that free-dom to move anywhere she liked, even those areas that would have been closed to her had she been wearing a gown and bon-net. She avoided the jockey's changing room, but not much else. Nothing meant more to Katherine than being able to *be* there, to see it all, to smell the scents of the stable, to hear the colorful language of men at work and play, to be able to often guess how these magnificent runners would place at race's end. Even backing a pack-trailer, a loser, was a part of the thrill, for what was a wager without risk? The risk was part of the game, the challenge.

What was watercoloring, or stitching, or playing the pi-anoforte compared to standing at a race rail, cheering on your favorite, flushing with pleasure when the longshot came in to collect the winning plate or purse?

Still, even if they had not been caught out by Papa, eventually their sport would have ended. Nature turned Katherine's body from that resembling a lad's into a woman's, and time only made her more and more fetching to look at. The three brothers had grudgingly known for a while what Katherine had not wanted to believe: that her days in lad's clothing were at an end.

Shortly after they firmly told her as much—refusing to budge even one more time despite her tears, arguments, and plans to better hide her womanly form—Jeremy had joined the army. Something in the brothers' alliance had broken down then, and that had been the absolute end of their race-sharing ways.

One day soon after, Lewis had asked Katherine to predict a race just from the news sheets—and she'd leaped at the one connection she had left. From that day forward, she'd never again been allowed to see the horses run, with only the news sheets and brothers' reports to keep her keenest interest alive, but it was better than nothing.

Her brothers might have been surprised, even a little ashamed, to know how much it had hurt her when her place in the world had shifted from under her feet. Seemingly overnight, despite being able to recite the entire ancestry of half a hundred horses and the immediate lineage of hundreds more, she'd had her favorite sport removed, whether she would or no. It counted for nothing that she'd cheered at her brothers' sides for a hundred victories. It did not matter she had been the undisputed source of monies that had long padded the allowances granted the boys by their father. No, against all she'd come to know and love, Katherine had suddenly taken on a new shape, and that newness must be protected, sheltered, and kept clear of the language and "rough sorts" that peopled the turf.

For the next three years she had fought to find a way that she might return to the races—but Papa and her brothers had never wavered, not even when she was clearly now a young woman capable of a measure of comportment. Other girls went to view the races, but not Katherine—it was judged too much a temptation.

When Jeremy returned from his military service to nurse a leg crushed under his fallen horse, she thought he might take pity on her and at last hold some sway over Papa's determination to keep his daughter away from the racing world—but Jeremy had gone on to the races with only his brothers at his side.

She could have gone on her own—but that would only have resulted in her coachman being punished, and she would not transfer her chastisement to an innocent party.

That was when Katherine first started to dream of living apart from her family—perhaps with a new family of her own choosing. Marriage. The right man would understand her interests. He would be as eager to see the races as she was. They would attend the races together. Or, as a married woman, Katherine could attend the races by herself, so long as she stayed in her carriage. And, who knew, perhaps the right man would not mind, too much, taking his wife on his arm that they might *occasionally* wander among the racers or speak with the trainers. . . .

The problem, however, was finding such a man.

When Katherine was nineteen, the neighbors began to query why she was not more in Society. Sir Albert had reluctantly admitted he must deal with his daughter's marriageability. He had—with obvious reluctance—hired one Miss Irving to replace the clergyman who had tutored Katherine until now. While Vicar Harntuttle had taught Katherine all the basics of mathematics and history, not to mention healthy portions of Latin, Greek, and French, he had not, of course, been able to teach her a single thing about being feminine. Miss Irving had been acquired—and Katherine's feminine imprisonment had only deepened.

Miss Irving meant well, and indeed did her duty as she had been hired to do it. Katherine was grateful to learn most of the things a mother would have taught her, such as pouring out tea, playing the pianoforte, dancing, and arranging a dining event for the precedence of those in attendance . . . but Katherine could not help but pine for the lad's life she'd once led.

Fate seemed cruel toward females—but Katherine was a calculator of horse racing and so not a believer in fate. Odds yes, fate no. She would make her own future, would set up a household with a man who took her as she was. Or no man at all, if that's how it was to be. It only required that she bide her time, for at the age of one-and-twenty she stood to inherit a tattered cottage on some land that she was assured could probably be made viable. It would not be much, but it would be all the world to Katherine, for in her own home she could do just as she pleased. In her own home, she would not be denied—most especially not denied the singular thrill of attending any and all horse races she desired to attend.

But first she had to reach the age of her majority.

She'd gone about in the small circles that made up local society, determining she would decline any offers of marriage should they be offered, no matter how advantageous, unless the man were the very fellow she hoped she might one day find. She would have no one but the one special man who would tolerate the life she wished to lead. She feared her tiny community was unlikely to host such a man, for he must understand, must embrace, her love of racing and all things equine, and must not ask that she change as she'd been forced to change before.

Now, here she was, twenty years old—in a month she would be twenty-one, the age of her majority. One month stood between her and the freedom she sought. She was soon to be mistress of her own fate—which was even more important than finding that one special man who would let her continue on the way she meant to go on.

But life enjoyed ironies, Katherine reflected with a small laugh and a shake of her head—for just as she teetered on the cusp of achieving her independence, that certain someone, that special man, had appeared.

That special man—he would look at her with deep amusement could he see her in these boy's clothes. He would not stare harshly at her as Lord Benjamin did now. It was ironic then, that for her gentleman's sake as much as her own, Katherine did not choose to push Lord Benjamin aside and flee. She had to make sure he did nothing to rob her of the freedom, the happiness, so close at hand.

She licked her lips and shook her head, denying Lord Benjamin's offer to take her home. She put on her most humble expression, the one that usually pacified Papa when he was in a temper.

"Lord Benjamin," she said, "I am afraid I must ask a boon of you—a promise."

Unlike Papa, Lord Benjamin immediately looked suspicious. So he was not only a pleasant-looking man, he was also at least a little clever.

Katherine put her hands together into a pleading gesture, as heroines often did in novels. She hoped it appeared appealing, as it seemed to with the heroes of such works. "Please, Lord Benjamin," she said, hoping she looked pitiable. "I know I have behaved curiously—even shamefully—by dressing as I have. The only excuse I can offer—" Her voice broke as real emotion threatened, but then she managed to swallow it down. "I . . . I love Fallen Angel. My father asked me to sell her, because she is not tame enough in his opinion for a woman. She has such fire in her—but Papa is correct. I could not keep her while not being allowed to ride her. She is a horse that must be ridden. She loves to run, so I had to give her up so that someone else can grant her what she needs.

"But I had to see her one last time before I let her go," Katherine said. "I hope you can understand that. Even if you cannot, I must ask, nay, beg that you say nothing to anyone about my masquerade today. Most especially not to my papa."

His upper lip actually curled. "I liked it better when you were curt and rude," he said. He flicked his forefinger at her, a dismissive or disgusted gesture. "This 'poor me' act is hardly swaying."

Katherine dropped her hands, blinking rapidly as if that would tamp down the rising anger that filled her. "Then what *would* be swaying, my lord?" she said, mouth tight.

"A kiss," he said, and for a moment a flicker of surprise crossed his face, as if he had shocked himself as well as her.

Chapter 2

"If I give you a kiss, you will have proof I am as coarse or vulgar as you already think me to be," Katherine said with a scowl.

"Then where's the harm, if I already think you vulgar?" Now he grinned, and it was not a very pleasant little grin.

"I am not vulgar."

"The point is, do *I* find you to be?"

Color flushed throughout Katherine's face, but more from anger than embarrassment. "That is not the point at all. The point is, will you say nothing to my papa or anyone else about finding me here dressed like this today?"

"I will not say one word—but for a price. You must give me the kiss I asked for." She stared at him. "Come, Miss Oakes, all boons come with a price."

"They do not," she stammered. "Not among friends."

"We are not friends."

"No," she said, the word drawing out as she experienced a sinking sensation, as if her anger sank into uncertainty. She probably could not win an argument with this man, not here and now. She was the one in the wrong; she wore the improper clothes, she stood in men's breeches and in a place she had been forbidden to venture.

She sighed deeply, the sound shuddering down her length, and then she closed her eyes. She leaned forward a little, and offered Lord Benjamin her pursed mouth.

"Ugh! No. Not like that," he complained.

Her eyes flew open, and she glared at him. "You said a kiss. You did not say how it must be administered."

"Administered? Like medicine? Come, Miss Oakes, you

wound me. No man likes to think his kiss is as disagreeable as medicine."

"It is to me," she flustered, and the fluster boiled upward, like a pot suddenly heated too much to contain its boiling contents. "Oh, this is foolishness!" she cried, straightening her shoulders. "Never mind! Say what you will, to whom you will." She put a hand to the side of his sleeve, meaning to shove him out of her way.

He had not let go of her sleeve, however, and his hand tightened on her arm. Of a sudden she was thrust backward a step, and then she was pulled up against Lord Benjamin's chest, his arms quickly encompassing her. He lowered his mouth to hers at once, as a scold was forming on her lips. The scold was lost to the pressure of his mouth on hers.

Katherine had been kissed before, a number of times. She liked kissing. Over the past few years a handful of young men had wished to kiss her, and when she wished to kiss them back, she had. Some kisses had been tingling good fun, and some had been as repulsive as pressing one's lips to a dead fish. Most importantly, though, her certain someone special had pleasant kisses—and it was to him that she now found herself comparing Lord Benjamin's kiss.

Although, truth be told, the two kisses did not compare at all. Katherine could not be sure why, but Lord Benjamin's mouth on hers caused more than a little tingling, making her toes itch and a shock race up her spine. He had to feel the ripple that coursed up through her, and he certainly had to hear the rather strangely hungry sound that involuntarily formed in her throat.

His response was to press her length to his more fully, and Katherine suddenly was no longer thinking, or comparing, or trying to find him loathsome, but clinging to him as if for her very sustenance.

He lifted his head just as she began to tremble, and Katherine almost wished he had not stopped . . . and then she gasped at herself for having had that thought.

"You have been kissed before," he said. For once the amusement was missing from his gaze as well as his voice.

She shoved against him, using both hands against his chest, but gaining only an inch of space between them for all her trouble. "What if I have?" she cried. How had he known? Did one begin to kiss differently if one had . . . well, more practice at it than her papa would approve of? "Ugh!" she cried now, her mouth turning down. She lifted a hand long enough to wipe her mouth against her wrist.

"Don't you dare spit as if you did not like it," Lord Benjamin said. For a moment Katherine thought he was angry, but then she saw a dancing devil in the depths of his light-blue eyes.

"You . . . you rogue!"

"Rogue. Yes, that is as good a word for me as any."

Her anger flared. "I could say worse—!"

"I have no doubt you could. No, do not bother. I have been called a hundred insults, and all to my face. But this is a tender moment I'd rather not have ruined by allowing you to cast unladylike words at me."

Katherine pushed away from him for real this time, putting space between them and forcing him to release her.

They had shared warmth where their bodies had touched, and it annoyed her considerably that she was instantly aware of the loss. "You, sir, are no gentleman," she said.

"Alas, I am. That is my problem."

Katherine scowled at him, wondering what he meant. His birth? He was the second son of a marquess, a lofty birth indeed . . . but even a high birth could not necessarily make a cad into a gentleman. Society's whispers said the man was found wanting, despite his superior position in life. His rank ought to have made him a much sought-after caller, but despite his presence now in London the *haute ton* did not have his name on their lists. Whatever sin or crime he had committed, it had been foul enough for the *ton* to treat him with the barest modicum of respect, and certainly not with a warm welcome.

He must have seen something damning in her gaze, because for just a moment the dancing light in his eyes died back, replaced by something that looked suspiciously like a lament. What a curious word!—but "lament" was the one that suited.

Lord Benjamin blinked, and the gleam returned to his eyes, hiding anything else they might have betrayed. Still, for just a moment Katherine had seen beneath the façade, had glimpsed the man himself. She would swear it. The usual gleam in his eyes was a trick, a ruse to keep the world at bay.

She softened toward him, just a little, for Katherine knew

what it was like to have to present a false front to the world. Whether in boy's clothing or woman's, there was ever a side to her that must be kept hidden.

"You've had your kiss, so now I get your word," she said. "You will not speak of this encounter to anyone."

Lord Benjamin gripped his hands together behind his back, and tilted his head a little to one side. "You are too eager. Why is that?"

Katherine twined her hands together, not to be beseeching but to keep from striking the man in his broad chest now accentuated by the backward pull of his sleeves. So much for softness, so much for empathy. She grit her teeth, working to bank this latest flare of her temper. "If you must know, I am betrothed. It is important to me that my fiancé not hear of this . . . little event."

"Ah! A fiancé!" he said with that annoyingly sly grin of his.

"Your word?" she prompted. "That you will not tell?"

"In exchange for a future favor, I will do you this one," he said with a nod.

Her mouth fell open. "But I gave you the kiss!"

"I *took* the kiss, it was not given. You owe me yet."

"I do not!"

"You do. Come, Miss Oakes, put your wrath away. It cannot possibly move me, nor would your tears because I simply cannot believe you would be the manner of woman who gives in to sobbing. So if tears are out, I would just as soon not have to quell a display of ire with my own—which I assure you is of late prodigious. Let us have a rogue's agreement between us."

A clatter at the far end of the line of horse stalls made Katherine jump. Another horse must have been sold and was being stabled until its owner came to claim it—the place might soon be awash in lads and trainers and owners. Time and an opportunity to flee grew short.

"I feel I am bargaining with Old Hickory," Katherine said. "And a bargain with the devil always ends badly for the bargainer."

"I am not evil, ma'am, just a mere rogue. I will not take your soul—only a promise." He did not laugh, but he might as well have, for his grin was ripe with laughter.

"What pleasure does this give you, my lord?" Katherine said, keeping her voice low.

"Entertainment, Miss Oakes. I have had far too little of it of late. I have, sad to say, been the victim myself of all the bon mots now circulating the morning parlors. I find I far more enjoy being the dispenser than the receiver. But cease stalling, my dear Miss Oakes. Just say yes, and then we shall have our agreement. Then your fiancé will never know from my lips what folly I think it that he means to marry someone like you."

She glared at him for the lack of gallantry, but she also chided herself for being so silly as to have expected any. Another rattle came from farther down the row of stalls, and one lad called to another, making Katherine squirm where she stood. "I will not do anything illegal or immoral," she cautioned, licking her lips and hating hearing the almost-agreement poised there.

"Nor would I ask it of you. I will want only a small favor, I assure you. An introduction, perhaps. Or that you would find me a dance partner to rescue me from some aging ape-leader."

"Oh," Katherine said with some relief. "I could do something like that."

"That is all I ask, Miss Oakes."

"Agreed," she said at once, before he could put forth any additional codicils.

He uncrossed his hands from behind his back. "A kiss to seal our pledge?" he suggested, and she longed to slap that practiced sparkle out of his eyes.

"The next time I let you kiss me, sirrah," she said, her jaw tight, "will be when my body lies cold and dead and in a casket."

He grimaced, but then his mouth quirked upward. "Am I correct in thinking you do not like me, Miss Oakes?"

She could not answer. It was not that she had nothing to say, but ladies did not say such things as the words that rose to her lips. Instead she lifted both hands, shoved him to one side, and swept around him out of the stall, her head held high in disdain under its boy's cap.

Disdain, however, does not work as well when the disdained party laughs aloud as you stalk away.

Katherine clenched her teeth, recalled that she had sworn to grant him a favor, and now swore she would "grant" him yet another: Someday, at just the right moment, she would return the favor of laughing at his humiliated back as he retreated red-faced and shamed.

Perhaps I could have avoided all this if I had followed Papa's dictates and never come here today dressed as a boy, one corner of her conscience noted.

"Be silent!" she growled aloud, making another stable lad stare after her, perplexed at the scolding he thought he'd just been handed.

Lord Benjamin Whitbury stared at the retreating back—donned in boy's clothing—of Miss Katherine Oakes, and wondered what had come over him. He was not normally given over to banter, and certainly not to taunting kisses out of young ladies. He'd been an officer in His Majesty's Royal Navy, for heaven's sake, and an officer had to maintain a certain code. Never mind that he'd had to leave his position—his only choices being to resign or be thrown out. Never mind that the world thought him as guilty as the Admiralty had—Benjamin knew better. And part of knowing better, of having a code of honor, was not inappropriately plaguing young ladies—even young ladies in breeches.

Benjamin reached out to the horse he'd bought not half an hour earlier, stroking his hand along the neck, just as Miss Oakes had done. Fallen Angel flicked an ear, but otherwise took no notice of her new owner as she nibbled at her rack of hay.

"So you were her horse?" Benjamin said aloud. What had she said? That she'd had to sell the horse because her papa thought it not tame enough for her. "Her papa does not know his daughter very well, I think," he murmured as though to the horse. "I suspect Miss Oakes could ride upon the back of Old Hickory himself, did she but wish to," he said, then gave a brief, bitter laugh. What could he know of Miss Oakes? Just because she had the audacity to don men's clothing and venture where she was not supposed to go, did not mean she had the iron will it took to handle a strong-minded horse. Still, he would be willing to bet his last four hundred pounds that this girl's spine had more steel in it than her papa ever guessed.

Perhaps that was why they'd struck up a repartee—even if it

was an admittedly rancorous one. Perhaps he had responded to the steel in her, for he had certainly long since shored up his own spine with the metal, forged by cruel experience.

His brothers, were he to call upon them, might plague him that he was now free to lose his military stance, that of chest out, chin up, spine ever straight—but right now that straight spine was all he had to fend off the world's blows, and he'd not retire the habit even if he *had* been forced to retire from his chosen profession.

Still, this to-do with his resigning, while painful, was not the first time he'd had to stand wounded before the world. He would survive now, as he ever had. He would, in fact, overcome his present circumstance. That was his plan, his scheme, his reason for not leaving London and all its staring, whispering faces. He *would* carve a new place for himself here.

Benjamin forced his jaw to unclench, glad there had been no one to see it tighten under the weight of his thoughts, and gave the horse a final pat. He stepped back out of the stall and whistled, drawing the attention of a lad at the far end of the stalls. "I am ready to take my purchase home," he called.

As Fallen Angel's bill of sale was checked for proper signatures, and the animal's lead secured to the back of Benjamin's hired phaeton, he found his mind wandering back to the puzzle of Miss Oakes. Her story aside, what could Miss Oakes have been thinking? To be caught at her chosen masquerade was to ruin her reputation.

She was young, granted, but not so young that she could possibly misunderstand what she risked, surely? And all to see a horse one last time? Why not simply arrive in her carriage and view the horse from there? While not strictly "done," it was far to be preferred to that of a woman wandering disguised, unescorted, and unprotected, in the rough environs of Tattersall's.

The girl had several brothers, Benjamin knew. Why were none of them in attendance upon their sister? The answer was obvious: They had not known Miss Oakes intended to come here. Not only had she planned this escapade, but she'd left her home, alone, to do so. Why?

No, that was not the question, at least not a question that Benjamin needed to worry about. The only question regarding Miss Oakes that ought to concern him was: When would he

claim the favor he'd made her promise to grant him? Well . . .
perhaps one other question was important as well: *Why* had he
made her promise him anything? Why had he extracted a kiss
and a promise from the chit? She was obviously a packet of
trouble—and Benjamin had all the trouble he needed right now.

And her kiss . . . it had quite literally made the hair on the
nape of his neck stand up. Miss Oakes had a certain air of in-
nocence about her, perhaps not refinement but also not the vul-
garity of which she had thought he accused her. Her manner
was innocent . . . but that kiss! It had been—to tell himself no
lies—delectable.

There was no real quandary here. He would never claim the
favor he'd demanded. That was the wise choice, and he could
not imagine why he'd even thought for two seconds that he
might wish anything from Miss Oakes. People of Miss Oakes's
ilk carried chaos around like a monkey on their shoulder—and
one small monkey could make a terrible mess. Benjamin was
tired of cleaning up messes.

Miss Oakes was exactly, utterly the very kind of person he
would make it his business to avoid. She was the opposite of
what he would look for in a woman should he ever look to
marry. He was too unsettled at present to think of marriage, but
when he was more plump of pocket and his name less tarnished
he would know to run, screaming, in the opposite direction of
Miss Oakes or anyone like her.

As he crawled up into his phaeton, he glanced back at the
horse he'd just purchased, the only horse he'd seen in a week
that he'd dared to think had the potential to one day fatten his
owner's purse. He realized he had Miss Oakes to thank that this
prize had been for sale—so she'd already done him a favor, albeit without having meant to.

For that matter, she'd no doubt done him an even better one:
by showing him exactly the kind of female he did not need in
his life.

Chapter 3

Upon first coming to London, four weeks earlier, Katherine had quickly discovered that when the entry hall of her papa's town house was well-lit by oil lamps in preparation for guests, their light plunged the head of the staircase above into deepest gloom.

Now, not even ten hours since she had been caught in boy's clothing by Lord Benjamin, Katherine blessed the stairway's shadows. She knew she blushed as she looked down on the man just arrived, even while relief washed through her that the blush would go unseen by anyone.

She blushed because it was Mr. Cyril Cullman who had arrived, a handsome man made even more striking in dark blue evening clothes and a waistcoat shot with silver thread. Mr. Cullman moved to greet his host, and Katherine shifted as well, to keep him in the line of sight. He bowed to Papa, and Katherine thought that perhaps there was just the faintest hesitation before Papa bowed in return.

It was probably wrong to spy down upon them this way, but Katherine took the opportunity all the same. It gave her heart time to stop racing, which it had begun to do at the mere sight of Mr. Cullman—the one man she'd once thought she'd never find—arriving in her home.

She considered that there was something about Mr. Cullman that flustered her a bit—she could not say why. Unlike Papa, who sported a head of thinning white hair and whose slender legs appeared at a disadvantage below a rounded belly that spoke of many and plentiful meals enjoyed, Mr. Cullman was trim and neat of figure. His appeal lay in his comely features, too, of course, but Katherine guessed it was also Mr. Cullman's polish that pulled her attention his way. *She* was not polished, she knew, and she sometimes had to wonder how it could be that he did not find her just a bit gauche. But he must not, for he *had* asked her to marry him—and she had said yes.

She had finally found "the right man."

What truly made her heart race tonight, though, was that she suspected tonight was "the night." That after the card party was over, after the other guests had left, he would ask Papa for her hand in marriage.

Mr. Cullman had already privately asked her to marry him, a little over four weeks ago, before she had been abruptly dragged away from the country for a Season in London. Her family had left Bexley so suddenly, Mr. Cullman had never had the chance to formally appear before Papa and request Katherine's hand in marriage. Despite recent calls here in London, he'd also not had the opportunity; Katherine suspected tonight he was going to *make* an opportunity even if one did not present itself.

Four weeks was a long time to be secretly betrothed, Katherine reflected on the darkened stairs as she tried to make her pulse steady. All the secretiveness was about to end, though—except perhaps the secret of why Papa had insisted on a Season so very abruptly and resolutely. Had he suspected a proposal was forthcoming? Had he objected to Mr. Cullman as a son-in-law? If he had, he'd made no declaration of it. He'd only said that he'd promised his wife, before she died in Katherine's infancy, that he would give their only daughter a London Season. Katherine had never heard that tale before . . . regardless, will she nil she, Katherine had been dragged to Town.

To Katherine's delight, Mr. Cullman had followed her, arriving so quickly that he clearly had left his country home as soon as he'd received her note that she must go to London. The eagerness of his pursuit since had convinced Katherine that she must soon be as *openly* betrothed to Cyril Cullman as she had allowed the odious Lord Benjamin to think she already was.

Katherine looked down on the man she'd promised to marry, and felt a flutter of . . . what? Anticipation? Eagerness? It was a jumble of a dozen emotions. The idea of marriage must linger in the back of every woman's mind, naturally, but now Katherine found that an idea was a far cry from a reality. It felt *strange,* this notion that if Papa said yes, Katherine would soon be Mrs. Cyril Cullman.

As she watched Mr. Cullman accept a glass of champagne with a smile—he had such a charming smile—Katherine felt her knees begin to shake, just enough to persuade her to lower herself to a seat upon the highest steps of the stairs. Surely all women on the cusp of becoming openly betrothed knew such nerves?

Four weeks ago, her secret fiancé may not have seemed the premiere choice as sons-in-law went, but four weeks ago Mr. Cullman had been only a country gentleman with some apparent money but very little else. He owned no land and there was no inheritance awaiting him. His father, a knight whose title was to perish with him, now had a good position with the Home Office in London, but until recent days had suffered from poor investments. He'd long since sold the country acreage his family name had once claimed, retaining only the modest Kentish stone cottage in Bexley where Cyril, his son, had come to live in the past year.

Katherine felt a new flutter in her stomach, remembering the Cullman cottage and the fence surrounding it, over which she had shared a first kiss with Cyril Cullman. It had been a fine kiss . . . albeit not as stirring as Lord Benjamin's. Was she disloyal to even think in such a manner, to even compare the two?

"No matter," she whispered aloud, but then she frowned, for she was not much of a liar, not even to herself. Truth was truth . . . and in this case, it was true that Lord Benjamin had delivered the superior kiss.

"Humph!" Katherine tried to scoff, the small sound covered by the chatter that rose from the gathering below. Even as she stared down at the back of her fiancé's head, Katherine found herself wondering how one kiss could be superior to another. Was it a matter of technique? Of a certain placement of the lips? A certain pressure? Perhaps it was unexpectedness that made all the difference . . . ? Regardless, she could not deny that one man's kiss had pleased her, while the other had *thrilled* her.

She shook her head and stood, dusting off her skirts with her hands, as if she could as easily dust away thoughts of the breath-stealing kiss she had shared with Lord Benjamin. She

...liberately turned her gaze back down toward her fiancé, and her thoughts back to having met him that first time.

It had been at a soiree, she recalled, feeling her lips turn up at the memory, a simple country affair that had hosted the most interesting gentleman, a man of great good looks, filled with witty *on-dits,* just come from Brighton. A man named Cyril Cullman.

The good people of Bexley had welcomed him, for his fresh news if naught else—but, too, he'd been counted as something less than a stranger since his family had once been of some importance in the area. To judge from his clothes, carriages, and spending habits, it had been evident enough that the Cullmans must have fallen on better times—and a man willing to spread his coins was always welcome in a small town.

In the end, it was universally decided that the son had been sent to see if the old cottage was worthy of habitation once more. If he'd also been sent to see if the residents would welcome the Cullman clan back among them, the answer had surely proved a resounding yes.

Katherine, for one, had been pleased to meet Mr. Cyril Cullman—and soon had realized that Cullman was the one man she'd ever met who did nothing to try to change her, or modify her behavior. She liked Mr. Cullman immediately—and within a few months, had concluded he liked her, too.

It had not been difficult to decide to accept the offer of marriage he had whispered in her ear one night, four weeks ago. She'd finally found the man she'd half feared would never cross her path, a man willing to allow her to be exactly who she was.

She felt a thrill at that thought, still unused to the idea of approval. Her father and brothers loved her—but they had despaired, often enough, of her ability to ever attract a mate. "You are too outspoken, Katie!" her papa had said often enough, and it had been difficult to argue against the statement.

But now, Katherine felt sure that tonight would be an end to the secret she and Mr. Cullman had been keeping. His request would be spoken aloud, Papa would consent with more or less good grace, and then their betrothal would be announced to the world.

Papa *would* accept the betrothal, Katherine thought as she

worried her lower lip with her teeth, surely? He could hardly object to Mr. Cullman as a son-in-law, not now that Cyril had come to London and become Society's darling.

In a few words: Cyril Cullman had become of the highest fashion. He was wanted everywhere. He'd charmed all the high flyers, those of the *haute ton* who disdained even the company of the better-born Lord Benjamin Whitbury. Where the marquess's son could not gain admittance, a lowly Knight Bachelor's son had, by dint of his charm and, undeniably, his dark handsomeness. Inside of a couple of weeks of arriving in London, matrons with eligible daughters had noticed the same glibness of tongue, flow of pretty manners, and charming laughter that had caught Katherine's regard while she had been Mr. Cullman's neighbor in Kent. His name was now on every guest list in the capital.

She almost hated to admit it, but Katherine welcomed such acceptance, such accolades. Heaven knew she had not garnered any on her own. In her four weeks in London she had not favorably impressed the *beau monde*. Even she could see she had been too much herself, too outspoken, not ladylike enough. She could finally see that having been raised without a mother had put her at a disadvantage, for half the time she did not realize she'd even faltered socially until the deed was done.

She had begun to understand some of her chaperone's—Miss Irving's—dictates. Too late she had begun to wonder if she ought to refrain from speaking on too many subjects or with too much opinion. Whispers had grown and been scarcely hidden behind fans, and backs had been turned. By the time Katherine had comprehended Town life was different from the easy manners of the country, her reputation had already lost its luster, and she knew she had been dubbed a hoyden in need of both polish and manners.

So now, even though it shamed her a bit to admit it to herself, if . . . when she became Mr. Cullman's wife it would, she prayed, give her a chance to start over again in this watchful, judgmental society. She would far prefer to escape to Bexley, where her outspoken style and disinterest in "womanly subjects" was more indulged. But if Mr. Cullman wished to live in London—and why would he not, when he was such a success here?—she could not help but hope his entrée would include her, his wife.

He'd even been granted a nickname by no less a person than the Prince's mistress (some said one-time secret wife), Mrs. Fitzherbert. Mrs. Fitzherbert had obviously enjoyed Mr. Cullman's flirtatious manner with her, for she had dubbed him "London's First Beau." She had hastened to add "First after our gracious Prince, of course," but the qualification was forgotten and Mr. Cullman's nickname was not; it preceded him into every party he attended.

"The First Beau is here," would come the whisper, and inevitably on its heel would come Katherine's blush of pleasure for the secret betrothal she had made with the celebrated Mr. Cyril Cullman, First Beau of all London.

It scarce signified that Katherine was not entirely sure she was in love with Mr. Cullman; she *was* convinced he was exactly the correct man for her to marry. Falling in love with him ought to be a simple enough "task"—he was handsome, fit, and dark-haired, with long, sweeping brows that drew one's attention to his dark brown eyes.

Above all, disregarding appearance or even feelings of affection, he had the one attribute she cherished, the one attribute that made him "the right man": Mr. Cullman gave every impression that he enjoyed her company.

He had never tried to stifle her. He had never glared at her, nor told her the subject matter at hand was inappropriate for a lady. He never made her feel gauche, and he often laughed aloud at something she had said or done. While some might argue such open amusement to be imprudent, it was like clean, fresh air to Katherine.

No, Mr. Cullman had not idly arrived at this card party of her father's, she supposed. She sensed her life would change tonight, and it was this awareness that made her wait on the stairs, hoping her knees and her pulse would steady.

She hoped, once they were married, they could remove to Bexley. The land she hoped they would live on when they married was hers, or would be in a month. It was a smallish patch in Kent that had been deeded to her from Grandmama Oakes, land Katherine would gain upon her twenty-first birthday. As dowries went it was not much, but the land had no debt attached to it, came with a small behest of funds, and it was not a part of the estate Jeremy would inherit from Papa—it was *hers,* which made it precious.

She felt another wave of nervousness—excitement?—course through her at the thought she would soon be free to live on her own land, and to marry the man *she* wanted, the man *she* had chosen.

She took one last deep breath, half assured her color and emotions were now under control, and gathered her skirts in preparation for descending the stairs. She'd only gone down one step when another caller was announced by the butler: "Lord Benjamin Whitbury."

Katherine froze, giving one soft, exasperated gasp as the sandy-haired man stepped into view. Lord Benjamin? At one of her papa's exclusive card parties?

At every card party he'd ever held in Bexley, Papa had only invited the prime of Society, those of good birth, good family. Papa's parties had a certain luster: The elite company was at least as important as the deep play. Which could only mean one thing: that Lord Benjamin had extremely well-lined pockets, for he certainly did not have the highest *ton.*

"I should never have guessed him to be well-heeled," Katherine murmured to herself, even as she thought back to their one and only meeting, in the horse stall. He'd been in gentlemanly garb, but had lacked any particular flair in his appearance. There had been no diamond stud to hold his cravat, no rings on his fingers, no fancy fob or watch tucked into his waistcoat pockets. He had not even sported a beaver hat or gloves—but those might have been left in his box or carriage, she'd been forced to concede.

He had looked . . . understated. Katherine had to admire understatement as being in good taste . . . but Lord Benjamin could learn a thing or two from Mr. Cullman on the subject of dressing so as to quietly proclaim the depth of one's purse. Mr. Cullman was always dressed to a nicety, even for a simple picnic. His waistcoat was always of the finest fabric, usually shot with silver or gold threads. It would not occur to Mr. Cullman to appear in public without some manner of dash about his person, Katherine felt sure.

Although, to be fair, there was more than one way to give a

first impression. Dress was not everything. Manner surely must be considered more important—and in that Lord Benjamin did not fare so poorly. In the horse stall, he had been gruff and critical, but there had also been an unmistakable flash of compassion in his eyes when he'd learned she'd had to surrender her horse, that she had agreed to give it up because giving it up would most benefit the animal.

Too, given the opportunity now to take a second glance at Lord Benjamin's more sober style of dress, Katherine admitted frills and furbelows would not have suited him, where simple lines and uncomplicated fabrics did. Whereas Cyril Cullman's masculinity was only accentuated by the lace at his throat, Lord Benjamin's plain stock better suited his square jaw. The highest shirt points would have covered that jawline, which was what provided balance in his face—so perhaps Lord Benjamin did not so much lack for style, as he chose his own.

Certainly something—or someone—had caused the man to be invited to Papa's first card party in London, a significant feat for someone whose name was being busily bruited about by the gossipmongers.

Katherine came down the stairs, and saw the answer to her question as soon as she stepped into the parlor now bedecked with card tables: *Mr. Cullman* was engaged making introductions for the newly arrived Lord Benjamin. It was impossible from their cordial air to think anything other than that Mr. Cullman had to be the man's sponsor tonight.

Her heart sank—for if she was right she could hardly avoid her betrothed's protégé. And how would she explain that she and Lord Benjamin had already met?

Before she could devise a scheme, Mr. Cullman turned and spotted her. "Ah! My dear, do come and meet my newest friend. Miss Oakes, may I present Lord Benjamin Whitbury. Lord Benjamin, Miss Oakes."

Katherine inclined her head and curtsied, and Lord Benjamin bowed. When he straightened, he said quietly, "Charmed, Miss Oakes."

"A pleasure," Katherine murmured, half afraid her relief must show on her face: It was clear he did not intend to claim a prior acquaintance. The only thing he did that might be seen as a bit out of the ordinary was to glance between Katherine and

Mr. Cullman—perhaps wondering if Mr. Cullman was the man to whom she had claimed to be betrothed. Thankfully, Lord Benjamin did not inquire.

Katherine followed in the wake of the two men, as Mr. Cullman made further introductions.

To her surprise, Lord Benjamin did not behave circumspectly only with her, but with everyone he met. He did not seem much like the man who had provoked her in that horse stall, for tonight his conversation was minimal, his statements restrained. He seemed . . . uneasy, not at all like the overconfident, even blustering man who had challenged her this morning to explain herself, who had demanded a kiss from her.

Perhaps he was as mad as the rumors claimed his whole family to be? Or, despite his birth, at heart a country bumpkin, nervous in august company? Or the kind of man who was a bully only when others were not around to confront him in return?

At any rate, if he had grown in Katherine's esteem by not mentioning their prior meeting, he again lost a measure of her admiration with this curious humbled act of his, for she could only think it had to be an act.

It was nearly half an hour later, when Lord Benjamin was occupied in greeting the Duchess of Dulaney, that Katherine found an opening in which she could pull Mr. Cullman aside to whisper a question in his ear. "How do you know Lord Benjamin?" she asked quietly, her hand on his arm to keep him for a moment close to her side.

"Met him at my club last night," Mr. Cullman said.

"Boodle's?"

Mr. Cullman nodded his dark-haired head. "Young Davison will put forth his name as a member, but Lord Benjamin will never make it, of course," he said with quiet certainty. "Bad *ton*. The family's mad, every last one of them, I hear. Add in that the eldest brother, the Marquess of Greyleigh, is married and the wife is breeding already, and it's clear young Benjamin here will likely never be the marquess. He has no expectations off which to live, and word is his quarter-day allowance amounts to a pittance. He must be at odds with his brother, to have so little a portion. Worse yet, it's said he did something dishonorable in the navy. Certainly he resigned, lending the rumor some credence. So you have to know the members of Boodle's will blackball him."

"What did he do?"

Mr. Cullman shrugged. "Something to do with smuggling, I think it was."

Katherine gasped. "A navy man? Smuggling?"

"Do not sound so shocked. Happens all the time. One has to suppose it is just that Whitbury was stupid enough to be caught at it." Mr. Cullman gave a sideways smile, Katherine's least favorite of his expressions. There was something worldly in that sideways slant—although she could hardly blame the "First Beau" for a worldly air. Still, she much preferred his large, open laughter.

"Then why have you made him your pet this evening?" she asked.

Mr. Cullman slid her a glance, but she could not guess what thoughts rested behind his gaze. "What makes you think I *willingly* took him on?"

"What—?" she began in startled puzzlement, but Papa interrupted the moment by clapping his hands together. At once a dozen servants flowed into the room, assuming their positions as footmen or croupiers. "Ladies and gentlemen, the tables are now open," Papa announced with satisfaction.

"Do you play at faro or whist?" Mr. Cullman asked Katherine as he pulled his purse from his pocket in preparation of paying for stakes.

She shook her head, more interested in the former topic, for she could not imagine Mr. Cullman taking on the task of introducing anyone *unwillingly*. Whatever could he mean? She parted her lips to ask, but before she could say a word, Mr. Cullman placed his hand on her forearm, the gesture somehow intimate in this crowded room. "Miss Oakes . . . Katherine. A kiss? For luck?"

His mouth came down upon hers at once, but not before she saw his eyes dancing with an odd emotion—humor? Nervousness? The kiss was over almost before it began, and he had moved away before she could chide him softly for the public kiss. Luck? At cards? Or in asking for her hand?

It did not matter. What mattered was he had all but declared for her by kissing her like this, openly, in front of guests, in her father's house.

She felt her knees start to tremble again, and she had to sit down in the nearest chair. She felt a dozen pairs of eyes upon her, and knew she was not alone in thinking that Mr. Cullman had just made a public declaration.

But why did she feel so . . . peculiar? Not elated, not anxious, not even on the verge of a nervous giggle. *I feel . . . numb.* It had something to do with the look he'd given her—why had that quick, sudden kiss seemed rather like a . . . well, like a *farewell*?

Or had he just been embarrassed by his own daring? Was he just behaving as nervously as she ought to be feeling? He would not be the first man to grow tense at the idea of presenting his suit to a father.

Something had happened, but Katherine was not at all sure what it was. She lifted her gaze, searching the room for her secret fiancé, and found him laughing with a group of men in front of a faro table. He looked calm—but she would vow he lacked the usual polished, sanguine air about him. He seemed . . . excitable? Agitated?

She would go to him, would stay at hand until another opening occurred, one in which she might take him aside and inquire further. . . .

Katherine sighed, seeing her fiancé swallowed within a veritable horde of gentlemen, who in addition to gaming at the tables seemed intent on learning the First Beau's opinion on everything from the latest cut of frock coats to Parliament's debate today. She suspected it would prove a very long evening before time and opportunity provided a chance in which she could get him alone for a moment.

It would surely be even later into the evening before Mr. Cullman could take her papa aside and ask for her hand. A very long time, with a very steady fraying of her nerves.

Chapter 4

Benjamin shook his head as he was offered the dice, which then moved on to the richly bejeweled woman standing next to him. As she threw the dice, eliciting moans of disappointment from those who had bet against her chances, Benjamin glanced down at the decreased pile of money in front of him. He had just lost another quid, which took his losses to a total of fifty pounds. He was keenly aware that fifty pounds would be considered a mere sneeze in this gathering; these people thought nothing of risking a sum that could have rented a cottage in the country for half a year. Their play ran deep, deeper than Benjamin had hoped.

However, he was far more keenly aware that, with the exception of the three ladies present (the duchess, Miss Oakes, and the ancient bejeweled creature next to him by name of Mrs. Huddleston, who kept cackling a need for "more ratafia!") the men gathered here tonight were the very men he needed to position himself among. He had birth, but no appointment, no waiting billet, and—undeniably—a tattered reputation. Unless he could find a sponsor, his hopes for worthwhile employment in London were dead.

So go home to Severn's Well, he told himself, just as he had a dozen times before. But the reply was the same as ever: No, he would not go home in retreat.

He had left home to make his own way in the world, to leave the shadow of his father's cold ways and his mother's undeniable insanity behind him. He'd gone to become a man, taking with him no more than the small quarterly allowance his brother had put in place for him. Gideon would have gladly given Benjamin more, but that was not how a man found himself. Benjamin would earn his wages, and grab life with his own two hands, son of a marquess or no.

Gideon had understood—even if he'd not truly understood that he, too, was part of why Benjamin left. For too long, Gideon had ministered to everyone in his home. He'd played the part of father, brother, minister, and master to a score of people, siblings and servants alike. His caring heart had caused him to take the weight of the world on his shoulders, had nearly crushed his spirit under the strain of it. So Benjamin had left his brother's home in order not to continue contributing to Gideon's woes.

Never mind that Gideon had since found his redemption, in the love shining forth from the eyes of the woman he married—for by going Benjamin had stumbled onto his own path to fulfillment.

He vowed he would become his own man. He would not return home until he'd achieved at least some measure of that goal. He knew that was pride speaking, but he also knew that when a man has little else, he tends to cling to his pride.

He'd wanted to reestablish his family's honor as well . . . but that, he thought with a wry, embittered laugh, might be too far beyond his abilities just now. It was enough, for now, if he could find employment, could start again to build a life for himself.

And now, tonight at Sir Albert Oakes's party, he could feel eyes on him, the eyes of these important men, assessing him, wondering what Mr. Cyril Cullman had seen in him to play the part of sponsor for Benjamin tonight. As well they might wonder, because Benjamin was hard-pressed to say himself. Mr. Davison, his host last night at Boodle's, was someone Benjamin had known as a friendly face since they were both lads living near Bristol, and so might be counted upon to render the service of introductions. Mr. Cullman, on the other hand, was a complete stranger.

Perhaps Cullman—who was called by the epithet "the First Beau"—was testing the waters of his own popularity, by seeing if he could sponsor a black sheep successfully.

Cullman was jovial and friendly enough—but Benjamin was cautious of those who were too cordial; they were too often either charlatans or fools, in his experience, and it was not the wisest choice to be backed by either.

Yet, in the end, Benjamin had let himself be persuaded to attend this assembly with Mr. Cullman as his patron. If he was a fool to trust Cullman, he would have been a bigger one to decline an invitation to the most exclusive party he'd been offered, and with such a noted companion to hand. His reputation was shattered—but he was the son of a marquess, and the First Beau had decided to deem him worthy company. This was a place to begin building anew.

So far the important personages whose company he shared tonight were cautiously accepting of him. There was speculation in their eyes—and not all of it was negative. If Benjamin could but make it through the evening without a misplaced word and with a measure of good manners, he would have done much to make them question the tales of his leaving the navy, much to improve his chances of later invitations among this most advantageous crowd. Invitations, it was to be hoped, that might result in finding another sponsor, one with a position to offer.

So Benjamin slipped into a manner he was familiar with, that all young seamen were familiar with if they wished to avoid extra patrols, polishing, or swabbing: that of silent observation. He spoke when spoken to, smiled at the right moment during a joke, and played at the cards and dice with a casualness designed to make it seem he was only incidentally interested in the results.

"What's this, my good man?" Mr. Cullman said with a broad smile as he returned late in the evening to Benjamin's side. "Is that your wager there? A shilling?"

Benjamin nodded. "Until this good lady took up the dice the table did not fare well," he said nonchalantly.

"Mrs. Huddleston has changed the luck, has she? Then we must celebrate," Cullman said, placing a stack of five-pound notes on the table. "Match me!" he urged Benjamin with a wink. "The good lady and I will bring you luck."

Benjamin loosened the strings of his purse to pull out some pound notes, uneasy with the wink and with himself for being so readily led, but in this company, this place, he had to play along. He had to face the likelihood that he would gamble away half—or, God have mercy, more—of all he possessed in this world. Besides the recently acquired horse, Fallen Angel, every last penny he held to his name amounted to the contents of his purse: just three hundred and fifty, down from the four hundred with which he had begun the evening.

It was a shock of pleasure when Mrs. Huddleston rolled her point and the four five-pound notes Benjamin had placed on the table were doubled to eight. "I told you!" Mr. Cullman said, then he laughed and everyone at the table laughed with him, even the servant who served as croupier. Champagne was called for and the wagering went on.

The spirit of gaming, the champagne, and a slightly intoxicating thrill of sensing he had somehow managed to carve out a small accommodating space in this elite crowd, gradually loosened Benjamin's constraints. He was a military man no longer, he reminded himself, and he need not cling to the stiff public image by which he was generally known. His brothers fondly called him a prig, which was true compared to their haphazard concern for their own reputations. But for an officer his demeanor had been completely what it ought to be: somewhat aloof, ready to defend his honor as ferociously as he would his King and Country, but hopefully with a sternness countered by compassion. Still, this was not the time and place for military formality. He forced his stance to relax, and he allowed himself to tell a humorous story, which brought about the laughter of his table mates.

He even let himself flirt a little with the duchess, five decades his senior, contentedly aware that her flirting back was just another sign that he had managed to be accepted, at least for this night.

Tomorrow he would have to thank Mr. Cullman. If he belonged to a club, it would have been fitting to offer the man supper there—perhaps he'd soon belong to Boodle's. For now, he must at least thank Cullman for granting him this night's entrée.

Late in the evening, his wagering having happily restored his purse to its original four hundred pounds, Benjamin found himself approaching a table that also hosted Miss Oakes. Unlike the cordial nods most of her guests had adopted toward Benjamin this evening, Miss Oakes gave him a cool look across the table as he took a seat. He lifted a brow in inquiry.

"You are less . . . reserved than you were earlier tonight," she surprised him by saying. She had not bothered to lower her voice. Her father, two chairs away, cast her a chastising glance.

"You have found me out. I am a mercurial creature," Benjamin said lightly. A young man to his right chortled.

"You do not surprise me," Miss Oakes said, and something in the way she said it made Benjamin glance down at the cards being dealt him, giving him time to school his expression away from a frown. Why that tone of censure? And who was she to question his moods? He had watched her on and off throughout the evening, had seen a half-dozen humors cross her features tonight. A new one had seemed to grace her face every time he glanced up and spied her across the room. He'd seen confusion, doubt, attraction, and even hope upon her visage, and always when she gazed upon Mr. Cyril Cullman.

It had hardly been difficult to suppose this was the man to whom she claimed to be affianced, the man to whom she had not wanted it revealed where and how Benjamin had found her this morning.

If his conclusion was correct, why had the two of them spent the evening a room apart? *Benjamin* had spent more time at Mr. Cullman's elbow than Miss Oakes had this night. That seemed odd behavior for a betrothed couple . . . but not as odd as the mixed hope and uncertainty that Benjamin had surprised in the young lady's gaze every time he'd caught her gazing toward Cullman.

It did not take a genius to divine that her betrothal—if it was real at all—was a secret one, one of which her papa knew nothing. They *had* to be a room apart, or else reveal their secret despite themselves.

Perhaps emboldened by the rest of the evening's success, or this insight into Miss Oakes's state of mind, Benjamin parted his lips to ask how it was that his mercurial nature did not surprise her—but before he could, she excused herself.

"The hour is late," she said as she placed her cards on the table and rose. All the gentlemen stood as well. "I am for bed. Good night, gentlemen. Papa."

"Good night, Katherine," her father answered.

She gathered her winnings from the table, curtsied to the table's occupants in general, and then surprised Benjamin by making her way directly across the room to Mr. Cullman's side. Between his play at the cards, Benjamin watched as Miss Oakes placed a hand, lightly, briefly, on Cullman's arm and spoke to him, saw the man answer. Cullman then gave her a wide smile and took up her hand, the palm of which he pressed to his lips. Miss Oakes took her hand back, her color high but her expression once again buoyed by whatever assurance the man had murmured to her.

As she mounted the stairs, she stopped once and glanced down at the man she had claimed as fiancé, but Mr. Cullman did not look up in return.

She turned away, the angle of her head turned down, perhaps in worry or uncertainty, or perhaps she merely looked to find the next step up. Either way, the angle of that bowed head pulled at something in Benjamin's chest. Perhaps it was a trick of the candlelight, but he thought he saw dejection cross her features, thought she moved with a slow step that owed more to unhappiness or dissatisfaction than to simple weariness.

When Benjamin turned once again to his cards it was with a scowl. He was convinced there was some emotional connection between the two—was he right to think it a secret betrothal? Was it merely that they played at liaisons late at night? Something. But where had been Cullman's loverlike glance? If Benjamin had wondered at it, Miss Oakes most certainly must have done.

The uneasy sensation did not quite leave him, not even through the next three hours of late-night play. But perhaps that was merely a sensation that came with the advancing of the hour. A glance at the longcase clock chiming in the corner revealed that it was four in the morning. Most of the other gamblers had already called for carriages and retreated home, but Benjamin had deliberately lingered, to be the longer in what company remained.

He had sewn seeds tonight, he sensed it, seeds that well might bloom into a smattering of approval, a slight correction for the better in his reputation, perhaps even an occupation. He would like to work at a government position, in the Home Office, or perhaps in the Courts.

Beggars cannot be choosers, he thought wryly. He would gladly petition for any of the occupations the two men still at the table with him could provide. Sir Lowell was a senior man with the Jockey Club, which society could surely use an inspector or a recorder. And Mr. Markey was in the House of Commons, where another clerk or assistant surely would be welcome.

Benjamin was a dab hand at his numbers, knew his Latin and his Greek enough to have made a decent physician's attendant, and could read French at least as well as he could speak it. The navy had taught him much about shipping, not to mention a smattering of Italian and Portuguese, and life had taught him to scent a poor deal before he plunged his money after it. He did not come to the trough empty-handed, and were it not for his tattered reputation, he knew he could have asked after a dozen occupations and been at leisure to choose among them.

Now, however, he could not be so cavalier.

He was tempted to ask about employment with these gentlemen who sat across from him, gently drunk on smuggled French champagne—there was bitter irony in that, for smuggling had cost him his capacity in the navy—but it was too soon. Tonight had been for connecting. The next week would be for re-proving himself, for melding into this strata that was the London elite. Later, a week or two from now, he would ask, and he just might be successful.

Sir Lowell and Mr. Markey rose, thanked their host, and tipsily made their way to the hall to await their carriages. Benjamin began to stuff notes and coins into his purse, gently pleased that in the end he had come out ahead by some three pounds this night of gaming.

The guttering overhead candles of a small chandelier provided a tall shadow, one that crossed the table surface. Benjamin looked up to find Cullman had sat down across from him.

"Come then, Lord Benjamin. Agree with me. I've done you a favor this night, have I not?" the man said in a pleasant tone as he settled with a smooth grace into the chair.

Benjamin cocked his head, a bit puzzled at the question, for the answer was obvious.

Cullman glanced at the croupier and motioned the sleepy-eyed servant away. "Now you will do me one. I wish to play a hand or two. Between just you and me," he said to Benjamin as the servant bowed and departed. He picked up the deck of cards the croupier had left behind.

Benjamin fought down the impulse to frown, the scowl a result of a sudden prickling at the nape of his neck. Cullman's gaze was level, but there was something wrong in the set of his mouth. Was that a smirk?

"Thank you, but the hour is late—"

"You are not afraid of a few turns of the cards?"

"No," Benjamin said, his tone short and clipped. He allowed the frown to spread and become obvious, pulling at his brows and his mouth. "I am not afraid to play, sir, but I fear you may be foxed, and I should dislike taking advantage of a man in his cups—"

"My worry, Lord Benjamin, not yours," Cullman said as he began to deal out cards. "I am content enough. Should I lose, I will not cry out tomorrow that I was fleeced because I was drunk. Come now, a hand or two more. What is that? Here then, there are your cards. Let us play."

In short order, Benjamin had won slightly over a hundred pounds from the other man. He squirmed in his seat. "Truly, Cullman, I should like to find my bed this night—"

"Very well. The hour does indeed grow late. After one last hand, shall we say?"

Benjamin sat back, resigned. He did not sigh aloud, remembering that until this curious interlude, Cullman had done him a large favor this night. "One last."

"Just so." Cullman leaned forward, and it occurred to Benjamin that perhaps the man was not as foxed as he'd let on. His eyes gleamed, but not with the glitter of drink, but something darker, deeper. "Since it is to be our last, it must be special, must it not?" Cullman said on a smile.

Benjamin felt his scowl deepening.

"But I insist! I insist, for if you will not give me the satisfaction of one last chance to win back my funds, I shall have to say you are no gentleman and I shall have to withdraw my fellowship. When I, the First Beau, declare you unworthy of gracing my company, your reputation will loom blacker than it did before tonight."

Benjamin froze. He had the fleeting thought that were Miss

Oakes here, she would note a return to his more usual, sterner demeanor, for he certainly felt it creep over his shoulders, pulling him to sit up a little straighter. He looked into Cullman's eyes, and concluded the man was not drunk, not at all. And Cullman probably did not brag—he probably could taint Benjamin's already shaky reputation, perhaps beyond all redemption.

"I knew something was amiss between us. I should have trusted the sensation that crawled up the skin of my neck," Benjamin said, his tone as chilled as an icehouse.

"You should have," Cullman said, and he almost smiled. "But the cards could go your way, you know! I am a good player, but not exempt from fate's touch. Have you not already won some hundred pounds from me?"

Cullman laughed then, telling the tale: He'd lost to Benjamin on purpose, to draw Benjamin into this moment, this one hand. Even now Benjamin felt the pull of the man's laughter, some small part of him wanting to succumb to the charming sound of it. The man could spit poison and almost win your thanks for his efforts. A fitting description, for he fascinated even as he dismayed, not unlike a cobra.

"The wager then!" Cullman went on, rubbing his hands together, some dark glee making his eyes glow. "If you win, I will match the entire contents of your purse there and thereby double your ready. How much do you have?"

"Five hundred pounds, more or less," Benjamin answered, his mouth gone dry.

If he doubled the money, his time in London would be an easy one, allowing him plenty of freedom in searching for just the right position. But if he *lost* the wager . . . what was the penalty for that?

"Too, if you win," Cullman proceeded, "I will continue to sponsor you and lend my entrée to you. Unless I am much mistaken, there is nothing you want so much as employment to replace the military career you've thrown away."

Benjamin's jaw tightened, but he did not bother to correct the man: He'd thrown away nothing. His actions had been deliberate. But a snake such as Cullman could never believe that Benjamin had *chosen* disgrace because the alternative had been even less acceptable.

"—And if *I* win"—Benjamin's attention refocused on the man as Cullman's smirk grew broader—"I take your five hundred pounds, and you agree to become publicly betrothed to Miss Katherine Oakes, thereby ending a secret betrothal I have already made with her. I do not care if you actually marry the hoyden, so long as I am left free to pursue other more . . . let us say, *profitable* associations."

Benjamin stared. There *had* been a hidden betrothal between Cullman and Miss Oakes! And Cullman was handing it off, giving away a bride—! More than that even: He was abandoning this other human being into the arms of a near stranger, to him, to Benjamin. As if his fiancée were less important than a pair of old shoes or . . . words failed Benjamin, as he sat and stared at a smiling Cullman.

He could not have heard right. What kind of a man could wager away a betrothal, let alone do so with such calculation?

"This is a poor jest," he said, hoping Cullman would laugh, would say Benjamin had caught him out.

"No jest," Cullman said coldly, his dark humor erased in a moment. He tapped the cards dealt out in front of Benjamin. "Now, play."

Chapter 5

I will not play," Benjamin said, using just the tips of his fingers to push the cards back toward Cullman.

"Unfortunate," Cullman said, still with that pleasant polish for which he had so quickly become renowned. He stood, seemingly unruffled, but there was a dark light in his eyes. "I hope you enjoy the exile you are about to know, for there will not be a single door open to you when I am through tarnishing what is left of your reputation." He flicked one negligent finger at a tiny speck of lint on his coat sleeve.

"Damn you," Benjamin said, feeling his color rise along with his temper. How dare this upstart threaten him?

The answer to that came quick and bitter: The man dared because Benjamin was vulnerable. His birth was superior—but Cullman's reputation was untainted. He *could* do just as he threatened.

"Tell me, why would I be willing to wager the bulk of my purse? If I lose, it is gone and I gain a fiancée! Why would I risk such a thing? And I cannot believe Miss Oakes would wish to be any part of this . . . this travesty! This is madness. No man would agree to a wager like this!"

"Oh, some man will," Cullman said, his expression bland, even jaded.

Benjamin stared, feeling a chill creep down through his very center. He shook his head. "Why do you not simply cry off from the girl?" he demanded. A servant glanced their way, absently scratching his chin.

Cullman noticed also. "Keep your voice down, Lord Benjamin. And you know the answer to that," he said quietly. "No gentleman can cry off from a betrothal. It must be the lady's idea."

"Then why not ask the lady to comply?" Benjamin asked from between gritted teeth.

"Perhaps the lady will not. Perhaps she has made up her mind not to change it."

"No." Benjamin looked into the other man's face, then shook his head. "No, it is something else. A betrothal that is a secret between just two people can be broken easily enough—it has to be that someone else knows about the betrothal. Someone important. Someone who would be disappointed if the wedding did not go forward."

Cullman said nothing, but the angry flush that filled his face spoke for him, confirming Benjamin's assessment.

"A superior . . . no. A parent! Your parents have demanded you marry or . . . what? What is it, Cullman? Have they threatened to withdraw all funds if this betrothal does not go forward?"

Cullman's eyes narrowed, but he surprised Benjamin by responding. "As pedestrian as it all sounds, that is the case. With two exceptions. It is only my papa who insists, for my mama has passed on. Secondly, I am to marry *someone* by the Season's end. It need not be Miss Oakes, necessarily."

"Not Miss Oakes," Benjamin mused, understanding dawning at last, "not necessarily *her* if someone else can be made to take your place as bridegroom."

"My papa can scarcely demand I honor my promise to Miss Oakes if someone else publicly claims her affections, now can he?"

"But why become secretly betrothed in the first place?"

"When my father would no longer support my living in Brighton, I was forced to abide in the country," Cullman said with a shudder. "I had to obtain funding, or perish of ennui. I thought Miss Oakes could provide that funding for my escape. Marriage, I thought at the time, would be the price I must pay."

"But you found your way to London through other means," Benjamin made it a question.

Cullman inclined his head. "Some money fell into my hands, yes, enough to bring me to Town." Cullman sat back and spread his hands. "Now that I am here, I am more than welcome. And I, the First Beau, find the pigeons of London are plumper of pocket than their country cousins." He shrugged, an elegant gesture. "I would be a fool to continue my betrothal to Miss Oakes. So she must be got rid of, and in a way in which my parent cannot object or insist otherwise. If I win the play tonight, sir, *you* will make my necessary freedom possible."

"You are mad."

"Mad enough to make a game of this entire circumstance," Cullman said, sitting up once more. "To give you a sporting chance."

"Again, why would I risk my five hundred pounds? If I am to have the 'penalty' of undoing an engagement for you, why would you even ask for my money as well?" Benjamin stared at the other man as Cullman's mouth slowly formed a very small, very cold smile.

"Because I can," the dark-haired man said.

Benjamin just stopped himself from pressing a hand to his forehead, feeling stunned as he frantically searched for the idea's fatal flaw, the one that would turn Cullman away. There must be a way to force Cullman to withdraw the challenge, to make moot his threat to destroy Benjamin's teetering reputation.

This simply could not be! It was untenable. He wanted a wife—someday. But not while his fortunes ebbed as thoroughly as they did at present. And any wife of his would have to be just the right woman. She'd have to be quiet and calm and easy in her manner, in order to be in accord with his unusual family. She'd have to have the best of *ton,* to help the Whitbury name recover from tales of insanity and dishonor. In fact, any wife of his would have to be everything he already knew Miss Oakes was not.

Benjamin could not accept this fool's wager . . . but to refuse it was to embrace defeat. He did not doubt Cullman would do as he claimed he would—and the man might not stop there, but also attack Benjamin's entire family.

His thoughts seethed. Very well then, he'd just have to go home to Severn's Well, pride or no pride. He'd have to admit he was unable to make a place for himself in the world. He'd have to return to his newly married brother's home and . . . Benjamin shuddered, feeling the edges of savage determination begin to crumble. Not because he thought he'd be unwelcomed at home, but quite the opposite: Gideon and his new bride, Elizabeth, would be all that was warm and hospitable—and Benjamin would be the proverbially useless fifth wheel. How could he possibly build a life, a purpose for existing from such meager offerings?

He glanced at Cullman—and his heart sank farther in his chest. The dark, amused gaze Cullman returned was enough to convince him the wager would not be withdrawn.

Benjamin shook his head, then looked with a narrowed gaze once more across at the other man, now with loathing. There was no way for him—or Miss Oakes, for that matter—to walk away unscathed. If he abandoned Miss Oakes to this man's schemes . . . he knew what Cullman would do. The blackguard had made it clear he would not surrender his sordid little scheme, that he'd find another dupe.

"If not me, then you will simply find another fellow to tumble to your contrivance," Benjamin stated with flat assurance.

Cullman nodded, a dark amusement making his brown eyes dance. "Naturally."

Benjamin saw the man's mouth twitch, just holding back a laugh. He watched several moments more, aware that Cullman still stood, poised to leave but not leaving. No doubt he hoped that Benjamin would accept his terms, erasing the need to cozen someone else into the same predicament.

Everything boiled down to one inescapable reality: Miss Oakes was the one who stood to be the most injured in this sorry little affair.

While she had clearly found wanting the idea that he might understand, let alone hold any gentlemanly standards, the fact was Benjamin had only told the truth when he'd said his problems all came from being a gentleman. She had no way to know that he'd accepted disgrace rather than watch a friend's life disintegrate, that he let everyone believe the fault was his, because to do anything else was to nullify the sacrifice he'd been positioned to make.

He'd saved a friend's family, and he would not undo that, not even to clear his own name. Especially *this* name, already long tarnished by the time of his birth. Perhaps, after all, no effort in his lifetime could ever wipe the tarnish clear. It must be simple vanity—a legacy from Papa?—that kept alive Benjamin's hope this long that one day the Whitbury name would be said with warmth and approval rather than the suspicion it now occasioned.

Just as he could do nothing about the family he'd been born to, now he would hardly blame Miss Oakes if she doubted his behavior stemmed from any notions of nobility. After all, he *had* demanded a kiss from her in return for his silence—hardly proof of his usual ethics. He *did* have standards however. Praise God, Gideon had defied their father, the son becoming the worthy man the father had been incapable of being. Gideon had taught his brothers to look beyond narrow views and snobbish constructs, to see where privilege ended and obligation began.

Miss Oakes might doubt it, but Benjamin knew one of the obligations of his birth was to—where he could—help protect the innocent.

A shudder coursed through him—not for his own sake, but for the true innocent in this affair, the woman in his thoughts: Miss Oakes. Truth was, Cullman was doing her a favor by breaking their secret betrothal, albeit a cold-blooded favor.

"Do you play and keep what reputation you yet retain, or do I find another pigeon to pluck?" Cullman demanded.

Benjamin gave him a steady look, one he hoped did not show the anger and spill of resistance that spread through him. He detested being manipulated like this. Worse, he felt trapped. But what choice did he have?

Go home. But he couldn't. He wouldn't. His brother had too recently conquered his demons. Benjamin could not be the one who disturbed Gideon's newfound happiness with his bride, the woman, Elizabeth, who had freed Gideon's trapped soul. He could not bring yet another round of cares home to Gideon, could not be yet another problem his brother must solve.

If not home—then what?

He must accept the wager.

And how to do that with any shred of honor or dignity? He'd have to find a way to make it right with Miss Oakes. . . . Could he pay her to cry off? No, no, she probably had more as pin money than he had total in his purse this night. It seemed evident that her father, Sir Albert, was flush with the ready. Money would not move her; it was never the way to make things right with her.

Perhaps, if she'd have him, he should go ahead and marry

her? Even though she was the exact opposite of what Benjamin would choose in a wife?

He nearly offered an oath aloud, but his eternal pride kept him silent before Cullman's obvious amusement.

"Come, come, it's not so bad as all that grinding of teeth would suggest!" Cullman chided. "All I want is that, should you lose to me, you become publicly betrothed to the chit," he reminded Benjamin, one finger pushing the top card slightly right and left, the motion faintly taunting. "Recall I do not care how you break away from the harridan, so long as it has nothing to do with me."

Benjamin sat forward, shaking his head. "There is an immense problem with your plan, Cullman. Miss Oakes will not have me," he stated. "Why should she?"

"Give her no choice! Announce your betrothal publicly tonight. Compromise her. Or take her to Gretna Green. There are a dozen ways to get a lady to accept the protection to be had in a betrothal." Cullman clucked his tongue, chiding. "You merely stall now, my lord."

The words were true enough; there was nothing else to be said. There were only two choices: accept the wager or not.

Benjamin reached for his cards with fingers that felt numb, as if they belonged on the hands of another man.

Cullman smiled. "I see you are going to be reasonable. I would wish you good luck, but the truth is I hope you lose."

As Benjamin lifted the cards to read them, he frantically thought how he could sell Fallen Angel, retrieve his money there. He could leave now, before playing out the cards in his hand. He'd have enough money to go home to Somerset, to Severn's Well, to . . . what? Buy an apprenticeship? At the age of three-and-twenty? To be beholden to another until the age of thirty? And as what? Who would want such an aged apprentice? Anyway, who was there to become apprenticed *to* in the small village of Severn's Well? Or even in nearby Bristol? There was no one, no task to fulfill . . . except being the marquess's brother. There was no shame in being Gideon's brother—but there *was* shame in being his *useless* brother.

Worse yet, Benjamin would not be alone in his shame. Miss Oakes would be shamed, too. Today, tomorrow, or whenever Cullman cornered someone else to fall into this scheme, when the cards played out badly—her shame was unavoidable so long as Cullman was connected with her.

She was not Benjamin's problem. . . .

Benjamin lifted his hand once more and reevaluated the cards he'd been dealt, his blood chilling as he read there his future. No matter. He had to play the cards out, had to accept that he was not going to turn his back on Miss Oakes's abandonment by this cur.

He lost the play. Cullman laid the final card with only the smallest of smiles, displaying the *savoir faire* that most men who aspired to dandyism would sacrifice a year's income to be able to emulate. Benjamin stared at the played cards on the tabletop and although he was not surprised, felt the numb sensation spread up from his fingers toward his brain. Cullman reached over, emptied Benjamin's purse on the table, and counted out five hundred pounds. The cards had been played, the wager decided.

When Cullman had satisfied the monetary part of the wager, three pounds, one shilling, and tuppence remained for Benjamin to pick up with a hand he forced to remain steady. That was all he had left in this world: three pounds, one shilling, and tuppence. Oh, and a horse—which must be somehow fed and stabled.

Cullman stood, stuffing the banknotes into his coat pocket. "My condolences," he said over a yawn. "You should compromise her, or however you plan to get her agreement, as soon as possible. No later than Wednesday. I will give you two days." He consulted his pocketwatch. "Lud, it is nearly half of five. Perhaps I should go straight to my club for breakfast."

Benjamin stared at the tabletop. God save him, what had he done? Had he really just "won" a fiancée? How could he ever tell her . . . or, worse yet, her father?

Cullman yawned again, and patted Benjamin on the shoulder in seeming fellowship. "I know you will keep your end of the bargain, Lord Benjamin, being a military man."

"I am military no longer," Benjamin said flatly.

"Some things get into your blood." Cullman dismissed his protest. "Notions such as honor, and all. Besides, if the deed is not done, and publicly so, by Wednesday, I shall simply then withdraw my sponsorship and proceed to destroy you. And, by

association, Miss Oakes's reputation, such as it has become, as
well. What honor will not propel you to, I think that knowledge
will."

Benjamin looked up then, his defeated air evaporating under
a kind of awe at the man's audacity and that damnable calm.
Another man might have been tempted to strike out with a fist
or a cutting word, but another man would not have known what
Benjamin knew. The knowledge of it filled him, kept his fist at
his side. Cullman would never know, never understand—but it
was something Benjamin would have to be sure to convince Sir
Albert Oakes was true.

He watched as Cullman walked away humming contentedly
to himself, and then Benjamin stood slowly to his own feet.

He had bluffed the man. Cullman had thought he could control Benjamin through fear and intimidation, but Benjamin had
dealt with bigger scoundrels than Cullman, and had—after a
sense—conquered after all. His own father had been a bully, an
immutable threat to the peace of any given day. So Benjamin
knew when a bully was too powerful to be attacked, too unkind
to be ignored, and too stupid to see that triumph could be had in
more than one way.

Cullman thought he had caught Benjamin with threats—but
it was the thought of seeing despair in a pair of pretty brown
eyes that had made Benjamin pick up those cards, had made
him play them out below his actual ability, made him assure it
was himself who lost that hand of cards.

Cullman had been too thick or prideful or uncaring to realize
he'd been gulled. And why should he care? He'd got what he
wanted; he'd traded away a burdensome fiancée.

Fiancée. Benjamin must make an offer for Miss Oakes's
hand, even if it happened that they never married. *Come, be my
bride, and we shall live like kings on my three pounds, one
shilling, and tuppence,* he thought bitterly. *That is, if your papa
does not shoot me first.*

Benjamin looked up, saw his host returning from the front
hall where Sir Albert no doubt had bid good-bye to a leave-
taking guest, and crossed to the man's side. "Sir Albert, may I
have a quiet moment of your time?" Benjamin asked, hearing
the strain in his own voice.

Sir Albert looked him up and down, his own smile fading,

presumably at the serious expression on Benjamin's face as well as the tone he could not help but hear.

"I'm thinking you should," Sir Albert said, and led the way into his bookroom, where he closed the door behind the two of them, not bothering to hide a worried frown.

Katherine spread her hands, her fingers tracing along her forehead as though to smooth away a headache, and slowly looked up from her seat at her father from between the arch formed by her hands. "I do not understand," she said. "How can I be betrothed to *Lord Benjamin*?"

Her papa compressed his lips, a grim line in his full face, and she knew he was losing his patience. He had already twice stated his outlandish announcement.

He did not chide her though. Instead he said rather gruffly, "Lord Benjamin asked for your hand. I said yes. I have decided. That's that. That's just the way things are going to be, Katherine."

He spun to face Lord Benjamin, leaving Katherine to watch in a fascinated dismay as his shoulders worked under his coat. Papa was highly agitated, an emotion usually reserved for serious offenses Katherine's brothers had offered to a schoolmaster or parson. Was he angry with her—at what offense?— or Lord Benjamin? But again, why?

"I shall place a notice in the news sheets as soon as may be tomorrow," Papa told Lord Benjamin firmly. "Today, I mean," he said, sounding weary. "The sun is up already."

Lord Benjamin glanced toward the window as though to verify the dim light creeping in there, but Katherine just stared up from her chair at her father, trying to make sense of all that had happened since Papa had sent a maid to fetch her from her bed. She had been urged to dress quickly, and to come down to the bookroom "as quick as may be, miss." When asked for details, the maid had shaken her head, as bemused as her mistress. Upon entering the bookroom, Katherine had been perplexed to find Lord Benjamin also waiting there in candlelight, his expression strangely blank. The grate had not been swept out since last night, and no new fire burned there, leaving the room cool in the predawn air. A shiver had run up Katherine's spine, but she'd thought it might owe more to the somber faces staring at her than the room's lack of comfort.

Papa had proceeded to announce with a deepening scowl that Lord Benjamin had asked for Katherine's hand in marriage, and had received Papa's blessing. Katherine had turned, startled, to stare at Lord Benjamin. *Lord Benjamin* had asked for her hand?

Under her astounded stare, his expression had not changed except for the small muscle that worked in his jaw. Muscle or no, smile or no, he had hardly radiated the aspect of a satisfied suitor.

Had Papa somehow misunderstood what the man had requested? No matter. A betrothal between her and Lord Benjamin was impossible.

"Papa," she now proceeded to explain with a logic that largely sounded calm, "I cannot marry Lord Benjamin because I am already promised to Mr. Cullman." She felt blood rising into her face, and cursed the coloring she'd been born with that so easily revealed when she was embarrassed or excited. "Secretly promised," she added when she saw the dark wave of disapproval on Papa's face.

Lord Benjamin must have told Papa much the same, must have guessed Mr. Cullman was the fiancé she'd claimed, for Papa did not appear wholly shocked. "Katherine!" His tone changed from angry to hurt. "I would have thought you'd come to me and tell of any such proposal. Not to mention the man himself! He should have come to me and—" Papa cut himself off with an impatient gesture. "No matter! Even if you had some manner of understanding with the man, that is at an end now," he declared.

Back home, she had suspected Papa did not like Mr. Cullman, and his disapproval now glittered quite clearly from his gaze. In that light, the family's sudden journey to London made sense, having little or nothing to do with a promise Papa had once made to Katherine's mother.

But did it make any sense, was it at all like Papa, to suddenly betroth his daughter to some man unknown—except superficially—to them both?

"You do not care for Mr. Cullman, is that it?" Katherine asked Papa now, desperate to understand. "Is it so offensive to you that his betrothal to me was in secret? Have you rejected him because of that?"

"I have rejected him because he is not the one here asking for your hand!" Papa growled, his neck remaining red above his cravat, making Katherine half afraid he would have an apoplectic fit. "Now, listen here, this is enough quibbling and spitting, my girl," he said very gruffly, in the same tone in which he'd irrevocably declared she must sell the high-spirited mare, Fallen Angel. "Everything is settled. All is set. No arguments! You should go on back to your bed now, as it is so early. I would not have awakened you, except I felt you should know the news before you saw it in print in the afternoon papers."

"The papers—!" But, Papa . . . I mean, this is . . . this is simply mad!" Katherine declared, coming to her feet. She glanced at Lord Benjamin, as if he might take up her argument. *Someone* had to speak reason to Papa, whose expression and tone of voice boded ill against any pleas—however logical or reasonable—from his daughter.

"No offense to you, my lord," Katherine said in a quick aside to Lord Benjamin, "but I say, this is . . . is hasty and ill thought-out, and—! Papa, I will *not* marry Lord Benjamin!"

Both men stared at her, and alarm began to grow in her where a moment earlier only confusion had reigned. While this was mad, and growing madder by the moment, still she got the terrible, sinking feeling that rational protests would not stop events from closing around her with all the reality of a trap springing shut on an unwary fox.

"I mean"—she sank back down into her chair, pivoting toward Lord Benjamin—"I thank you, my lord, for your kind offer, truly I do. But I must inform you that my affections are engaged elsewhere—"

"Confound it, girl, this is not a matter of affections!" her papa cried, his hand to his forehead like an exasperated schoolmaster. "This is marriage! And I've done well by you, agreeing to this match. You'll be the wife of a marquess's son! Lady Benjamin Whitbury. That's an end to it. The matter is not open to discussion. Now go up to your bed!"

Katherine lifted a hand to the ribbon tied around her throat, her fingers anxiously closing around the cameo that hung there, a small but lovely trinket Papa had given her for her last birthday. Where were his smile and his understanding now? She stared at her parent, unaccustomed to her father raising his voice like this. Yet it had happened several times of late. He had shouted four weeks ago that they were going to London and that was the final word; then last week he had demanded she not only stop trying to ride "that wild-eyed heathen of a horse," but that she must sell the lovely and high-spirited Fallen Angel "before she breaks your stubborn, willful neck!" And here he was again, shouting down the roof—and, more importantly, avoiding his daughter's gaze.

Something was wrong, terribly wrong.

"Do you owe Lord Benjamin a great deal of money, Papa?" she asked, her voice sounding hollow to her own ears. It was the only thing she could think of that made any sense of this affair.

Papa and Lord Benjamin exchanged glances, a gesture of shared guilt more telling than words. The hand at her throat began to shake, as if responding to the heart beating there with the steady rhythm of a death knell.

Papa froze for a moment, but then, slowly, he began to nod. "Yes," he growled, his eyes dropping to the carpet, his posture the essence of guilt. "Yes, you have guessed what . . . that something provoked these circumstances, Katherine. I have promised you to Lord Benjamin in exchange for settling a debt. A very large debt." Papa's neck turned a deeper hue, looking very red in contrast to his white hair. She assumed this time his color had risen more from embarrassment than anger.

He looked up from under his brows at Lord Benjamin, whose expression had lost its neutrality and grown dark and forbidding—the man must not have wanted Papa to reveal the truth. Indeed, what man would want his potential wife to learn such a sordid reason for a betrothal?

Still, this made no sense. Large sums had been lost by Papa before. Katherine had always thought he'd used funds not vital to the estate to settle them. But he must have dipped far too deeply this past night—for why else would he now be in such straits? The wager's sum must be bad enough, large enough, to threaten the estate. That was the only thing that explained Papa's willingness to accept this proposal . . . well, that and the significant rise in standing his daughter would take were she to become the wife of a marquess's second son. She would become Lady Benjamin, losing her own Christian name, having to adopt her husband's style, no more to be known as Katherine except to her most intimate of friends.

Papa would not be unmoved by such an elevation in his hoydenish daughter's rank in life. He would, in fact, be delighted with it.

"But . . . why *me,* Lord Benjamin?" Katherine spoke directly to the marquess's son as she rose again to her feet. The muscle in Lord Benjamin's jaw was working again—she would swear anger filled him, not passion. "Why marriage? You do not love me. You do not even like me, as you do not know me well enough *to* like me," she said aloud the questions to which she could think of no sensible answers. "Your precedence . . . we all know you could do better than to marry me, a lowly knight's daughter, little known for her polish. Oh!" she cried, thinking again of the debt her papa had claimed. "It has to do with money! You require money! That is why you are willing to marry so far beneath you!"

She almost felt relieved, for at last she understood. "But there has to be another way to settle this. I assure you my person, my dowry, is far less valuable than, say, a piece of land Papa might deed to you, or perhaps some of the horses and a carriage or two from his stables—"

Lord Benjamin cut her off by abruptly turning away. His hands gripped together behind his back; he had posed much the same way after kissing her—although now his wide shoulders were held stiff, and any banter was erased. "Only a betrothal will do," he said over his shoulder to her, his tone flat, brooking no argument.

Then he must need a *wife* to go along with the money. That was the only explanation that seemed logical.

Equally clear, he did not have time to court someone. What could cause such haste? Did he need to be married to fulfill some codicil of a will? To reestablish his name via a connection to an unsullied female? But none of that stood to reason! As far as unsullied females went, a man could do better than to ally himself with the "peculiar Miss Oakes. . . ."

Whatever demon drove him it was not her concern. She was betrothed to Cyril Cullman. Not even Papa's unexpected dictates could change that reality or her allegiance, because in a mere month she would be of age, and she would marry as she wished. Papa could lock her in her room, but he could not stop time from moving forward. He could not insist on this betrothal.

Still, curiosity filled Katherine. Papa had to know his daughter could not be made to marry where she did not wish, and Lord Benjamin had done nothing to woo her. So whatever could have made them call her from her bed in the dawn hour in hopes of achieving such an improbable result as her agreement?

She drew herself up, looking down her nose at the back her "suitor" had turned to her. "Lord Benjamin," she said with icy calm, "I believe I deserve to know why you are so anxious to marry me, and in such a hurry. Please explain."

Chapter 6

Papa groaned and settled heavily in a chair, while Lord Benjamin turned and stared at Katherine. Merciful heavens, what was the man thinking to create such a searing light in his gaze? What could have driven him to take the bizarre step of asking for the hand of the woman he had scolded yesterday, a woman whom he obviously disliked?

To her surprise, he blinked as he turned to face her and the anger died back. He even gave a laugh, the sound more angry than amused, but a laugh all the same. Perhaps his shoulders relaxed a little.

"Miss Oakes, could it be that there is a wager? One that stated I could not be betrothed by cock's crow?"

"Another wager?" Added to whatever folly in which Papa had entangled himself, and her? *By cock's crow . . .*

"The sun is already up," Katherine pointed out, relief surging at the thought. "The cock has already crowed."

"And your father has already granted me your hand."

Katherine winced, as one does when one has been struck, unable to deny his claim.

"You would do . . . *this*? Become engaged, for the sake of a wager? Is it not enough that you have forced my father's hand through gaming?"

He shook his head, not at what she'd said but some inner turmoil of his own, she presumed. *He is not pleased at this either,* she thought with a tremor of surprise.

"You will recall that you owe me a favor—that there was an agreement between us," he stated.

Papa threw her a baffled look from where he sat, his elbows on his knees and his hands twined together. "You have met before tonight?"

"Very briefly," Lord Benjamin said, sounding banal, as if their first meeting had been nothing, had been *normal.* "Through a mutual acquaintance."

A mutual acquaintance named Fallen Angel, Katherine thought, grateful that Lord Benjamin made their only other meeting sound as if it had occurred in a crowded ballroom. Certainly Papa's expression relaxed.

"I now call in that favor, Miss Oakes," Lord Benjamin went on. He lifted his chin, the gesture silently demanding she pay his words heed. "I ask that you agree to be publicly betrothed to me for a month. Then, if you wish, you may cry off and I shall disappear from your life forever. You need not truly marry me. That assurance must put your mind at ease, to where you can agree that it is hardly an unfair favor that I ask?"

"Not unfair, no," she said, meeting his light-blue eyes squarely, as if she might understand if only she could see there into his soul. However, his steady gaze told her nothing. "But it is a favor that makes no sense. I can understand a need to marry—but a need to merely be betrothed for a month?"

His mouth worked for a moment, and he cast a quick glance toward her father. "All that is important is that I be betrothed."

She nodded, a shadow of tranquillity returning to her as she considered that her questions held no real purpose, for she would not concede to his request. How could she? She was betrothed to Mr. Cullman. Still, she wanted to understand before she gave this man her complete refusal.

"But I must ask you again, why *me*? Did you hope this particular family would lose to you? Did we appear grasping and eager to advance our precedence through marriage? Or would it have served to gamble against any woman's father, so long as he had a marriageable daughter?"

Lord Benjamin scowled at her—confusing her even further, for why should he want to be betrothed to a woman he could look at with such daggers, even for only a month?

Because not many women would agree to a false betrothal, she answered her own question. Papa's debt to this man had put her in a uniquely vulnerable position.

"Your father's involvement was . . . what circumstances dictated," he said through a tight mouth.

It was not much of an answer, but all the same Katherine felt another wash of relief. She understood that something larger, something beyond this one foolish wager, was transpiring. She understood that the matter *involved* her, but it was not *about* her.

"You asked for a betrothal of one month. Why? No, you need not answer that." She made a little discarding motion with her hand, cutting off the comment he'd parted his lips to offer. "I know already. You said you needed to be betrothed, but that marriage is unimportant. Clearly, you want me to play a part, in public—for reasons that you are reluctant to reveal. I see that much. But, Lord Benjamin, what would become of me after that month?"

"You will cry off." He looked as if he'd sipped bitter wine; the words were unpleasant for him to utter.

"Ah!" She considered, a finger to her chin, as she began to pace. "I could do that, of course. No harm in that. A lady is allowed to change her mind."

"Exactly."

"Exactly," she repeated, still pacing. She wondered if he heard the derision in her voice.

She came to a halt, turning to her father. "Let me see if I have this correct. We pretend to be betrothed for a month, then I cry off," she said succinctly. "We do not marry. I am not to know why we must be betrothed in the first place, nor how it is that Lord Benjamin stands to profit from this peculiar arrangement even though we part at its end. All the same, Papa's debt to *you*"—she glanced toward Lord Benjamin—"is then considered settled. You will be free to do whatever it is you wish, as will I, matrimonially or otherwise. Do I have this correct?"

Lord Benjamin nodded, relief shining through his gaze despite the continued frown that had settled between his brows.

"But it seems to me that I am the only one who would not profit in any particular way from this arrangement," Katherine said. She raised her left eyebrow, the gesture meant as a challenge.

"Katherine—" Papa said in warning tones, but Lord Benjamin waved his objection down.

"She is correct. She should gain something from this as well, since it must be agreed that crying off from a betrothal does not . . ." He fumbled for the right word.

"Does not enhance my worth on the marriage mart?" Katherine supplied crisply. The words ought not sting, but they did. A lady had to have some pride of self, after all, lest she be slovenly or lacking any spirit. And self-pride did not welcome questions as to its integrity.

"Exactly," he said, the sound almost a sigh. "Name your price."

"Ah. How tidy," she said, not quite able to keep the acid from her tone. "A business arrangement."

He made a small noise, not quite a laugh but more like derision. "What betrothal is anything else?"

"There is love."

"Foolishness!" Papa said.

Lord Benjamin merely shook his head.

"You do not believe in love?" Katherine asked.

She was not a romantic. She certainly believed in love, but she knew that life was made up of more than the curiously delicious sensations awakened by kisses and notions of love. Choices that would affect the rest of her life, a potential marriage, potential children, were vitally important and must be made with care. "Love" did not lend itself to care or caution. Love was a thing given over to acts of spontaneity, to giddiness, to regrets or perhaps relief if all went well despite a hasty choice. Love was irrelevant to marriage—especially in this instance, where a marriage was never meant to go forward.

Lord Benjamin's answer to the question of love was also irrelevant now, since she'd not accept his suit—but his hesitation intrigued her. Why should it? No matter what he said, she meant to stand by her betrothal to Mr. Cullman—a logical, appropriate choice. Why would she care for one moment if Lord Benjamin believed in love?

"Love?" Lord Benjamin repeated. "Do I believe in it?" He blinked twice, and it was clear his vision had turned inward, toward memories. "No," he spoke slowly. "That is, once I did not believe that love could last between a man and a woman. I was sure marriage was only a contract, long and binding and terrible."

Katherine fell still. Of whom did he speak? Whose marriage had left such a legacy? His parents'?

"Once?" Katherine shivered ever so slightly, for Papa had

asked the question that had risen to her own lips—as if the answer was important for him to hear as well.

"Then I saw my brother and his wife," Lord Benjamin said. He blinked again, and he was back in the moment, and spots of color appeared along his cheekbones as he realized the other two occupants of the room stared at him. "They love each other. I do not doubt it," he said very low.

He does believe in their love, Katherine thought, feeling slightly dazed. She might not be a romantic, but it astonished her to find that at least some small part of Lord Benjamin was. She never would have guessed such a courtly sentiment could reside in this man.

He nodded, swallowed, and his expression shifted, making it clear that he would offer no more elaboration on the matter.

He folded his hands together before him. "What say you, Miss Oakes? Will you have the false betrothal?" A quick denial was poised on her lips, but he went on. "Will you save your papa from the debt he says he owes me?"

The two men exchanged yet another long, speaking glance, and Katherine felt her throat tighten around the single, firm negative she'd meant to utter.

The debt. She had pushed aside looking at the catalyst to all of this foolishness. She'd all but forgotten that Papa was deeply, perhaps even ruinously, in debt to this man. Too, she'd tried to ignore a keener, more awful understanding: that Papa had done what she never would have believed he'd do. He had traded Katherine's hand in marriage in exchange for release from this obligation he owed Lord Benjamin.

It was not merely her future being decided this early morning, nor even Mr. Cullman's, but the future as it included Papa. What affected him, affected her brothers.

"Papa, is there no other way?" she pleaded, her hands balling into fists within the folds of her skirts.

Papa shook his head, and refused to meet her gaze as he sank into a chair positioned before the fireless grate. "Reputations are at stake, Katie," he mumbled.

Not just money, but reputations, too? How large was this debt, to make Papa behave this way?

"Miss Oakes?" Lord Benjamin asked quietly, even politely. "Is there to be a betrothal between us?"

"Yes," she said, her decision made in a moment's time, because there was no other answer to give. She would not ruin her family, not for the mere loss of one month's time. She only had to playact for a handful of weeks, and then her future would be hers once more to direct. For Papa's sake, for her brothers, for the good of the family, she must comply with the situation.

Lord Benjamin nodded, but he did not look particularly gratified. *How curious,* Katherine thought.

"For Papa's sake I will be betrothed to you, Lord Benjamin," she elaborated. "I will *not* marry you, ever. No matter the consequences." She glared at him. "Just so we are entirely clear on that specific point."

He gave another nod. "Entirely clear." If anything, he now looked faintly startled, as if she had surprised him. It would seem Lord Benjamin had not been completely sure of his ability to gain what he wanted. Good. She liked that he was not completely complacent, and that at least in this one matter she could read his feelings on his face.

His face—that was one thing she could credit him with: an open face. It might be filled with censure, or outrage, or disappointment, but at least he did not hide his thoughts. That betokened a kind of honesty in his nature, if not nobility. Too, she admitted reluctantly to herself, there was something rather winning about a face not schooled into what she had come to call "Town sophistication," a kind of urbane ennui, such as she saw daily at London gatherings . . . and even sometimes written across Mr. Cullman's features.

Staring into the face of the man to whom she'd just promised a thirty-day betrothal, it struck Katherine anew that while Lord Benjamin might not hold a candle to Cyril Cullman's handsome face and stylish mode, he had a kind of rugged, unflamboyant good looks. *A woman could go about town on the arm of a dozen less appealing men,* she thought, startling herself with the observation. She lowered her gaze from him, a little shocked at herself for having stared so long at him and for the thought that had come unbidden to her mind.

If she was to think of appealing faces, better to think of Cyril's—and to fret how it would appear when he heard this news. Katherine shuddered, trying to imagine how she would feel if their roles were reversed and she must hear that he was betrothed to someone else, albeit "only for a month." She closed her eyes, letting out a silent breath meant to help calm the agitation she felt.

There was no point in thinking that way. It would not be the same. As the woman, Katherine had every right to cry off—and she would, the very moment she could. Until then, she could only try to see that Cyril heard the news first from her. She'd explain how false it all was to be, how fleeting. *He will understand,* she told herself—and shuddered again, not entirely sure of her own assertion.

"Katie?" Papa looked up from his seat, concern etched on his face. She shook her head, silently telling him nothing was amiss. Not amiss? How droll! Everything was amiss—and it would take a month before it could all be put right again.

Plundering the depths of her nature for something that might pass for poise, she turned with at least an outward show of calm to Lord Benjamin. "I will do this," she told him, "but for my own sake I demand one thing you *must* do for me. If you do not, and not to your best ability, I will immediately terminate this charade of a betrothal. I will shout out the truth to all of London, with no consideration for this month of pretense you demand."

He grimaced over a nod of comprehension. "I understand. What would you have me do?"

At least he did not insist on pretense among themselves—his directness was something to his credit. He sounded reasonable, even . . . rueful. Rueful? It must be her imagination, for what could motivate a man to arrange a false betrothal and also make him regret the need? If indeed he regretted any of this lunacy he'd fashioned.

"I want for you, as my supposed fiancé," Katherine stated, "to act as my representative in business matters."

"Business matters?" Papa scowled. "I can conduct any business matters for you, Katherine."

"Can, but will not," she said, the demand in her voice giving way to something softer. She hoped her words would not sting too sharply if they were more gently said. "You will never do what I wish, Papa."

"I—!" Offense colored his features as he sprang to his feet. He blustered for a moment, roughly stuffing his thumbs in his waistcoat pockets, but after a brief struggle he managed to suppress his exasperation. "So then," he said in a voice stiff with hard-won control, "what is this that you wish I would do for you but claim I would not?"

Katherine sighed. "Papa, I love you and the boys, but . . ." She lifted her hands, palms up, her fingers spread as if she could thereby make her father open his ears to her words. "But much as I have loved sharing a home with all of you . . . I want to live in a house of my own."

Papa stared. "It is unseemly in one so young. A female, living alone! Besides, you will have a home of your own when you marry. Er, really marry—"

"No, Papa. I do not want to wait for marriage. Besides, that would be my husband's home, not mine. I am one-and-twenty now, nearly, and I want my own home. I want to develop the property on Meyerley Creek—"

"Meyerley Creek! It is a swamp!" Papa cried in horror.

"It need not be, with proper drainage. Grandmama always hoped I'd build a farm there someday. It is mine, or will be when I have come into my majority in a month." Her voice wavered, and she had to swallow down a feeling of apprehension, for she knew Papa would not want to hear what she had to say next. "Papa, I want to develop my property so that I can train and sell racehorses from there."

Papa paled. "Sell and—?" He sank back into his chair, passing a shaking hand over his face. "Katherine, my child, you'll ruin your name! Ladies do not do such things—living alone, and managing a stud!"

"Lady Farnworth does. She manages her own horses—"

"She's a harridan, and ancient besides. And her son lives with her, acting as her steward. You're a child—"

"Papa, this is not open to debate," Katherine said. Now that the words were said, she felt a little giddy with defiance and a dawning delight in this scheme she'd hatched today. No, not hatched—birthed from pain and distress. It had been a dream long in the nurturing—now unexpectedly, even wondrously, to come true. "This is my demand for pretending to be betrothed. Lord Benjamin must do what I know you would not, no matter how prettily I begged, and you must do nothing to interfere now or later. You will sign control of the property over to Lord Benjamin until the date of my twenty-first birthday, the sixteenth of June. It is that, or nothing. Those are my terms."

"But your reputation—!"

"Is mine to hold or lose," Katherine said firmly.

Papa bowed his head into both his hands. "Why did your mother have to pass away? She'd be able to explain to you why this is a terrible idea."

"No, she would not, because it is not a terrible idea." She really *ought* to think it was as awful a pact as Papa clearly found it to be, but Katherine had an opportunity here. She would seize on the idea's merits rather than its faults.

"I agree to these terms," Lord Benjamin said, looking very serious, very sober.

Papa issued a groan, but did not lift his head. "I agree"—the words were dragged from him, very low.

"Agreed." She was amazed to find she was smiling.

Lord Benjamin stared for a long moment more, his thoughts his own. "Well then. All is settled." He seemed nonplused for a moment, then he thought to bow. "Your servant," he murmured to Katherine, clearly in preparation of leaving.

"Lord Benjamin," she said, to keep him from going just yet. "I wish to be absolutely clear. It is my intention to have you do all that is possible in the next month to forward my plans. Please understand that I mean to ask that you complete a great number of tasks as my representative."

"I understand." His tone lacked contentment, but at least he sounded sincere.

"Well then, we are clear," she said with a crisp nod, thinking that was an end to their meeting this day.

Lord Benjamin, however, had a point of his own to make. "And, just so we are clear, you must understand that we must pretend to be happy. At first anyway," he said, his mouth still held tight, but with some emotion other than anger. Tension, perhaps? Disinclination? "At some mutually agreed upon time, three weeks, shall we say? We can begin to quarrel or ignore one another. As you wish, just so it is believable by the end of a month that we will not suit."

"I understand," she repeated his own phrase.

"Good."

She rose, moving to put her hand on her papa's shoulder,

where he still sat slumped in the chair. She did not say anything, instead merely squeezing his shoulder. Papa lifted his head, she offered him a smile, and he managed to give her a twisted, pained one in return. "Off to bed again?" he questioned, unhappiness rife in his tone.

"I doubt I could fall back to sleep," Katherine said, and now it was her turn to give an uneven smile. She glanced around at Lord Benjamin, hoping her irritation that he seemed inclined to linger did not show. "I am not sure how we go on from here. When will I see you next? And do we"—she gave a shrug of her shoulders and made a questioning gesture with one hand—"do we attend balls and soirees together? Drive together? Visit museums?"

"Yes, of course." Lord Benjamin cleared his throat, perhaps giving himself a pause in which to ponder a moment. "I will speak with your father and see what events we have been invited to in common. We will compose a list."

"Good," Katherine said on a nod. "Well then. Good night—" She glanced toward the sun-filled window. "I mean, good morning."

"Good morning," Lord Benjamin said politely.

That was another point in his favor: Even if he made appalling bargains, at least he undertook them with a show of manners.

She started to move again, but a sudden thought made her turn back to Lord Benjamin with a sway of her skirts. "Please, do not think me rude, but I feel I must state clearly that we have an agreement, one that cannot be changed merely because I have left the room. I expect both of you men to honor our agreement, unaltered."

To her surprise, Lord Benjamin smiled at last. He had a nice smile, not meltingly beautiful as was Cyril's, but it flattered his features. "A cautious lady," he said, and she was surprised to hear the edge of a tease there.

"Wiser than her years," Papa put in bitterly.

"Well then," Katherine said, displeased to be blushing yet again. "I will see you soon then, Lord Benjamin."

"Soon." He bowed again. Katherine curtsied in return, and then left the two men alone in the bookroom.

She walked up the stairs whose shadows she had hidden in

last night, and marveled at how the oddest of events could be twisted into a touch of good fortune. She must dance to a tune the two men below had played—but in the end she was the piper who would be paid.

It will all turn out well, she thought. All this would end with her having a home of her own, from which she could begin to make her own choices in life. And she could surround herself with horses! As many horses as her purse and her hopes of developing a stud would allow. No one would ever again force her to sell what she loved, go where she did not wish to go . . . and all it would take to earn such freedom was one month of play-acting. She could do that. She *would* do that.

Excitement at what she had arranged carried her up toward her room, which door she reached before it occurred to her that one important factor had yet to be dealt with: her betrothed. Her *true* betrothed, Mr. Cyril Cullman.

Katherine slipped into her room, her heart beginning to pound painfully. She had not exactly forgotten him—in the back of her mind she'd pictured living on the stud with someone who adored horses, or at least adored her, horses or no; Cyril would feel that way.

Cyril, the man who liked her as she was, who made her feel discomposed whenever she glanced up and saw his handsome face. The man who had asked for her hand—not as a ruse, as Lord Benjamin had, but for real. Cyril wanted the real Katherine. He had even been to see her property, along Meyerley Creek outside Bexley. He had *asked* to see it, and she had not thought herself vain in thinking that he asked to see it in order to please her.

Cyril—a better man by far than Lord Benjamin could ever hope to be, she thought, attempting a sniff of disapproval. The problem was, how could she possibly explain to him, the better man, that she had to be betrothed, publicly, for a month to someone else?

Chapter 7

"The Repository is betrothed to whom?" Jeremy cried.

"The Repository" glared up at her eldest brother, and cursed the rapidity with which tidings flew through London. Mercer had brought the "news" of her betrothal home from his morning's ride in the park. Here it was only eight hours since Katherine had been summoned from her bed to agree to Lord Benjamin's fatuous scheme, and clearly the man had *already* spread his tidings to the world.

"Kate's hitching herself to Lord Benjamin Whitbury!" Mercer asserted from where he and Lewis slumped in a pair of the parlor chairs. Mercer was the only brother to come close to having the same auburn hair as Katherine, but his was a lighter red with hints of gold, never so dark as hers. "I said to Jamie in the park that it wasn't true, that her brother would know. I said she'd not have such a jackanapes. And now she tells me it's true!"

"But . . . the Repository's only a child! She does not need to be betrothed to anyone, let alone that scoundrel!" Jeremy protested.

"I do not appreciate your speaking as though I were not in the room, or as if I lack a proper name," Katherine said crisply. "And I am hardly a child. I will be one-and-twenty in four weeks," she informed Jeremy. "I ought to have been out of the schoolroom at least three years ago."

"Well, that is my point exactly! Perhaps you ought to have been, but you were not. Miss Irving acts as much the tutor as she does the chaperone, and it has . . ." He tapped his foot against the carpet as though to jar his thoughts, clearly searching for words that suited and yet would not offend.

"And this continuing pursuit of education has made me seem

younger than my years, is that what you mean, Jeremy?" Katherine said crisply.

He gave a grimace and a small nod.

With a heavy sigh, Katherine tossed aside the embroidery at which she'd been pretending to work. Stitchery was not a craft at which she excelled. Instead, normally she would have had any number of news sheets spread out on the floor, and would have been on her hands and knees reading the race news and adding the information she garnered to the books of racing results she kept. Today, however, she was expecting a visitor, and it would hardly serve to be caught either on her hands and knees or compiling racing figures. Her caller might then think her as rash or undisciplined as Society dubbed her to be.

Truth be told, Katherine did not comprehend why she'd been branded as such. Why was it wrong, anyway, to tell someone they had their facts about Napoleon's childhood wrong, even if that someone were a viscount? Napoleon Bonaparte was not an only child, and that was simple fact! Or for that matter, why was it wrong to laugh at a joke if one divined the ending before it was completely told? No one at home in Bexley bothered to hide their mirth if they were quick enough to see the humor in a tale being told!

Katherine sighed to herself; London had a hundred rules that defied reason or even simple enjoyment—and she was fairly certain she'd broken most of them already.

"I know you will not like to agree with me," Jeremy went on, avoiding her gaze as he began to pace. His limp from his war wound had long since become scarcely noticeable. "But, yes, damn it, Katie, this being your first Season and all—you *do* seem to me to be too young for marriage!" Jeremy turned, seeking his brothers' support.

Lewis, the middle in age yet the tallest of the three, just shook his head as though puzzled. Mercer rubbed his upper lip and nodded. "She does seem youngish for marriage," he agreed.

"Enough!" Katherine stood, pressing her hands into her skirts to keep from curling them into fists. "Regardless of my age or what you all think about its suitability, I am betrothed to Lord Benjamin! I do not care if any of you like it or no. Papa knows, and Papa . . . approves. For now, I am expecting a caller. I want all of you quit of the room before he arrives. So go!"

"I am not leaving you alone with Lord Benjamin," Jeremy declared.

"My caller is not Lord Benjamin." Katherine tried to keep the asperity from her voice as she reached to neatly snag Mercer's ear and give it a pinch. He cried out, clapped a hand to his head, and leaped to his feet as she'd intended. Lewis followed suit, clearly not wishing to risk his sister's inclination to pinch a second time.

"Then who is your caller?" Jeremy demanded, but he, too, danced away from his sister.

"It is none of your concern." She made shooing motions in the air, herding her brothers before her like geese. "Miss Irving will be down in a moment to serve as chaperone, so you have no more excuses to linger and play big brother on my account," she said as she forced them across the parlor threshold.

"I am going to discuss this Lord Benjamin matter with Papa!" Jeremy warned.

"I shan't stop you!" Katherine shot back as she closed the parlor door between them.

"That could have been worse," she said aloud to herself, even though she had difficulty imagining how.

Her brothers had heard unpleasant rumors about Lord Benjamin—probably far worse than Katherine had herself. She could hardly blame them for thinking it an unbefitting match—and clearly Papa had not revealed the reasons why it had gone forward. A wise decision. *She* would not tell her brothers either, and not just about the size of the debt Papa must owe. Were she in Papa's place, she would fear what the three might attempt against Lord Benjamin, out of revenge or anger. Revenge would never do, not when only a month's time and a little pretense could resolve the financial difficulties and no one the wiser.

She gave another sigh and turned her back to the door and leaned on it for a moment, as if to draw strength from its solid oak build. At least her brothers' consternation at the betrothal could serve as a warning. She was not sure if she was grateful to them for a peek at how Society would react to the news, or not. One thing was certain: The next month would be a volatile one, full of moments she would have preferred to do without.

For that matter, so would the next hour, for Mr. Cullman had agreed to call on Katherine.

She'd sent a footman with a note early this morning—but Mr. Cullman's reply had not come back until nearly noon. Now it was quarter past two, and him due to arrive at half past. Had he heard of the proposal yet? She prayed he had not. And if he had not, how would she find the words to explain? At least he had been willing to come to see her today, not forcing her to wait and worry through a long, restless night.

A knock sounded on the door at her back, making Katherine jump before she realized the lack of a butler's announcement meant it had to be Miss Irving. Katherine opened the door to her chaperone, and after murmured greetings each lady moved to fetch a bit of stitchery, an art Miss Irving had been trying to teach her charge. Katherine chose a chair near the door; Miss Irving moved across the room to take advantage of the window's light.

The stitchery could not possibly hold Katherine's attention, of course, she realized with a sigh as she put it aside. Not while she was waiting for this particular caller. Not while she wondered what to tell the man who had stolen a kiss from her, all but announcing to the world that he loved her.

A minute later, when the butler announced that Mr. Cullman had arrived, Katherine silently thanked Miss Irving for choosing a seat with better light—for Katherine and Mr. Cullman would be able to speak in low tones that would not reach Miss Irving's ears, where she sat by the window. Life would be easiest, Katherine had decided, if, like her brothers, Miss Irving did not know or even suspect the falsity of the betrothal to Lord Benjamin.

The butler retreated, and Mr. Cullman moved into the room, coming to Katherine's side with his usual grace of movement. She spied a folded news sheet tucked under his left arm.

Katherine offered her hand to Mr. Cullman as he approached, but to her utter astonishment, he seized her proffered hand and held it against his chest instead of bowing over it as she expected.

"My sweet! My dear, dear lady," Mr. Cullman said, the look on his face anguished.

He must have heard already, Katherine thought, her heart abruptly feeling as heavy as lead. Certainly Mr. Cullman was aware that something was astir.

"How can I explain my sorrow at my folly? At that cur's cunning?" he cried.

Katherine pulled her hand back, and she sat once more, for her knees were definitely unsteady. "What . . . ?" she asked, her voice faint.

He took the news sheet from under his arm, unfolding it once and laying it in her lap. Katherine took it up with both hands. It was one of the afternoon papers, and there beside the crease where it had been folded, she read: "Sir Albert Oakes of Oakes Hall in Bexley, in the county of Kent, lately of Wigmore Street, London, announces the betrothal of his daughter, Miss Katherine Oakes, to Lord Benjamin Whitbury of Severn's Well, in the county of Somerset. Bridal plans have not yet been announced."

"You are betrothed to another!" Mr. Cullman stated, his mouth turned down.

Katherine's hands began to shake as she set aside the paper. Papa had done as he'd said he would, putting a notice in the afternoon papers, making this moment even more difficult for his daughter. Her mind went blank, just when there was no excuse for silence.

"Mr. Cullman," she said around lips gone dry—but no explanation came to her, just as it had not in the more than eight hours since Lord Benjamin had secured a token betrothal to her.

"Tell me what occurred," Mr. Cullman said, the voice of reason. He sat beside her, the knee of his dove gray breeches brushing her skirts. He gathered up her hands again, both of them within his own. The look he gave her was compassionate, not hostile.

The words came then, because his expression was kind, not severe. She stared down at her hands clasped within his, speaking low so Miss Irving could not hear. She told him all, down to the falsity of the betrothal to Lord Benjamin, that it was to last only one month.

"And at the end of the month?" he asked gently.

"I am to cry off, and that will be an end to the matter." She dared to look up at him through her lashes. "At the end of the month I will be free again. I will be one-and-twenty, and I can then rebuild the old cottage near Meyerley Creek."

He made a face. "Meyerley Creek? That is a very wet place, my dove, and that house half crumbled."

"The house is solid enough despite its outward appearance," she told him, just as she had the day they'd driven to view her admittedly meager dowry. "Still, I would like to rebuild it, of course, and I have been assured by my father's steward that drains could be routed into a pond. That would make it so the lower land could—"

"Could, could, could," Mr. Cullman chided lightly with a small crooked smile. He had a wonderful smile, even when it was touched with rue. He placed a finger to her nose. "But 'could' is not for today. Today, unfortunately, is for this new betrothal of yours."

She did not quite know what to make of the mix that showed on his face, of sorrow and something like amusement.

"I did not know what else to do," she explained. "I would have thought Papa could settle any debt, so this must be very large. I had to help him. I did not think Papa was that imprudent in his gaming . . ." Her voice faded away; the idea had been nagging at her. Papa had gambled extravagant amounts before, she knew from other prior black moods, but never outside his ability to settle. This was . . . odd behavior on his part, to say the least.

"I think, my dear, your papa thought you could do far worse in marriage. Myself, for instance."

Katherine leaned toward him, knowing her eyes were rounded by surprised disbelief. "You also think Papa knew about you? That he guessed we were . . . becoming close?"

Mr. Cullman nodded. "He must have guessed. To give him his due, he was only thinking of you, Miss Oakes, when he thought to make other arrangements for you. After all, Lord Benjamin *is* the son of a marquess."

This must be the truth, since Katherine had also wondered if it might be so! She recalled that faint hesitation before Papa had bowed to Mr. Cullman last night—Papa did not approve of the man. It was obvious.

He had thought to do better for his only daughter . . . but *Lord Benjamin*? And, she realized with an internal gasp, the luck would have to have run the opposite way: The man must have lost a fortune to Papa, not Papa losing to Lord Benjamin! It must have been an amount large enough to force Lord Benjamin, in effect, to sell his name, his self, in exchange for release from the debt.

But, why then only make Katherine promise to be *betrothed* for a month, with no marriage pending at the conclusion of the designated time? How could a *betrothal* settle a debt between Lord Benjamin and Papa? Papa would demand marriage, for only a wedding could serve to better his daughter's social standing.

Had Lord Benjamin seen the refusal in her eyes, and realized he must keep her at his side if he were to have any chance of persuading her otherwise? Did he secretly hope to woo and win her?

"I do not know . . ." Katherine said slowly, doubt and confusion reigning no matter how she turned the puzzle of this betrothal before her mind's eye.

"Miss Oakes."

"Katherine. Call me Katherine," she said a little breathlessly, her thoughts churning yet.

"Katherine," Mr. Cullman said softly, and he smiled at her. His smile was enough to draw her focus away from the enigma of Lord Benjamin's offer, to gaze into Mr. Cullman's dark eyes, so unlike Lord Benjamin's.

"You must call me Cyril, when we are alone like this," he said, his voice a caress.

"Will we be?" she asked, knowing the question was coy, but wanting an answer. "Alone like this, in a month?"

"It is my dearest wish, now that you tell me how things go on." His hands squeezed hers, and she wished she could unfold her cupped hands to squeeze his back.

This was wonderful! She could settle the debt between her father and Lord Benjamin—whichever way that debt ran—and Cyril was not offended. He would not be driven away by the ruse. He understood! He meant to call upon her. She could have her cottage at Meyerley Creek, and quite possibly restore her betrothal to Mr. Cullman—Cyril—as well. All it required was the passing of a month's time, regardless of who had lost to whom. She had an agreement with Lord Benjamin, and she would see that it was kept, but she would not, could not be wooed by him.

What had been a disaster early this morning had evolved into a matter of utter satisfaction. Lives could be built around that idea, around the aspiration to find satisfaction.

But what of love? Katherine heard the tiny question in the back of her thoughts.

She looked up into Mr. Cullman's eyes and she thought . . . it was difficult to be sure from his expression, but she thought

Cyril was trying to tell her he would wait for her. He must be at least a little wounded—but he did not chide, or scold, or demand. He did not speak of feelings at all. Of course, by choosing silence, he also did not speak of love. . . .

But he was without doubt correct—this was not the time for such declarations. It was enough that Cyril was tolerant of this bizarre circumstance. His willingness to perceive this betrothal for what it was and to take no lasting offense that Katherine must play it out, was enough for today. Really, the man was almost too good to be true—and it was Katherine's great good luck that she had caught his eye back in Bexley.

Cyril rose, but not before pressing the back of each of Katherine's hands to his lips. "My dear, until we meet again," he said, and his gaze lingered flatteringly on her mouth. Then his gaze dropped lower, to the fichu she had pinned carefully low within the bodice of her gown, that her "charms" not be too obscured by the gauze folds. He'd never given her such an openly . . . *invitational* look before. What was she to make of the frankly appreciative caress of his gaze but to reaffirm he wished the month were already gone and behind them?

"Yes," she said, a little breathlessly.

He bowed and exited, leaving Katherine in a warm fog of serenity that all would work out, all would be well.

Miss Irving looked toward Katherine with open curiosity, but Katherine felt no compunction to comply with her chaperone's silent request for details. The less Miss Irving knew, the better, especially if Katherine wished to receive Mr. Cullman as a caller. And if Katherine wished to be alone again with Cyril, with no chaperone at hand at all, there were ways to achieve that end, too.

What would Miss Irving say if she knew Katherine had two fiancés: one public and false, one secret and real?

She picked up her stitchery as Miss Irving sat down nearby to do the same, but after a couple of stitches the tambour was put aside again and forgotten, as Katherine rose to move and stare out the window.

Gazing at nothing in particular, she tried to unravel the knotted sensation in her stomach. All was well. All was in place. All was set to turn out for the best . . . but if her gambling papa had taught her nothing else, he had taught Katherine that when things seemed their most risk-free and set for a golden out-come, that was the time when disaster fell.

His dictum had proven itself time and again at the horse races—all the predicting in the world, all the calculating and studying and knowing a horse's best times in hot sun or clinging mud could not mitigate the element of chance. Sudden calamity occurred. An ankle broke on uneven turf; or a usually timid horse jostled in the crowd just right so as to find itself springing ahead of the horde; or a jockey could not keep atop the horse's back. Chance made the unpredictable happen. It made unsuspecting losers rejoice, and broke customary winners' hearts.

Katherine stared out the window, and wondered at the vague sense of unease she felt. Cyril had not chided her nor given her his adieux forever. He had looked upon her with admiration, with—call it as she'd seen it—a kind of hunger. His had been a proprietary glance—like the glance any eager bridegroom extended to his beloved. All was as right as it could be, for now . . . was it not?

It was then that what Cyril had said repeated in her mind. "How can I explain my sorrow at my folly? At that cur's cunning?" he had said. He'd said it as soon as he'd entered the room, even before he'd shown her the bridal announcement. He'd certainly said it before she'd had an opportunity to explain how Lord Benjamin had come to ask for her hand.

Cyril had already known something of last night's events, Katherine realized with a gasp. Beyond what the news sheet had said. Even more, he had been *involved* in some way in last night's debacle, for he had claimed a part in it by saying he was sorrowed at his own folly.

Katherine leaned back in her chair, her thoughts whirling, her hands unsteady where they fell together in the folds of her gown. She saw Miss Irving glance at her, frowning just a bit before turning back to her stitchery.

Katherine saw that she was being handed the truth in little pieces, little moments of insight. She wondered fleetingly if she would ever really be told all, ever totally comprehend the goings-on of this odd affair? A few more things had fallen into place, because Cyril had shown he already knew a wager had taken her hand from his and placed it—however temporarily—in that of Lord Benjamin.

Clearly, Papa had arranged *something*. A wager? A *fixed* wager? Papa, who hated cheaters?

No! No, it was not possible. Papa would not violate his own rules of conduct—and surely not in the matter of a betrothal! Then again, Katherine had been willing to believe that he had overplayed his ability to pay, so how sure could she be of her papa's ideals?

What *was* possible, what seemed born of the particulars, was that Papa had somehow contrived to engage both men in a matter resolved by a wager. Had Mr. Cullman been deep in his cups? Was that the nature of his "folly"? Or had his folly been not seeing Lord Benjamin's "cunning," as Cyril had called it?

Cyril had lost this wager, clearly. Why did he not tell her? Katherine winced—how would one explain such a thing? Or . . . she lifted her head slowly, finding another explanation, one that made more sense of both Cyril's and Papa's actions. If Papa had wagered too deeply, to the point of ruining his estate . . . could Cyril have accepted the wager, even lost deliberately, in order to help Papa?

It was at least *possible* he had surrendered his betrothal for the month Lord Benjamin needed, in order to assist his fiancée's father. . . . Possible, but how likely? Surely such thoughts were half mad. . . .

But, no, wait. The pieces of this riddle were all there. They just needed to be sorted through. Think! Was it so impossible that Cyril could have lost on purpose? Cyril's losing on purpose even made sense of his lack of outrage over last night's events, his tolerance today.

He had to know Katherine would be hurt to learn Papa had treated her future as a chit in a game of chance. So . . . perhaps he acted as he had in order to protect *her*?

The lingering glance he had given her—that had surely been a silent promise, had it not? That their time together was not at an end? That one day he would explain, when the raw edges of this wound had healed a bit? Perhaps when he was actually the son by marriage and not just the hidden fiancé he had been until now?

He would be free to explain all, in a month.

Until then, she did not doubt he would hold his tongue on the matter . . . but she supposed she had the right of it anyway. Lord Benjamin, after all, had said that there had been a secondary wager, his being betrothed before morning—obviously that wager had stood between him and Cyril. But how had Cyril come to offer or take up such a foolish wager?

"How can I explain my sorrow at my folly? At that cur's cunning?" Cyril had said upon greeting her today.

There were only two answers: that he'd been protecting Papa somehow; or that Cyril had been deceived—and it had to have been Lord Benjamin who had done the deceiving; Katherine could not believe that Papa would condone cheating.

Then there was the biggest question of all, the one she came back to time and time again: Why?

Could there be some standing feud between Cyril and Lord Benjamin? Was taking away Cyril's betrothed an act of revenge on Lord Benjamin's part? Is that why he only required Katherine's playacting at a betrothal and not a marriage? To offend or humiliate Cyril, while never having to end the "game" with an actual wedding—which, she felt sure, was the last thing Lord Benjamin wanted with her.

But . . . how could this folderol be meant to embarrass Cyril, since no one knew of his betrothal to Katherine in the first place . . . ? And why such a nonsensical scheme? She'd heard of this manner of folly being wagered upon in the betting books at the gentlemen's clubs. . . . She shook her head, hardly able to conceive of it, even though she knew fortunes had been won and lost on something so inane as whether or not a certain raindrop would fall to the bottom of one window before another.

She'd have to ask Cyril to explain his part in all this. In a month—for she had no doubt he would hold his tongue until then, until Katherine had publicly ended this fiasco.

She rose from her chair and stepped to the shelf where she stored her journals, the ones in which she recorded racing results. She pulled out one of the large books, running her hands over the binding, seeking the comforting touch of the familiar. Early this morning she had settled her future—well, her ability to live at Meyerley Creek anyway—to her liking and she ought to be as satisfied as a cat who'd been at the cream . . . but she frowned down at the leather binding in her hands, and remembered the gambler's advice, and wondered what part of this tangled tapestry could come even more unraveled.

It could end with my never marrying Cyril, she thought with an interior wince. *It could end with me never being with the one man who is willing to take me as I am.*

"I do not *need* to marry," she reminded herself, her voice sounding disappointed even to her own ears.

"What is that, Miss Katherine?" Miss Irving asked, glancing up briefly.

"Nothing," Katherine said, chagrined she had spoken aloud. In this matter of marriage she must keep her own council. Papa had plans, Lord Benjamin had plans, Cyril had plans—everyone did, including Katherine. And her plan was to marry the man of her choice, or marry no man at all. She could live in her cottage on Meyerley Creek. Grandmama had deeded her a small income on which to live there, and perhaps Papa would contribute toward making the cottage more comfortable? Even if he did not, it could—would—be Katherine's home, a refuge, a place where she could be her own woman and live her own life.

She was fortunate, she saw that now. She need not be practical; she need not even fret over the details of this arrangement in which she was ensnared. Time would pass; the trap would open, and she'd be a free woman then. She could afford to fall in love then, to marry where she wished . . . or *if* she wished. She had choices, which was more than most young women could say.

I shall consider marriage after I am finished being engaged to Lord Benjamin, Katherine told herself, hearing the irony of the statement in her own mind, even as she tried to ignore yet another flutter of unease.

Chapter 8

Not three minutes later, Benjamin nodded as the front door of the Oakes's home was opened by their butler, Langley. Before Langley could even speak to greet him, another voice interrupted.

"Lord Benjamin!" Mr. Cullman said sharply from where he stood in the front hall, his hat and gloves already in hand. "I would speak a moment with you."

The butler looked from one guest to the other, clearly unsure what to do.

"Er, very well. Let us speak outside," Benjamin said.

Cullman nodded curtly, and swept past the curious-eyed butler. As soon as the door was closed behind them, Cullman whirled to face Benjamin. "You told Miss Oakes that we were engaged in a wager!"

Benjamin made a small gesture. "Which we were."

Cullman glared at him. "I confess it never occurred to me that you would be so maladroit as to tell the lady what had truly occurred. But I should have known, given the family from which you sprang."

Benjamin's tolerance evaporated and he grabbed the other man by the cravat to slam him up against the wall next to the front door. "You know nothing of my family."

"I know your mother was mad, and your father a ruffian—just as you appear to me. Unhand me, sir."

"Listen closely, blackguard," Benjamin said, never loosening his grip. "Any collusion is ended between us from this moment forward. I have played your game once, and I will not play it a second time. As to Miss Oakes, I told her what I could of the truth, because she is not a mere toy to be tossed aside lightly at a man's whim. She had to be told something that made sense to her. Her father and I allowed her to believe Sir Albert is in debt to me and that I require a temporary fiancée. She agreed to the pretense, but only for a month, until her birthday.

"*You*," Benjamin shook the man as best he could, so that Cullman's head repeatedly struck the wall, tipping his hat forward over his eyes—"will tell her nothing otherwise, or I will be forced to remember this moment and take offense at it. I will not be afraid to stand opposite you in a duel. Do we understand one another?"

"Plainly enough," Cullman said on a sneer as he reached to push his hat back into place.

"What we allowed Miss Oakes to believe protects you as much as it does her, so I assume you are intelligent enough to know it behooves you to hold your tongue."

Cullman reached up and after a brief struggle managed to bat Benjamin's hands aside. "You could have told her prettier lies so that you need not look the complete cur in her eyes," Cullman said as he straightened his cravat. "I think you a fool. But that is your affair, of which I will say no more. I prefer not to waste my breath on fools."

"Do not talk to your mirror then."

Cullman growled low in his throat, then turned to go down the few steps, but Benjamin stopped him with a call. "Cullman!" The dandy half turned, glaring. "Why did you come here this morning?" Benjamin demanded. "You had to have known you would be unwelcomed."

"The First Beau is welcome everywhere," Cullman said haughtily. He gave one last tug to his cravat, then looked down his nose. "Unlike some I could mention."

The hands at Benjamin's side formed into fists. "Do not call here again, Cullman," he growled after the retreating man's back, but he received no response before Cullman climbed into his waiting carriage and drove away.

Benjamin took several deep, steadying breaths, and tried to comprehend why Cullman had come here at all. If the man wanted to be free of Miss Oakes, why call at her home the very day after he'd traded her away?

Had the man tried to excuse his behavior to Sir Albert? Had Sir Albert asked the man to come, to see if Cullman's story matched Benjamin's? Benjamin had told Sir Albert the whole truth, for it had been the only way to win Sir Albert's support of this sudden betrothal.

No, it was more likely that Cullman had come to call on another occupant of the house: Miss Oakes herself.

But why?

Did he regret what he'd done? Could he have changed his mind so completely, now wanting to court Miss Oakes anew . . . ? Unlikely. So what game did the man play at? Or was he just so arrogant he thought he'd throw the wine out and still somehow have it with his supper?

Never mind. The cur had come, and now he'd gone, good riddance, and it was Benjamin's turn to face the occupants of this house. He turned back to the front door and knocked a second time.

The butler issued him into the spacious entry hall, took his hat and gloves, and left Benjamin long enough to announce his arrival. He returned promptly to lead Benjamin to a parlor at the front of the house.

To Benjamin's surprise, it was not Sir Albert he had been led to meet, but Miss Oakes. Another lady sat in the corner with an open book—a chaperone, to judge by the lady's clothing and demeanor. Miss Oakes, on the other hand, knelt on the floor, a large book under one arm.

"Have you fallen?" Benjamin inquired at once, as he rushed to her side.

Color formed on her cheeks as she rose to her feet. "Langley, you are too quick by half," she said to the butler, who murmured "Sorry, miss," as he bowed himself out. Miss Oakes patted a hand to her coiffure of red curls, obviously flustered. "You caught me just putting aside my . . . my pastime," she explained.

Benjamin glanced down at the floor, seeing several different news sheets had been spread about the floor. "Are you training a puppy, Miss Oakes?"

To his surprise, she laughed. "No," she said. She opened the large book she'd had under her arm, hesitated, then turned the book to hand it to him.

He ran a lingering glance down a list of names and figures, then glanced up at her again. "Racehorses?"

She gave a tiny shrug of her shoulders, but there was something less sanguine hiding in her eyes. "I like to track how they finish."

"Racehorses?" Benjamin repeated as he handed back her book. Really, he could not approve, not if this pastime were for real. "A woman?" he spoke his thoughts aloud.

Miss Oakes drew herself up stiffly, still some six inches shorter than Benjamin even though her aggravation made her seem to grow taller. "Yes, a woman. And it might surprise you to learn that I can also read and do sums."

"I meant no offense—"

"Men never 'mean offense,' but they offer it all the time anyway," she said with an angry toss of her short curls. Fashionably short, her curls were more of a fetching deep, dark auburn than he had remembered them to be—and her brown-eyed stare less friendly than he had recalled as well. Benjamin was at a loss to understand why she had taken such umbrage, but it was clear in the set of her shoulders. "So, now you know," she went on crisply, "that I can be a bit of a bluestocking."

The chaperone made a disapproving sound from her corner, but Miss Oakes did not seem to heed her. "So, tell me, Lord Benjamin, will a bluestocking serve as a temporary fiancée?" she demanded to know.

"Ah! I begin to comprehend." Benjamin folded his hands together behind his back. "You hope to put me off with all this bluster of yours. You hope to end this matter between us before it goes much further."

Miss Oakes looked startled, and her chaperone almost managed to hide a knowing smile behind the book she read.

"If that were my intent, I would state it," Miss Oakes said, not quite able to hide her pique.

"It will not do, Miss Oakes. You have seen the morning papers, presumably?" He glanced around at the news sheets on the floor. "You do read the social pages as well as the bits on racing?"

She nodded stiffly, with a tiny frown. The chaperone cast Benjamin a noticeably amused glance from her corner.

"Then you have seen your papa's announcement. For better or worse—" Benjamin paused, abruptly mindful of the unintended pun, and started anew. "Whether we like it or not, we are

now committed to behaving as though we are betrothed. That is
why I called today." He reached into his pocket and retrieved a
list, which he handed to her.

Miss Oakes read it swiftly. "This is a list of our mutual engagements."

"You will note for yourself that quite a few of my invitations
do not rank so well against those that you and your papa have
received." He did not lower his gaze, keeping it steadily fixed
to hers, but he did give a small shrug. "My consequence in London is . . . strained. At present anyway. These are the places
where we have both been welcomed. I hope they will suit you
well enough."

"Well enough," she answered at once, surprising Benjamin
into a sensation that felt suspiciously like relief. She could have
stood on ceremony, could have declared his acquaintances to be
inferior, socially beneath her reach—and she would have been
correct.

Without doubt the Oakeses' consequence surpassed that of
any Whitbury, marquess's sons or no, because the Oakeses
were seen as being respectable. The Whitburys were collec-
tively seen, at best, as eccentrics. The marquessate—the title
and the money that Gideon had inherited—opened some doors,
of course. But new and old rumors now sweeping through London—of familial insanity and Benjamin's dismissal from the
navy—had closed the majority of the most select homes to
Benjamin. Acquaintances from his brief time in public school
had not come to his chambers on a return call. Navy friends had
failed to see him on the street, even though he'd lifted a hand in
greeting. His birth was superior to Miss Oakes's—but his place
in the social stratum had slipped all the same.

It was rather . . . gratifying to have Miss Oakes so easily concede to attend these lesser affairs he proposed—until it occurred to him that she might have readily agreed because they
were lesser affairs. Those events on his list stood to host fewer
of the "correct" people whom she would later wish to associate
with—that is, when she was free of his company at her side.

When she looked up, he wondered if his expression was as
cross as hers was bleak. "But . . . there must be fifteen events
listed here. Must we attend all of these?" she asked in a faint
voice.

This response was more like what he had expected, only now it carried the obvious sting that what she really objected to was so much time in his company. "That is a customary number of engagements in a month, I should think," he pointed out, hearing the starch that had come into his own voice. "To do less would appear suspicious."

"Very well," she conceded, her frown remaining. "May I keep this list? Do you possess a matching one?"

He nodded, once again ever so faintly pleased by her easy—if reluctant—capitulation. Perhaps she was a trifle more sensible than her reputation would have it, and had determined that anything—anyone—might be tolerated so long as it all was over in a month's time.

"I truly must beg your pardon, my lord, and yours, Miss Irving," Miss Oakes said, glancing between them, "for not yet making the introductions. Lord Benjamin, this is my chaperone, Miss Irving. Miss Irving, Lord Benjamin Whitbury, my . . . my fiancé."

The woman stood to bob a curtsy, her lack of astonishment revealing she'd already heard the news. Benjamin offered her a bow of his head.

"I pray you do not mind if I continue to read?" Miss Irving asked, not awaiting an answer before she sat once more and buried her nose in her book, or pretended to.

Benjamin took advantage of Miss Irving's discretion, pretend or otherwise, and took a step nearer to Miss Oakes. "You will be well enough?" he asked very quietly, so that only she would hear. "Say, for dancing?"

"Well enough?" Miss Oakes also spoke low, looking puzzled.

"Your side. Where Fallen Angel kicked you?"

"Oh, my side," she said, appearing relieved. "I have a bruise, of course, but it hurts less than I feared."

"Good," Benjamin said. Really, when she was not frowning, Miss Oakes was pretty after a fashion. Her hair was a truly fetching color, deepest red, a color he'd seen in old paintings, a red that had darkened with time—only Miss Oakes's curls had a vibrant shine to them, nothing dull about them at all. Her gown was just the right shade of pink to complement her hair color, where another pink might have clashed. Her eyes were a rich brown, her lashes so long he wondered how he had ever mistaken her even for one moment to be a lad, and although her nose was perhaps a shade too small for her face, a pixie's nose, she had a fine mouth. Her lips were evenly matched and generous, a mouth made for smiling. Not that he'd seen her smile all but, what, twice?

He took a step back, putting distance between them, and lifted his voice for the chaperone's benefit. "You saw on the list that tonight we have the Bellord ball?"

She gave a wag of the list she still held in her hand, wrinkled her pixie's nose in a quick grimace, and nodded.

"It will be a bit of a trial, with the news of our . . . our betrothal so fresh," he warned.

She sighed. "I suspect you are correct." Now it was her turn to drop her voice, while doubt clouded her gaze. "I suspect I am not much of an actress," she cautioned him, barely above a whisper. "To appear delighted and all."

Benjamin glanced toward Miss Irving, who appeared to be mindful only of her book. He'd believe he could fly before he'd believe the chaperone was not noting with keen interest how closely Miss Oakes stood to her new fiancé. The thought, totally misguided, almost made him smile.

"Nor I an actor, Miss Oakes," he lowered his tone to match hers. "But we need not pretend at a love match. We must only appear contented, and the betrothal will be believed."

"Contented?" she echoed on a sigh, but the word was not really a question. Even if it were, he had no thought how to answer it.

"It might be a trifle easier if we were seen together before then. Would you consent to walk in Green Park with me at four?" he offered.

She nodded, her expression neutral but also notably lacking any open signs of pleasure.

"Very good." He took her hand, bowed over it as he murmured his farewells, and turned to leave. Out of defiance or ignorance of convention, Miss Oakes nearly let him see himself to the door, at least until her chaperone rose and murmured a few words to her charge.

"Oh!" Miss Oakes said to him, blushing as she approached

him once more. "We are very casual in the country, I fear. Please, do follow me."

It was a silly custom really, albeit a correct one, he thought as he gave her a nod and followed her to the threshold of her parlor. There she nodded in return, and then he murmured another farewell and turned to now follow her butler to the front door, to await his gloves and hat.

Sadly, the rumors about Miss Oakes's countrified manners seemed proved here today. She had not been demurely sitting when he was announced, but sprawled on the floor. And doing what there? Reading the racing results, for pity's sake! And she had not rung for tea—but that might have been deliberate, a way of letting him know he was not invited to linger. Then she had not thought to see him to the parlor door, to hand him over to the butler as every other young woman of decorum would have done. Poor creature. She was unpolished here in London—and the chagrin in her eyes had told him that she knew it. She knew she did not fit in.

The same could be said of you, Benjamin thought, before he thrust the idea firmly aside. He was untried in London, true, but hardly unpolished. He had even begun to cut a bit of a dash in the navy, had begun to think he might aspire to a lieutenancy did he but continue on as he had begun. Still, with such plans now destroyed, he told himself he would do well enough here in London, if only he could escape from under the clouds of the past. In fact, this connection, this "betrothal" to the respectable name of Oakes might even enhance his reputation. At any roads, it would do him no lasting harm, even when she cried off, unless she said something untoward about him by way of explanation for their falling apart. . . .

He turned back, thinking to request what blame she meant to use in the deed of crying off—only to spy through the doorway that she had once again sunk to the rug, her pretty blush pink skirts billowed around her. She scanned the news sheets spread before her, and then stretched to fetch ink and quill off a nearby table. As she settled back, testing the quill tip with her thumb, utterly absorbed by what she read, Benjamin shook his head. Poor creature indeed, with so few feminine graces.

Accepting his gloves and hat from the butler, Benjamin chose after all not to ask Miss Oakes the question that had occurred to him, but instead to thank heaven—for his own sake as well as the good of the family name—he would not truly have to marry such an unsuitable female.

Benjamin was stopped before he could leave the house, causing him to wonder in a twisted humor if one was ever allowed to simply come or go in the Oakes home without being verbally halted. Certainly not at the moment, for it was Sir Albert himself who had hailed Benjamin.

"If you could step into my bookroom?" Sir Albert asked. Without waiting for Benjamin's assent, Sir Albert retreated down his own hall, leaving Benjamin to trail behind him. Benjamin pursed his mouth for a moment, knowing that before the naval debacle he would have been afforded more deferential treatment, but also knowing that only time could favorably shift that tide once again. He returned his hat and gloves to Langley, and sighed before silently following in Sir Albert's wake. A month? It could not pass quickly enough to suit Benjamin.

When he entered the bookroom, Sir Albert was standing before an unlit hearth that gave testimony to the fine spring weather. He had a glass of port in one hand and thrust another toward his guest.

"Thank you, I believe I will," Benjamin said as he crossed the room and accepted the glass. He tossed down a large gulp before lifting an inquiring brow.

"'Tis this damned betrothal, of course," Sir Albert said. The older man's white hair was ruffled, as if he'd run a hand through it. "I mishandled telling my Katie things," he said, a sheepish quality in his tone. "She's got the wrong notion in her head, I am afraid, and it does not a paint a pretty picture of you."

Benjamin shrugged. "I could see at once that it would be . . . hurtful to your daughter to be told all."

"I asked you here to give you my apology for that, you see? And to ask a favor of you. A favor that I did not think of in my shock when you first came to tell me what Cullman had wrought." Sir Albert's stance changed subtly, as if he assumed a dueling position. Gone was the openness of entreaty, now replaced by a cautious posture.

"If I can grant it with honor, I will," Benjamin said carefully as he put aside his drink on the nearby table.

Sir Albert stared at him, as if he would read Benjamin's soul, and at length he nodded. "I believe you are a man of your word. Unlike another I could name."

"I am glad you now know that Cullman is not trustworthy," Benjamin said.

"Now? Why do you think I brought my Katie to London?" Sir Albert said on a huff, any reticence fleeing. "I knew she was partial toward the rascal, but I never thought she'd make an understanding with him, not without first consulting me! She seemed so young to me, so unready for marriage . . . well, I was blind, was I not? But, Lord Benjamin, I swear until she announced it last night, I never knew she'd pledged herself to that coxcomb."

Sir Albert scowled. "She's a . . . a forward girl, that one. Gets notions in her head." He looked up, alarmed, as if he'd said too much. "She's a good sort, though," he hurried to add. "Perhaps too clever for a woman, but even the Bible tells us not to put a bushel basket over a lamp, eh?"

Benjamin tried not to smile. "And some lamps flare higher than others."

"Exactly, my lord! You are a man of sense and reason, I see. Here then is the boon I would ask of you." Sir Albert looked down into his glass, frowned a moment, then gazed once more directly into Benjamin's face. "All I ask is that you do not woo her. Not unless you mean it! At the end of this whole sorry matter, her heart will have been played with enough. To be honest, Lord Benjamin, I fear she'll not come out of this unscathed.

"I fear her . . . repute has not seasoned well here in London. She'll have wounds enough to lick when I take her back home to Bexley, let alone those from this whole sordid affair. So, my lord, I ask that you promise not to add to her burden by wooing her. I would beg that you not play the pretty . . . er, to be franker yet, not seduce my daughter nor engage her heart."

Benjamin stared, and Sir Albert lifted his chin.

"I know that your intent is the very opposite . . . now," Sir Albert went on. "But these things tend to alter with time. And she is a lively sort, with some charm I tell you, even if you've yet to see it in her! So, my lord, I would have your promise."

"And if I would not give it?"

Sir Albert's jaw tightened. "The two of you would be chaperoned at all times, in all ways, by no less than her three brothers and myself. Day, night, and every second in between." His gaze narrowed. "And I would learn that you lack honor, just as the gossips say—something I had hoped was not so."

The two men stood silent for a long moment, tension palpable between them.

Benjamin broke the moment's mood by allowing a slow smile to form, careful it not appear mocking, but, really, this was too pitiably amusing. He hung his head, then spread his hands in a gesture of capitulation. "I fully expected such chaperoneage in any case," he said, his mouth twisting with humor despite himself.

Sir Albert's shoulders relaxed, but he still gazed at Benjamin, awaiting an answer.

"Sir," Benjamin said, "you have my promise. Beyond what small performances Miss Oakes and I must affect to convince others there is a betrothal between us, I will do nothing to woo or win your daughter."

Sir Albert nodded, slowly at first, but then with growing satisfaction. "See that you do not, Lord Benjamin." He tried to sound gruff, but his relief was obvious. "Do well by my Katie, and I will call you friend for life. That is all I can offer in return for this favor you have sworn to grant me and my daughter."

Benjamin inclined his head, his humor softening, becoming less bitter. "All, sir? Is not friendship a pearl beyond price?" Again, he was careful not to sound mocking—for the words were true enough, were indeed an axiom in which Benjamin believed. He could count on one hand the few friends who had stood by him in his recent difficulty—he would ever remember who had proved themselves the true friend, and who had not.

"By God, I could like you, my lord!" Sir Albert said, giving a brisk nod of his head.

"Could?" Benjamin grinned openly.

"You know how to convince another to put their trust in you. I pray I am not misled," Sir Albert said.

"As to the matter of your daughter, you may put your mind at rest and fear not."

"That I cannot do, Lord Benjamin. Only a fool fears not. I may be many things, but I am not a fool."

Benjamin cocked his head, silently acknowledging that the other man's caution was not misplaced—Benjamin would not trust fully either, were the roles reversed. "You know what is said of me, and yet you have taken my word. Others would not, and think themselves prudent," he pointed out.

"My Katherine came by her willful ways honestly, you see, for we Oakeses are a stubborn lot who prefer to decide things for ourselves." Sir Albert grinned as well, even as he shrugged. "Of course, sometimes we decide wrong."

"What is the punishment for disappointing a member of the Oakes clan?" Benjamin asked, meeting the man's gaze.

"Death by the Cut Direct."

"Ouch!" Benjamin pretended to wince. "But I should warn you that the Whitburys have survived the Cut Direct for decades now. We have grown inured to it."

"Perhaps in Somerset, sir, but I have to wonder about your stamina in Town."

Benjamin gave a crooked smile, and acknowledged the thrust with a bow of his head. "Only time will settle the matter."

"It will."

Benjamin offered a shallow bow, preparatory of leaving. "Since I have sworn not to woo your daughter, I could, if you like," he said as he lifted his head once more, "give your daughter a disgust of me, sir. She already half hates me. It would take but an unfortunate scratch of my backside here, a ribald joke there . . ."

The older man ran his tongue between his upper lip and teeth, not quite masking a responding smile. "Thank you, Lord Benjamin, but that will not be necessary."

Benjamin gave an elegant shrug. "As you please."

Sir Albert's expression sobered. "Thank you, my lord." The bow he offered in return to Benjamin was deeper and longer and said much.

Benjamin began to turn to leave, but then he hesitated. "You are welcome, sir. I would ask one last question, however."

Sir Albert spread his hands. "Yes?"

"If you do not care overmuch for Mr. Cullman's company, how is it he was a guest at your card parties?"

Sir Albert pulled a face. "He is the son of a friend. A good man, is Mr. Henry Cullman of the Home Office, formerly a squire of Bexley. We have been friends for many years. He asked me to receive his son, give him a leg up in our little bit of society in the country, y'know. It was only recently that I realized the son does not follow in the father's footsteps." Sir Albert shrugged, not responsible for a friend's less-than-shining offspring.

"Still, Cullman the Younger is where he belongs now, a dandy among the highest-flying of the fribbles. London is the place for him. I cannot regret that he has turned away from my Katie, even if I regret how he went about it. Even though it seems the man has a purse to support this high life he's chosen, I am glad he will not be the one to support my girl's comfort and well-being into her old age. For all I know, perhaps he is deep in dun territory, telling his creditors to wait forever as fashionable fools seem to do these days. At any rate, Katherine is well rid of him, I think. And her heart will mend." The last he said with less certainty.

"It is the way of young girls," Benjamin asserted.

Sir Albert grunted. "Young girls? I don't think my Katherine's ever been a 'young girl,' not as you mean, my lord. You'd do well to think of her as a woman grown, with a mind that rivals any of her brothers'. A mind that makes itself up and damn the consequences."

Despite the girl's reputation, Benjamin felt himself staring, for he'd never heard a father so describe his own daughter—*take that as a warning and learn from it,* Benjamin noted to himself. People called her a hoyden and a hellion, and her own papa said she'd "damn the consequences." The woman had named herself a bluestocking, in this case the more generous of epithets that could be tossed about—and he'd be wise to remember both her words and her father's.

Yes, Benjamin decided, he would do well to remember not to treat Miss Oakes like any other woman he'd ever met—but only for one month. Thankfully, after that, she would not be his concern.

Chapter 9

"I am Mrs. Cyril Cullman." Katherine tested the name while she gazed into her looking glass. "Why yes, I *am* the wife of Cyril Cullman," she tried. Her reflection appeared pleased.

Also reflected was the clock on the mantelpiece, showing it was twenty minutes to four, the hour Lord Benjamin had said he would return to take Katherine walking in the park.

"Katherine Cullman," she tried one last phrase, following it with a coy smile, only to see her reflection devolve into a scowl. Scowling was not an expression that afforded her well in the arena of good looks, but it was better than "coy." She did not do "coy" at all well.

"How do you wish your hair dressed, miss?" the maid inquired, already moving to pick up a yellow ribbon to match Katherine's yellow sprigged muslin gown, from the top of the chest of drawers. She paused. "Your hair has grown longer than usual, miss, since we come to London. Do you wish me to trim it first?"

Katherine glanced back at her looking glass, seeing that her hair was longer than it had been in many a year. Not for the first time, she wondered if she ought to grow it out—most women had long hair. Almost every woman back home in Bexley eschewed this fashion of short hair, taking pride in their long locks. Katherine had often been asked if she ever meant to let hers grow.

She thought of the many times she'd had to comb it back like a lad—and it occurred to her that she probably could let it grow now, if she wished, since she had sworn never to don lad's clothing again, at least while in London. The risks of exposure were too high here. But she did not wish to grow out her hair, not really . . . not yet. She wanted to reserve the ability to slip into her old disguise, just in case—she might want to visit Fallen Angel again, she thought with a flicker of defiance.

Only to sigh. The horse was the one creature on all the earth she could *not* visit, for its owner would not welcome this particular visitor, in women's clothing nor men's. For that matter, Katherine had no notion where Lord Benjamin had decided to board her—no, *his* horse.

She shook her head. "No trim today," she told the maid. "Can you do something stylish with it as it is?"

"Oh yes, miss," the maid assured her at once. "A ribbon woven through finger curls will do very nicely."

The maid set about her task, and Katherine let her mind linger, not on missing her horse, but on the rest of the day ahead.

She would walk in Green Park at four, as she'd agreed to do, and attend the Bellord ball tonight at eight. Beyond today, she would follow Lord Benjamin's list of places to go and things to attend, and she would accept best wishes for her supposed pending marriage. All the while she would somehow keep from screaming that it was a complete deceit.

She must remember to picture herself, in four weeks, sitting before the fire in her very own cottage near Meyerley Creek. Or, perhaps, sitting on the lap of Mr. Cyril Cullman before the fire in her cottage.

Cyril. As her husband. Katherine drew in a sharp breath and let it out slowly, and then had to assure the maid that, no, the girl had done nothing to cause Katherine discomfort. But . . . marriage. She'd planned to marry Cyril, for many weeks now. She had run many scenarios through her mind, from going to chapel together to lying together in bed. She'd lived too long in the country, in the company of men and horses, to be ignorant of the physical nature of taking a mate. She knew the pleasures of kissing—and hoped bedding would be all that and more.

It was not those intimacies that disturbed her composure so much as it was the idea of sharing most, if not all, of her waking hours with a man. A strange man. Papa and her brothers were known and familiar, and caring of the female among them. The idea of sharing hour upon hour, day upon day, with a man so unbeknownst and unaccustomed to her, and she to him—now *that* was daunting.

"Just as well we will be at Meyerley Creek," she told herself. Then she frowned, for Meyerley Creek was hers, but it was not home, no matter that it would soon be her new residence.

She had wanted freedom—and marriage was yet another way of getting it; it would be, inarguably, freedom from the familiar. But somehow in her mind "freedom" had meant she would be free to choose what to do, when to do it, or how to do it. She would make the decisions that needed making. But surely a husband would expect some say-so in her life, her decisions? Of course he would—just as she would hope he'd include her in deciding important matters.

Katherine frowned, and the maid gave her mistress a helpless look. "'Tis not you, Ginny, 'tis my own poor mood," Katherine assured her.

But, she thought the moment her contemplation turned back to marriage, in her concern she was forgetting something, something very important: Cyril was different. He *liked* Katherine. He encouraged her, and laughed wholeheartedly when she amused him, and never bid her change a thing about herself. He would be largely a stranger if . . . *when* they wed, but so would any man she had not lived with all her life. At least this "stranger" could be counted upon to take enjoyment from their alliance, to *want* to marry *her*. And, if she were right, Cyril had swallowed a great deal of pride in order to help her papa. He had taken a step back, had agreed she must be publicly betrothed to another, had not insisted on his prior claim—and the only reason to do so had to be that he worked to protect her papa. Surely that said much of the nature of Cyril Cullman.

If she were right. But she had to be—the explanation was the only one she'd been able to form that made sense, for Papa had refused to give her any other when she'd gone to him not an hour since.

"I cannot tell you why I agreed to Lord Benjamin's proposal, Katie," he had said, his expression so terse it bordered on misery. "You must accept that is all I can say on the matter."

His anguish, more than his words, had made her leave him be, made her not press for answers as it was surely her right to do. Whatever had happened, she guessed she ought to be grateful this mock betrothal would put it right.

"Do you like it, miss?" the maid asked, bringing Katherine back to the moment.

"Why, it is charming, Ginny!" Yellow ribbon peeked out be-

tween a riot of curls, a flattering look that even the ladies in
Bexley could not find wanting.

Ginny nodded with satisfaction. "'Tis all in how you pin it,
miss."

The maid helped her mistress don the rest of the late afternoon's ensemble. Katherine turned back to her looking glass to
be sure all was in order, from her half boots for walking, up to her
lace gloves and the shawl draped over her shoulders. Fashion de-
creed she ought to wear a bonnet, but Katherine was in no mood
to accede to yet another dictate. The ribbon would serve as decoration enough for her hair on this day blessed with fine weather.
Why work to keep her face from the sun when it already had too
much color in it anyway to be considered fashionable?

As soon as Langley brought Lord Benjamin to the parlor door
and announced his presence, Katherine felt a blush add to the
color in her cheeks. At least Lord Benjamin could not know what
it was that brought the blood rushing to her face. For when she
saw him anew, it was not of the false betrothal she thought, nor the
discredit surrounding his name, but of the way his finely shaped
mouth had touched hers only yesterday morning. Not anger at his
part in all this, not chagrin—but memories of his kiss.

Her reaction was understandable. He was a fine-looking
man, in his sober way, and when he smiled he was actually
quite attractive. He smiled now, ever so slightly, in a general
greeting sort of way, and it was hardly remarkable that his smile
should draw her attention to his mouth. The memory of those
lips on hers . . . his had been a breath-stealing kiss, quite literally. At first she had responded only with the shock of being
swept into his arms, but then the shock of the kiss itself had
coursed through her.

It was . . . style, or skill, or instinct. Something about the
way he'd held her . . . or the way he'd held his mouth—but his
kiss had not been something merely to be endured. Katherine
had, in fact, welcomed his mouth's touch with a readiness as
spontaneous as . . . well, as a laugh shared between friends. His
kiss had been on the one hand as enticing as a candle's glow inside a darkened room, and yet as comforting as pulling on a
warm pair of gloves when one's hands were tingly with cold.

Comforting? A kiss with Lord Benjamin? Impossible! And
yet . . . "comforting" was the only word that came close to de-

scribing why she'd not only lingered in his embrace, but so readily kissed him in return.

Despite her warm thoughts, or because of them, she felt a tremor of discomfort at knowing she was going to be alone with this man—Miss Irving had a headache but had said a walk in the park without a chaperone was utterly innocent and perfectly acceptable, especially as Katherine and Lord Benjamin were betrothed. Katherine had not liked it, but she'd had no recourse but her brothers, and quickly dismissed the idea of their open-eared company.

"Lord Benjamin," she greeted him.

"Miss Oakes," he greeted her in return. Was that humor in his eyes? "Are you ready to endure a walk through the park?" he asked.

His lightness of tone surprised her; she could almost appreciate his humor. A second glance into his face assured her that gone was the doleful Lord Benjamin who had attended her papa's card party, or the snappish man who had asked for her hand; here again was the banterer who had discovered her in lad's clothing and demanded a kiss in exchange for keeping her secret.

What a changeable fellow! If any woman ever married him in truth, Katherine would feel sorry for the pell-mell life that woman would undoubtedly lead. She would have to be a woman who liked change . . . and kisses.

Katherine looked down at her folded hands, thinking her cheeks must have reddened even further at the turn, yet again, of her thoughts to this man's kiss. Did she possess no circumspection? Better to reflect on how the world called him "rogue." Which thought reminded her that she wanted to ask him a question.

"Before we go, Lord Benjamin, I feel I have a right to ask you to tell me something."

His gaze did not waver, even if his slight smile disappeared. "Ask, and I will decide if you have the right to an answer, Miss Oakes."

She nodded; it was a careful reply, such as she might have given were she in his place. "Since my name is to be attached to yours, however fleetingly, I feel I have the right to ask what compelled you to leave the navy?"

Instead of looking annoyed or angry, Lord Benjamin

smiled—albeit a wicked smile, full of teeth like a shark's jaw that Katherine had seen at a scientific display.

"Plain truth, Miss Oakes?" he asked, his eyes glinting, although not with humor despite his smile.

"Indeed."

"I was forced to resign after I admitted to selling naval supplies to smugglers."

She gasped, even though she'd been told the same by Cyril. How could Lord Benjamin grin around the ignoble words he spoke?—although his smile reminded her of a stained-glass window she'd seen in which the artist gave the devil a brittle grin, as if the Fallen One knew tempting souls into the depths was but a false triumph.

"How could you?" she asked, hearing the aversion in her voice. "How could you sell supplies meant for your shipmates, for men who were going off to battle—!"

"These things are done for money, Miss Oakes." He cut her off, the smile erased, his expression turned sour.

"Did you do it? Sell the supplies?"

The sour look fell away, replaced by a superior lift of his chin, to her mind quite out of keeping with the dark deed he'd claimed. "I must have done, to have admitted to it. But, I do not wish to speak of this any longer. The misdeed was made and admitted, and it is time to move on."

Katherine stared up at him, and wondered why she saw under the smugness something like distress in his eyes. No man liked to be forced to revisit his misdeeds, of course. Could this merely be simple regret that he'd been caught? Or did he now realize what he had put at stake and belatedly regretted having risked it?

"You are buying respectability!" Katherine said, the thought coming to her suddenly. "This proposal—it is to make you appear respectable!" she declared. "You want to be seen being accepted by an old family with a good name."

Lord Benjamin neither nodded nor shook his head, but his lips thinned.

"Our wealth may not be extensive," Katherine said, completing the puzzle aloud, "but the Oakeses stand among the oldest families in England. We are imminently respectable—" She cut herself off, another point of confusion coming to her. "But if you are buying respectability, Lord Benjamin, surely a marriage would serve you far better than a mere betrothal?" she challenged.

His face darkened now, either from embarrassment or aggravation, but he merely shook his head.

"Oh!" Katherine regretted the cry the moment it crossed her lips, but understanding had dawned. Lord Benjamin stared at her. "You want to be connected with the Oakes name, but not at the cost of actually having to marry *me*! I see. Really, I do. I know I am not well regarded here in London."

It was her turn to stare back at Lord Benjamin. There was a sense of satisfaction at having reasoned out the situation, but that did not mean her pride went unwounded.

"And so our betrothal is to be broken, and no marriage was ever desired," she declared, resisting the impulse to let her shoulders sag. "Not with me."

If possible, his face darkened even further in obvious agitation. "You malign yourself unnecessarily, Miss Oakes. It is not you specifically—I do not wish to marry *anyone*. Not at this time," he said gruffly.

She could not imagine why his words lifted her spirits a fraction, except that perhaps it was possible he spoke the truth, not so much rejecting *her* as marriage altogether. She thought his scheme a poor one—why not make a betrothal to a more likely lady in the first place?—but the answer to that was *expediency*. She had to believe he had seen an opportunity, something between him and Papa and Mr. Cullman, and had seized it.

"Nor do I wish to discuss this any further," he said firmly. "Everything is behind us except the next month's work, and that is all we need concern ourselves with now."

"Yes." Really, it was a bit of a relief to know the worst of the man. At least she would not be surprised by any lack of scruples in him for the next month . . . assuming he'd just shown her his worst intentions.

"You are sure your bruise will not bother you if we stroll?" Lord Benjamin asked, changing the subject. It was clear there would be no more questions answered by him this evening, not about this betrothal. "We could greet people from my phaeton, if that would be better."

"Oh no. My side does quite well unless I apply pressure. Walking is fine."

This was the second time he had thought to ask after her health. It could all be pretended concern—but, really, she found it difficult to hold fixed in her mind the idea of him as a horrible scoundrel. . . . Perhaps it was the underlying edge of discomfort—regret?—in his manner that allowed her to think he must wish he had taken a more noble path in this whole, sordid affair.

That he even knew which path might be the more noble one meant he was not utterly without human feeling and, perhaps, a desire to change his ways.

Perhaps Lord Benjamin had come to London seeking a second chance? *I could wish for such a chance,* Katherine thought as she placed her hand on the arm Lord Benjamin offered her. Besides, their fates were not going to be bound together for long. His honor, or lack of it, was not her concern. She had only to be gracious and tolerate him as she would any stranger, and soon enough Lord Benjamin and his reputation would be out of her life.

Their walk through Green Park turned out to be painful, not physically but emotionally. After enduring a dozen snubs, Katherine was tempted to announce aloud that she and Lord Benjamin were actually well suited, having much in common, largely their barely tolerated existence at the edge of the *beau monde*—but good sense prevailed.

However, perhaps in their way even more painful than the snubs were those moments when someone made a point of coming forward to congratulate the couple, for Katherine found it difficult to look into kind eyes and lie about her intention to wed this man. Snobbery could be preferred to kindness, for the latter tended to bring tears to her eyes, tears that she had to blink away, or else explain away as "tears of happiness." The embraces she was given and the kisses on her cheek stung like salt in a wound, and it became increasingly difficult to smile and nod and play such a terrible game of pretend.

What would they all think of her when she "cried off"? At best, they would think her frivolous. Many would say she only ran true to her reputation. What would they think if . . . *when* she was betrothed a second time? She would not be the first woman to turn over one fiancé for another in a short period of time . . . but that thought brought little comfort, for she already knew Society did not like to welcome back wayward daughters who tried to play outside its rules.

But, did it matter? What use did Katherine have for Society? She hoped to make her home in Bexley, far from London. Taking a little comfort from that reminder, she found another store of smiles and chatter, and used them to get her past this afternoon's awkwardness.

When a congratulatory Mrs. Trundle and her daughter had made their adieux, it left Katherine and Lord Benjamin alone as they had not been since first descending from his phaeton at the park's gates. Katherine turned to look up at this man she was claiming, however temporarily, as her betrothed. His face was composed in bland—one could even say sanguine—order. If not for the tic of a small muscle along his jaw, Katherine would have thought him entirely at ease, entirely pleased with the day's events.

Somehow she liked him a little better for that small, telling tic. The short time she'd spent in his company had already taught her he was not a wholly horrible man—he had his moments when she thought him more human than beast. Not many, and too far between, but he was not so much an ogre as first impressions had implied. Besides, she would be wrongheaded to compare him to the matchless Mr. Cullman; any man would pale in that shadow.

Lord Benjamin glanced about, then lowered his gaze to hers. "I think we have suffered enough," he pronounced with the hint of dry humor, one she now acknowledged he was capable of displaying. "Are you ready to return home?"

"Yes, thank you," she said with heartfelt relief. She'd have to go through much the same scrutiny all over again at the Bellord ball, in just a few hours, but for the moment she'd had enough of stares and whispers—and she was gratified that Lord Benjamin had the sense to give them both a time of respite. He might be ruthless when he wanted something, but at least in small matters such as this he had already proved to possess a modicum of sense—and even, remarkably, tact. Tact from Lord Benjamin? *Wonders never cease,* Katherine thought wryly to herself.

Chapter 10

Later that evening, Benjamin stared at the funds atop the dresser drawers that had come with his rented room, amazed all over again by how little money was there. It was three weeks until his quarter day, when funds would go into his account at the Bank of England, as he'd arranged for them to do when he'd first arrived in London. Gideon's man of business would be sure the funds were paid on time from the estate. It would not be a large sum, but certainly welcome. As for now, with just a little over three pounds in his purse between now and quarter day . . .

At least three pounds was enough to see that he had bread once or twice a day until more funds arrived. Bread and an occasional beer—enough for life, if not for enjoyment. But he'd lived on meager rations before, for want of supplies on a ship too long at sea. He'd survive.

However, rent was due in ten days. Even if he could persuade the landlord to wait, that payment would consume half of the quarterly sum that would have just come to him.

It was sorely tempting to write home . . . but he would *not* ask Gideon for an advance, nor for an increase in his allowance. The estate could afford it, easily, but Benjamin would not ask. Pride had its hold on him again.

He did not even want to think how he'd pay the fees to keep Fallen Angel, yet he was determined not to support his choices through his brother. Truth was, he knew he'd have to sell the horse—the one thing he had managed to make his own since leaving home. He'd not even get to see the mare run before he lost her, too.

Benjamin gave a frustrated thump on the top of the dresser drawers, making the coins jump before he scooped them into his purse. If worse came to worst, he could move into the old family home on Seymour Street, which Gideon had ordered completely gutted and renovated upon his marriage. Benjamin had gone there, upon first arriving in London, but the unfamiliar man paid to mind the place of an evening had assured him the house was uninhabitable, a fact his own eyes had seen. Still, if so little as one room was capable of being made usable, Benjamin might end there yet. *Go home. . . .*

His pitifully thin purse now in his coat pocket, Benjamin shook his head and turned to his room's looking glass.

His black coat over a cream-colored waistcoat and charcoal-gray breeches was well enough for a ball, but his hair was growing out. It had a slight wavy texture to it, requiring that it either be kept very short or else grown out long to look its best. Despite the fact both his brothers preferred their hair long, Benjamin preferred his clipped and controlled. Could he cut it himself? His reflection frowned at the very idea of such folly.

"Guess I will not become a barber," Benjamin said to himself as he straightened his cravat, well aware he had no talent for physicking, or pulling teeth, let alone cutting hair. He just managed to scrape away his own beard.

He'd not hired a valet upon coming to London, knowing the money in his purse after leaving the navy was all that would keep him until he found employment. Besides, he'd learned how to maintain his own apparel while he'd been on board ship. He was not clever at it, but he got by.

He tugged at his cravat, trying to make the one side match the other. The cursed thing would not lie properly. "And so much for a career as a valet," he muttered, but not without a small, if slightly mocking, smile at himself.

The cravat would have to do even if it was not perfectly draped. Benjamin turned to collect his greatcoat, gloves, and beaver hat, at least the latter of which he knew how to brush until it looked just as it ought.

"You are in a fine mood this evening, my lord," the manager of the bachelor apartments, Mr. Finchley, told Benjamin as he came down the stairs toward the front door.

"Am I?" Benjamin replied, a little surprised by the observation. He would have thought an unpleasant expression might grace his visage. He could certainly think of more pleasant things to do than escort Miss Oakes to a ball—although it would scarcely be an onerous duty, nothing like keeping watch on a storm-washed night sea.

"I will need my phaeton brought around yet again," he requested, naming his only vehicle—and even that one meager equipage was only something he had hired out for a month. Yet another worry: How would he get about London if he could not afford another month's hire? He'd have to walk. Yet another step down in consequence.

To think, if only he would go home to Severn's Well he could use any carriage in his brother's stable; could have a valet; could have beer or champagne to his fill anytime he wished them, without a single penny leaving his purse.

He *could* go home. Perhaps he should . . . but, no. Not for a month anyway; he was to be at Miss Oakes's side.

Instead of discouraging him, that thought actually buoyed his sagging spirits; he had another month to possibly—if improbably—make something of himself.

He could leave such dire thoughts for another day. The only worry he had for tonight was that of maintaining a happy façade. He was tired, but he could manage the act even if today had already been a very long day, with too much high emotion crowded into it.

The latest, and worst, had been when Miss Oakes had erroneously come to the conclusion that he wanted a limited betrothal between them only because he had no interest in marrying *her* specifically.

Truth was, he did *not* wish to marry her, but neither did he wish his actions to make her feel belittled. While he would choose a wholly different kind of woman as his wife, there was surely someone, somewhere, who would appreciate Miss Oakes's . . . er, enthusiasm for life.

Miss Oakes had a certain amount of grace, even charm, when she was not outrageously dressed in lad's clothing or demanding recompense for a faked betrothal. Whereas he might have liked to tell her how to alter her behavior the better to suit London life, he had no interest in implying her hopes on the marriage mart were small. There was no reason to be cruel, after all.

Benjamin climbed up into his phaeton, accepting the reins.

He signaled the horses to proceed, even while he uttered a tired sigh. Yes, it had been a long day. Besides everything else that had subsequently occurred, this morning he had gone straight from Sir Albert's home—where he'd just proposed to Miss Oakes—to the club where his old friend, Davis, was likely to be found breakfasting.

Davis, stout friend that he'd proven himself to be, wrote out a letter of recommendation, and had introduced Benjamin despite some dubious gazes thrown their way. Over breakfast, six men of importance had been met, six bows exchanged—but no employment offers had been tendered.

"Sorry, my lad, but I already have a capable fellow clerking for me," had been the typical response to Benjamin's not-so-subtle inquiries.

Still, tomorrow would be soon enough to renew the pursuit of employment; Benjamin just hoped he was not so tired as to accidentally offend tonight someone he might wish to impress tomorrow. All he had to do tonight was to pretend he was happily on the edge of wedded bliss.

All? he thought with a small, ironic smile.

He had been right to doubt the task would be a simple one, Benjamin thought an hour later. He had to stifle an annoyed sigh, watching from a few feet away as his supposed fiancée became so caught up in stating her opinion—that Green Park was meant to resemble woods and adding flowers along its paths would detract from its deliberate countrylike flavor—that some of the wine in her glass sloshed onto the Bellords' carpet. Hardly the kind of female to which he wished his name attached.

Her chaperone, Miss Irving, came from a nearby chair to dab at the carpet after murmuring something in Miss Oakes's ear that caused the latter to put down her glass.

Only to have Cyril Cullman pick it up again and place it back in her hand with a smile, even as he signaled a footman to come and refill the glass. Miss Oakes smiled brightly at him in return, and Benjamin just managed to keep his lip from curling.

It was now abundantly clear that Cullman sought out Miss Oakes's company. It made no sense at all, but the man had been at Miss Oakes's side since the moment she'd entered the room. And, unlike the chaperone who tried to curb the more flamboyant aspects of her charge's nature, Cullman encouraged Miss Oakes by grinning at her, and asking her to "please, go on," and giving every impression he listened intently to everything she had to say.

Why? Why desert the girl, hand her over to another, only to come back to her side? Why gaze upon her with what strongly resembled approval, even admiration?

The answer, perhaps, stood on Cullman's left: Miss Violet Mansell. Miss Mansell was quite pretty, and a brief acquaintance had led to an impression that she was well mannered and intelligent. Were Benjamin truly in the market for a bride, he would look for someone very like Miss Mansell. She was soft-spoken, demure, and pleasant. He liked her blond hair, which would be long and straight once unpinned from atop her head. The large pearl earbobs at her ears were a silent testimony to style, as well as an announcement that her papa had a few coins to rub together. Her gown was cream silk, adorned with furbelows the color of her Christian name.

Miss Mansell, Benjamin supposed, must have a greater dowry than did Miss Oakes. Cullman would have made the same assessment as well. Logic went further, to suggest that Cullman was using Miss Oakes as a foil, to attract the attention of the real target in this campaign, the wealthier, more socially adept Miss Mansell.

Benjamin looked up at a long case clock across the ballroom, and ground his teeth in impatience to see an hour had not yet gone by. The dancing was not set to begin until ten, until after most of the guests had arrived and partaken of the food laid out at one end of the room.

He thought to ask Miss Oakes if she would promenade with him, but then she flushed with pleasure at yet another compliment Cullman spewed forth, and instead Benjamin merely turned away. If he lingered here, he would say something terse or impolite, and Miss Oakes would demand to know why. Better just to step away, to let his irritation dissipate a bit. Then he would return to fetch his "fiancée" and play the pretty with the evidently easy-to-flatter Miss Oakes.

Though, really, the poor creature was to be pitied—how would she feel if Cullman did not renew his offer when the month was over? How would all this flirting and conviviality on Cullman's part now make her feel then?

A glass of port, Benjamin decided grimly, was what would suit him best just now.

Alone in the Bellords' bookroom, Benjamin tipped the port he'd found into a glass, but when he went to lift it, instead he just stared down at the liquid and frowned. How was he supposed to act enamored of Miss Oakes if she was going to ignore him and make eyes at Cullman?

He felt his annoyance rising again, and told himself to concentrate on something else, anything other than Cyril Cullman and his contemptible ways. So what was the first thing to come to mind? Miss Oakes's demeanor while he had kissed her, there in the horse stall at Tattersall's.

Even now, hours later, the memory struck him nearly as hard as a blow. The startling truth was: Miss Oakes was eminently kissable. She slid into a man's arms as smoothly as a counterpane settled atop a mattress.

When he had kissed her, her mouth had yielded to pressure, but not in a weak or frail way, but with an aspect of welcoming. Her lips had met his while slightly parted, an invitation almost as intoxicating as the body that had conformed and accommodated every tension he brought to bear against it. Her hips had tilted up toward his own, her breasts had been pressed without restraint to his chest, and when his arms had slid around her waist, she had drawn nearer yet, closing a paper-thin distance he hadn't known had remained between them until that moment.

Yet there had ben something *guileless* in that kiss, despite all signs to the contrary. Her body may have longed to be held, and her lips had proved they had surely been tried before, but still Benjamin would swear Miss Oakes was an innocent, not quite sure of the fire with which she played. She promised so much with the way she allowed herself to be held, how she allowed him to test her mouth with his tongue. Yet when she had pushed away there had been only anger in her eyes, not fear. Anger at him for presuming, but not actually for what he had done, how he had touched her.

Miss Oakes had been designed for making, sharing, giving love—yet despite her own nature, remained an innocent. If asked, Benjamin would have to answer that he did not believe Miss Oakes had ever been in love, no matter how she blushed when Cullman threw his flattery her way. Curious! But Benjamin began to understand why Sir Albert had made him promise not to woo the woman—she was a plum ripe for the picking, and it would be far too easy for an unscrupulous man to bruise her, perhaps beyond redemption.

Benjamin took up the glass of port and sipped as he considered: Cullman was unscrupulous.

Why, not long after he'd handed the very same lady away in a card game, had Cullman come to call on Miss Oakes this morning? Did Cullman now regret having abandoned the woman? Was he as ruthless as Benjamin thought him to be? Could he be playing at some deep game, making one woman jealous of another?

Benjamin finished the port in his glass in one gulp.

"Lord Benjamin," a voice interrupted his reverie, the last voice he wished to hear right now.

It was Cullman, standing just inside the bookroom door. A cool smile shaped his lips. "You have held up your end of the bargain. I am come to say I am contented."

"I am not sure I understand you," Benjamin said, putting down the glass and turning to face him.

Something in Cullman's smile spoke of duplicity, of cunning, of amusement at another's expense. The man did not even bother to hide his smugness.

In that moment Benjamin was certain he was right to despise the man. "Do you mean you approve my being so public in the matter of the betrothal with Miss Oakes?" Benjamin said, shoulders stiff with caution.

"I mean just that. Too, I am curious how you got her to agree, and so promptly. What threat did you use?"

Benjamin stared across the room at the man, marveling others could not see that beneath whatever appeal Cullman exhibited, the man was a snake.

"No threats. I just told her as much of the truth as I could," Benjamin said with cold disdain.

"The truth? You told her you are all but penniless, with no expectations?" Cullman said, his amusement growing. "You have a unique courtship style, I will give you that."

Cullman glanced over his shoulder, apparently satisfying himself that no one was at hand to hear. "Are you going to see this betrothal through? Do you crave her land? She *did* tell you about that worthless swamp she thinks she can manage a stud on, did she not?"

Benjamin looked sharply into the other man's face. "Why do you say it is worthless?"

"Ah, so you *are* interested!" Cullman appeared pleased with his conclusion. "I understand. That land is half of why I asked for her hand in the first place. Then I went to see it for myself— I tell you, it is all but worthless! The girl has the most pathetic dowry known to man."

Cullman must have seen something in Benjamin's face that urged him to go on. "Her papa saves all his pennies for his gaming, not for his sons' idle hours, limiting their allowances. Nor does he offer any cash money as part of his daughter's dowry. She's only to receive that water-logged patch she thinks will someday be tillable, that and a token strip belonging to her papa, atop the ledge that abuts her swamp. A small, narrow strip, mind you. Sir Albert's not so foolish as to grant anything of size for the girl to mismanage. She could have a hundred acres of the estate, with him scarcely missing the revenue they'd generate, but he's given her only three." The man spoke with a cruel glitter in his gaze, evidently thinking himself clever to have escaped tying himself to Miss Oakes and her forlorn dowry.

Benjamin knew what it was to own no land; a woman who could bring land with her was a woman who would garner a second glance from him. Land was equal to money and power. If land was not got through the wife, how then was a second son to gain any? Still, Benjamin liked to think, when he went to consider a potential wife's earthly worth, he would not prove so thoroughly bankrupt of human feeling as Cullman clearly was.

"She claims the swampy part might be drained, but even the piece of land from Sir Albert that *is* usable is raw land. It is untilled, unbroken. Once worked, it will still be at least several years before Papa's portion could yield any income, let alone the swamp below it."

"But it always takes a few years for newly broken land to be of full worth," Benjamin pointed out, perplexed by Cullman's sneer. "Anyone who would farm knows success is measured in years, not months. And wet land can be drained and made usable, sometimes."

"Are you a farmer then?" Cullman shuddered, as if something foul had crawled across one of his highly polished boots. "Well, *I* am not! I haven't time to sit about waiting for what may or may not grow, dependent on the contrary weather and if a bit of bog can be drained."

The dark-haired man hesitated, but then his scowl dispersed, replaced by a dawning comprehension. "Come to think on it, Lord Benjamin, I can see where a second son might crave any land he could get his hands on. Ah, yes! I see now that Miss Oakes might not be so poor a match for you after all! What *I* personally must deplore might not look so poor a match for you after all! What *I* personally must deplore might not look so poor an investment to such as you. I, on the other hand, crave the birthright of the firstborn. I find I can marry better, and richer, than Miss Oakes, and I shall."

"You are blunt, sir." Benjamin could not quite keep the sneer from his voice.

"When I wish to be." Cullman laughed, not kindly. "And glib with honeyed words when they would better suit."

"You have a gift," Benjamin said, no longer even trying to hide his contempt.

"I do," Cullman agreed with a flash of teeth.

"Why did you tell me this, about Miss Oakes's dowry?" Benjamin demanded as he crossed to stand before Cullman.

Cullman just stared at him, one eyebrow lifted, perhaps in mirth.

"Do you want her back?" Benjamin asked, wanting to doubt his own question.

The man offered an elegant shrug, nonchalant, but there was humor in his eyes, and something darker than amusement.

"You want her back," Benjamin said, sickened with understanding, "but not as your wife. You want to dally with her!"

"So would you, if you had ever kissed her," Cullman said. "She was made for dalliance."

Benjamin took a step back, as if the man had struck him. He knew exactly what Cullman meant, knew because he had held Miss Oakes close, their bodies fitting as one, had kissed her luscious mouth, a mouth made for kissing.

"You think to scare me off with tales of how poor her dowry is," Benjamin accused. "You do not want this betrothal to become real, because then Miss Oakes would feel compelled to resist your attempts at seduction."

"Yes, and yes." Cullman did not even bother to look abashed. Indeed, he smiled at Benjamin as he put a hand to his own chest, as though to swear out a vow. "Although, to my credit, the bit about her dowry is all real. God's truth, Whitbury! I have never seen a more miserly portion set aside for the daughter of a man who clearly has funds at his disposal. I must have a liking for you to give you that information, and for free. I had to spend hour upon hour talking to every sapskull in Bexley to find out as much myself, Lord Benjamin. Think of it as a bridal gift, from me." He grinned. "Or, rather, a *non*bridal gift, because I know you could not want the girl now, knowing how useless her land is."

"She will not have you," Benjamin said, but even to his own ears doubt was evident in the words. He did not know Miss Oakes, except superficially. He could not predict what she might do—and she had already demonstrated a willingness to linger in Cullman's company despite the fact she ought to have been in Benjamin's. Her preference was clear, a preference Cullman would cultivate. . . .

Cullman shrugged again. "We will see if Miss Oakes will want me. Enough, do you think, to share my bed if not my name? I happen to think so." He cocked his head to one side, his smile erased. "But, then again, the girl is not really your concern, is she? She is not really engaged to you. She can do as she likes, particularly after a month."

Benjamin took another step away, as if he feared catching a disease from the man.

Cullman reacted to a sound behind him, stepping back into the hallway outside the bookroom. He glanced back in at Benjamin. "Alas, our conversation must be at an end for the day. Miss Oakes and Miss Mansell have come to find me." He deftly turned to greet the ladies. "Miss Mansell, Miss Oakes, your beauty assaults all my senses anew."

Benjamin took a deep breath, struggling to stifle fury under a veneer of composure. He followed Cullman into the hall, and could feel the rigid set of his own shoulders.

"Miss Oakes, we should be going," he said to her as soon as she met his gaze, obviously surprising her with the pronouncement. Perhaps she began to speak, but then she stopped herself. To his surprise, she did not argue.

He waited while she collected Miss Irving, and while the ladies made their adieux to Miss Mansell and Cullman, and then to the Bellords. After taking leave of their hosts himself, Benjamin promptly escorted Miss Oakes out the front door, a firm hand under her elbow.

After handing the chaperone and Miss Oakes up, Benjamin walked around the phaeton to its other side, contemplating in agitation the idea of telling Miss Oakes exactly what Cullman had said, what the man's intentions were . . . but how could he? Perhaps once the chaperone had been dismissed for the night? But, even if they had a moment or two alone, what could Benjamin say? "I believe Cullman means to seduce you, and I am afraid you are likely to comply with his wishes?"

And in a way Cullman was right: It was no real concern of Benjamin's what became of Miss Oakes. It was her father's duty to protect her—and her own duty not to allow herself to be seduced. Cullman had an unfair advantage, in that Miss Oakes did not know he had coldly gambled her away, did not know that any affection she felt toward him was *not* reciprocated and never really had been—but her virtue was still her own to protect.

Miss Oakes's future was not Benjamin's problem. It was not his concern that she might fall into a dalliance with the very man who had abandoned her. Miss Oakes's well-being, beyond the thirty days, was not a dilemma that Benjamin must solve. . . .

But, by God, Benjamin vowed with sudden ferocity, for the time Miss Oakes was publicly known as his intended, he *would* protect her. He'd do all in his power to see that churl, Cullman, never had the chance to be alone with her, let alone seduce her. For thirty days, Benjamin would protect the foolish creature, even from her own desires.

"Can you tell me, Lord Benjamin, why we needed to leave the ball so suddenly?" Miss Oakes asked him after a long, strained silence in which the only sound had been the clopping of his horses' hooves on the cobbles. "I did not get to dance even once." Disapproval filled the already crowded phaeton.

"I have a headache," he said. He'd sounded terse.

"Oh," Miss Oakes said, only then glancing up into his face. He must look the part, for her tight-lipped displeasure lessened. "I am sorry," she said. "It *was* a bit of a crush. No wonder you left the ballroom, to get some air." She said the last with enough inflection to make it a question, and he nodded, allowing her to believe that was why he'd left her side.

That would change; there would be no more leaving her on her own, particularly not if Cullman were in attendance, not from now on. Benjamin would serve as a guardian to her, for these four weeks that he was pledged to her.

That decision made, Benjamin felt a sense of purpose displace the outrage with which Cullman had left him. Miss Oakes looked up at him with gentle concern, and he felt his shoulders begin to relax.

With an effort, Benjamin put aside any lingering testiness and did his best to engage her in conversation.

By the time they turned onto her street, he was faintly surprised to realize that he had not been bored, nor had to struggle for something to say. Miss Oakes was many things, but a tiresome companion was not one of them.

As soon as the phaeton rolled to a stop, Miss Oakes was already turned to face him. "Thank you, Lord Benjamin. I will see you tomorrow," she said hastily, and just as quickly turned away from him. Without awaiting his assistance, she leaped down from the phaeton, a drop of some three feet. The effort clearly did not vex her at all, for she strode away without so much as a backward glance. Miss Irving of the other hand, gave an exasperated sigh and a shake of her head before allowing Benjamin to hand her down.

Small wonder all London called Miss Oakes a hoyden—leaping unaided from a high carriage! What if her dress had caught on something?

Benjamin opened his mouth to call after her and tell her next time she was to wait for him to come around and assist her descent, but then he pressed his lips together and smothered the comment. His only role, for one month in Miss Oakes's life, was in keeping her safe from one specific danger: Cullman. All other choices were hers to make. He'd be wise to keep that ever in mind.

*   *   *

Katherine went straight up to her room, waiting until she saw Lord Benjamin's carriage already halfway down the street before she opened her window. She leaned out, inviting the touch of the cooling night breeze.

Nature's caress did as she'd hoped it would, giving her a kind of peacefulness in which to take one last look at all that had happened since early this morning.

Aside from all the madness of the false betrothal, there had been something else, after leaving the Bellord ball. There had been a shift of Lord Benjamin's mood—or had he in truth just had a headache? He had seemed . . . discontented? Perhaps . . . determined? But determined to do what?

She could only guess he had not approved of how she'd leaped down from his phaeton unaided. He probably thought she did so all the time, even though skirts made it a poor choice. What if her hem had caught on something? She could end up with her chin on the ground and her backside in the air! But, from dawn to dusk, she'd been in this man's company three times today. She'd suddenly wanted free of any attention from him, even something as expected and casual as his hand on hers as he helped her down from a carriage.

She sighed into the night as she considered that if he had not before, he must now be thinking her very gauche. She ought to have waited, tolerated, the few more seconds it would have taken to be helped from the phaeton—she'd only proven she was as mindless of decorum as all London had already claimed her to be. Truth be told, she could hardly argue the point.

She purposefully and with deliberate effort turned her thoughts from Lord Benjamin—only to recall yet another strange moment, although this one had been with Cyril: He had given her a wink as she'd bid him adieu tonight.

At first she had felt her lips part in utter surprise at receiving something so common as a wink from the most polished man she knew.

Since, she'd half wondered if she'd imagined it, for wondering was easier than deciding how to interpret its meaning. Flirtation? Connection? Thoughts of the future?

In the end, she had decided the wink was pure Cyril, another sign of his usual lighthearted self—a self that was capable of being just a bit unruly.

Like me, a bit unruly, Katherine thought, deciding she was glad she'd been given that wink after all. It reminded her that Cyril waited for her when all this nonsense was behind them.

Despite best intentions, Katherine's thoughts wandered back to Lord Benjamin. She could not argue that she and he had accomplished something of what they'd set out to do this evening: letting London know about their supposed intent to wed. On the drive home, Lord Benjamin had made it clear he intended to do more to be sure that impression was firmly established.

"I thought of something public to attend tomorrow, during the day," he had offered.

"What is that?" Katherine had asked.

"To see Fallen Angel race at Epsom Downs. Would you like that?"

She had been careful to keep her gaze fixed open, for she feared if she blinked, tears would form and fall down her cheeks. He was offering to take her to see her horse again? The one she'd longed to keep? The one that had slipped away before Katherine had possessed any reason to think she might soon achieve her dream of training racers?

"I would like that. Very much," she managed to say. He probably had not meant to offer something so wanted, so sweet—but he had.

He glanced at her again. "It is just a horse. Just a race."

She pursed her lips, any feelings of gratitude fading. She wondered if he knew what it was to really care for anything outside himself, and decided it was unlikely.

"I would like to go to Epsom Downs all the same," she had said from between tight lips.

"I will come for you at one o'clock," he'd said.

So what if his offer had been made for some reason other than merely to please her? He probably had no idea how much Fallen Angel had meant to her. How could he know that Katherine had once hoped the mare would be the first block in the horse-racing stud she'd dreamed for years of someday building? He could not know.

All the same, she was delighted she would get to see the mare run, even if Fallen Angel was no longer owned by her. It would be gratifying if the horse raced well, a vindication of her eye for judging horseflesh.

Katherine sighed again, and stood away from the window, reaching to pull from her hair the pins that held the yellow ribbon in place. For just a flash of a moment she recalled Miss Violet Mansell's long blond tresses, so cleverly arranged and pinned beneath her bonnet. She also recalled the admiring look Lord Benjamin had given her.

Katherine turned to her looking glass, and was a little surprised to see a small frown sitting upon her wearied features. "Being betrothed is exhausting," she said to her reflection. It was less exhausting being betrothed to Cyril, even working to keep it a secret, she silently added.

Her reflection regarded her, and stuck out its tongue.

She gave a small, self-deprecating laugh, and decided that, in reality, it was fighting against the situation she was presently in that was so wearying.

"Then stop fighting. It will only last for a few weeks. You might as well try to have what enjoyment the situation allows," she advised herself.

Her reflection lost the small frown, and nodded in agreement.

Chapter 11

"**P**apa has offered the use of his coach, as that will sit five comfortably," Miss Oakes told Benjamin when he came the next afternoon to take her to Epsom Downs.

Benjamin nodded, a quick glance telling him the other occupants of the coach would be Miss Oakes's three brothers.

Jeremy and Lewis were a few years older, and Mercer born later in the same year as Benjamin; it was hardly a strain for the coach-jostled party of five to find common matters to discuss as they rolled toward the racing course. In fact, Benjamin soon came to the conclusion that Miss Oakes's brothers were all fellows of obvious goodwill—and then he wondered if their goodwill would yet extend toward him if they knew he was never going to marry their sister. *He* certainly would not mention the fact.

Already used to the more casual manner the entire Oakes clan seemed inclined to follow, nonetheless Benjamin did not know quite what to make of it when their driver pulled the coach beside the racing course rail, and the Oakeses all then went into a flurry of activity. From the basket they had brought along, Jeremy brought out quill and ink, Lewis produced a folded collection of news sheets, and Mercer brought out a largish journal that he handed to his sister, along with an ink-stained apron.

Benjamin stared, a little nonplused and a little fascinated, as Miss Oakes donned the apron, a full one that covered most of her gown, and her brothers proceeded to read the racing information aloud, practically shouting over each other. Mercer held the bottle of India ink, in which Miss Oakes frequently dipped her quill, in order to scratch quick notes into the now-open journal on her lap.

"On this horse in the third race? Devil's Pride?" Lewis said, glancing up from a news sheet to his sister.

"Out of Devil's Folly and Much Heart," Miss Oakes responded at once, without looking up from her notes.

Benjamin blinked in surprise, for Miss Oakes was exactly right regarding the horse's sire and dam.

She shook her head. "Bad choice, I fear. He will be in the rear of the field. He ran Friday last. He has no stamina for two races within a week."

"Sanctuary?" Lewis inquired with a doubting grimace, pressing a scrap of paper to his leg and snitching his sister's quill long enough to jot a quick note there.

"Sanctuary? Out of Scourge and Maybelle. Ran five times, all in Ireland. Brought over by the Earl of Donbury. Has a new jockey, Sam Dean—but Mr. Dean is good and his horses tend to respond well for him. Sanctuary's history is a bit uneven." Miss Oakes gave a little shrug. "Good for a long shot, but at no more than a third place finish, I would wager."

Jeremy looked up and grinned sheepishly as he caught Benjamin's eye. "Do not mind us," he said with a crooked grin. "We are deciding how to place our wagers. I know it's not very ladylike and perhaps we ought not encourage, er, this, er, activity . . . thing is, Katie's very good at predicting. She really is. You'll see."

Apparently Lewis required no more input from his sister, for he scurried out of the coach and skipped off with paper scraps fluttering, in pursuit of an oddsmaker.

"What did the Repository say about the fifth race again?" Jeremy asked Mercer in a low voice.

"I am writing, not deaf or dumb. Ask me," Miss Oakes said without looking up from her notes.

"I was trying to leave you alone. But since you are inclined to be curt, I shan't mind my manners either. So who'll show in the fifth?"

"Tempest to win, Windblower to place, and Lasdun to show," Miss Oakes rattled off without glancing up, her quill pressed to her lips as she considered some facet of her notes.

"Lasdun it is," Jeremy said, then also climbed down from the carriage.

Miss Oakes finished making her notation, blew on the fresh

ink, then closed her journal. Her lips were still pursed from blowing when she looked up to once more observe Benjamin, the shape of her mouth reminding him he had once kissed those lips—and had enjoyed it far more than he ever would have expected.

"The Repository?" he asked, one eyebrow lifting high.

"'Tis her nickname," Mercer, sitting next to Benjamin, supplied. "'Cause she remembers everything. She's like a walking repository of information, you see."

"Charming."

"How much did Katie tell you to put on Fallen Angel?" Mercer asked Benjamin as he recapped the bottle of ink.

"She did not tell me anything. I chose for myself how much to wager."

"Oh." Mercer looked dubious. "Well then, how much?"

"One pound. To place," Benjamin answered. *One pound too many,* he thought sourly. Earlier in the day, he had pawned a set of carved deities he'd brought back from his one and only voyage to Jamaica and his second best pair of Hessians, more than doubling his purse's weight by adding almost three pounds to it. He'd known he could hardly attend the race and not wager on his own horse, so he'd found a way to raise the necessary blunt.

Actually, he *longed* to make at least the one wager on her, while she still belonged to him. Even if he lost the pound, he knew there would be a day when he would look back and be glad he had backed her. He'd know that for one day he had played at the gentleman's game of owning a racehorse, bought by money no one else had earned but him.

"I am glad you did not wager on her to win," Miss Oakes said. "She has great potential, of course, but she's untried in paying races. Where a purse is concerned, sometimes the jockey begins to communicate all the wrong signals to a horse. Fallen Angel might be uneven to start, but I dare to hope her record will even out with experience."

"Truly?" Benjamin asked. If Miss Oakes noticed any skepticism in his tone, she did not indicate as much.

"Although, I must say," she went on, "if you were to run her at the Helmman in Kent three days hence, I would expect her to outdistance the other horses likely to appear there. Helmman's is far enough in the country that it tends to attract more of the new or minor racers. I predict Fallen Angel will not long be among that set."

She spoke with such utter confidence—like a man, but in womanly tones. It was disconcerting, and hardly feminine. If she had shown this . . . acumen in front of other gentleman, it was no wonder that she had been dubbed a hoyden. "Blue-stocking" almost hit the mark as well, although her passion was less for Greek and Mathematics than the unlikely matter of racing horses.

Benjamin felt his mouth thin with annoyance, but he was not entirely sure why. Miss Oakes's intense study of horses and how they placed in their races was irksome, yes . . . but he sensed that most of his restlessness really came from *dallying* like this. He ought to be spending his waking hours seeking employment, not discussing races.

He'd given his whole morning over to calling on his brother's London solicitor, and beginning the promised process of readying Miss Oakes's land. Only to learn the land that was promised to come from her papa as dowry could not be touched, as he'd more than half expected despite the betrothal agreement.

"When you are married, the land is under your control then of course," the solicitor had told him, and gone on to explain that until that time only the land directly inherited by Miss Oakes via her grandmama could be altered in any way, and that only to make improvements.

So he had begun what he could. A steward was to be hired to oversee that drainage paths were dug and a new receiving pond built. And if there was to be any hope of growing feed for horses from Miss Oakes's own crops, as a careful list from her had specified, they would have to plant before the summer was too far advanced.

Benjamin had felt a small, nagging scruple at informing the solicitor that all costs were to be directed to Sir Albert Oakes—but that gentleman had said it was to be so. Her father had told Miss Oakes she could pay him back "when you turn a profit," and if his daughter had seen the doubt in his eyes, it had unquestionably only served to double her desire to prove him wrong.

Expending so much energy on the lady's business and not his

own was what had really provoked Benjamin's sour mood, of course, but knowing that and being able to put it aside were two different things. He had made her a promise, so he would fulfill it, but that did not mean he had to pretend to like it. When Fallen Angel's race, the fourth, had been run, he would insist they return to London. He had work to find. He did not need to be sitting here, idle, wagering money he could ill afford—and being told how to wager it by a mere slip of a girl who liked to pretend she had an expertise at calling winners.

"I must walk," Benjamin declared suddenly, the coach suddenly feeling too close a confine. He remembered his manners enough to belatedly offer, albeit reluctantly, "Would you join me, Miss Oakes?"

She put aside her journal. "I would like it indeed, Lord Benjamin."

He'd rather hoped she would say no, but was starting to realize that Miss Oakes was unlikely to ever do what *he* would have her do.

All the same, as they strolled along parallel to the carriages and people lining the railing that surrounded the racing course—exchanging nods with those willing to acknowledge them—Benjamin felt his tension lessen. After all, he was used to far worse than simple snubs—he was used to being called a madwoman's son, and his own captain had called him a "coward and a thief" when he had accepted responsibility for the crime he had not committed. What was a turn of the head or the presentation of someone's back against those more egregious insults?

"I am sorry," Miss Oakes said at his side, with a wistful smile hovering around her lips. She had donned gloves to cover her ink-stained fingers, her right hand now lightly on his arm. She had left her apron in the coach, once again revealing her gown of fetching palest green, almost white in the sunlight, which looked fresh against the far darker green of the grass at their feet.

"Sorry? For—?"

"That my character is so contrary that half of London offers me the Cut Direct. It cannot be pleasant for you."

He did not respond at once. Miss Oakes? Taking the blame for the snubs they received onto her own shoulders? And not with a martyred air, or a great gnashing of teeth, or tears of self-pity, but only a simple apology.

"Alas," he said, pushing aside his own ill humor and striving for lightness, "my own contrary nature has offended the other half of London. How shall we go on?"

She looked up, searching his face, and then she gave a small laugh, an inviting sound. "I suppose there is nothing to be done but to separate, each to their half of London," she offered, tilting her head so that the brim of her chip bonnet managed to shade her eyes from the afternoon sun, but which left her mouth sun-kissed.

A strange pang went through Benjamin, some curious emotion that tangled with a sudden urge to lean down and kiss her upturned mouth in imitation of the sun's caress.

He came to a halt, the impulse filling his thoughts, blotting out a reasoning voice that wondered if there would be much scandal if they shared a public kiss, here in the sunlight.

Miss Oakes stopped beside him, her body turning toward him in that invitational manner he'd swear she scarce conceived, let alone did on purpose.

"Lord Benjamin—?" she started to inquire, but her words stopped abruptly. She stared up at him, and he down at her, and for some absurd reason it felt entirely right to take her face between his two hands. He did it because he wanted to and be damned the reason. He wanted to know if he had imagined the sweetness of her kiss, and suddenly he knew he meant to find out.

He slowly lowered his mouth, giving her time to retreat if she wished, but she remained still, a questioning look deep in her brown eyes. He brought his lips to hers, meaning only to lightly press there.

Her mouth yielded to his, and with a sinking feeling that ought to have been despair but was something else entirely, he stopped thinking and only felt. Felt anew that she had been kissed before; then he longed to kiss her in such a manner that all other kisses would be forgotten by her. What had been meant to be only a mere brushing of lips, grew deeper, hungrier. It sent a shiver not only to the nape of his neck but also down his spine and spread in his belly as a kind of warmth.

A horn blew in the distance, announcing the first race was about to run. Abruptly a sense of time and place came back to him. He stepped back, his hands springing from her face as though she had suddenly gone aflame and burned him. He just managed to swallow a gasp.

"I . . . It is my turn to say I am sorry," he managed, his voice a touch unsteady. "But I . . . this makes the betrothal look true enough . . ." His voice trailed away as he tried to read her reaction from the wide-eyed stare she gave him.

"Oh," she said on little more than a breath. "Oh yes, I see." She gave a quick, self-conscious glance around. "I think it worked to a nicety."

Benjamin looked up, seeing many eyes turned their way. He swallowed hard. "I hope I did not embarrass you."

"No!" she said, turning away quickly in the direction of the coach. "No, but . . . I would like to sit down now." She turned at once, and did not look to see if he followed.

He *had* embarrassed her—devil take him, he'd embarrassed himself. Not five minutes earlier he'd been filled with animosity toward her, letting her know in how he moved and spoke that her little pastime annoyed him. He'd been annoyed that she was so relentlessly singular in her behavior. Too, that he'd been forced to conduct her business. That he was forced to use up precious time, time better spent seeking employment.

Then his annoyance had given way to something else, to the point where he had kissed her in a field, before an audience of hundreds. Worst of all, kissing her anew had not realized his hope that their first kiss had been but a fluke of sensation and reaction. He would swear his nape and his fingers and toes were tingling—*tingling,* for pity's sake.

Benjamin shoved his hands in his coat pockets, trying to ignore the sensation. He just managed to resist the impulse to kick out at a clump of grass—but he'd be hanged before he'd go back to the coach, to sit across from Miss Oakes and her damnably kissable mouth.

He spun in the opposite direction, moving his thumbs to reside in the empty watch pockets of his waistcoat in a falsely casual pose, and strode as quickly as he could, without actually running, away from Miss Oakes.

Miss Violet Mansell was prettier than Miss Oakes, Benjamin decided not an hour later as he smiled across the table between them. *She has a larger dowry, too,* he thought as he glanced from Miss Mansell to her escort for this race day, Mr. Cullman.

At Benjamin's right sat Miss Oakes, thanking Mr. Cullman for inviting them to join him and Miss Mansell for refreshments beside the race railing.

"It was my pleasure, Miss Oakes," Cullman said, smiling at her, using that smile to flirt with her again, to seduce her by degrees. "These race days are always so tediously dull between runnings. The least we can do is refresh ourselves with a little wine, a little bread, and thou. Your delightful company, that is."

Miss Oakes smiled and blushed, and Benjamin forced his features to remain politely blank, not to register the tendril of repugnance that snaked through his belly.

He might not have thought to bring wine—even if he could have afforded it, let alone the servants to serve it as Cullman had arranged—but Benjamin knew he served Miss Oakes a better dish: He was here to be sure the lady did not end up as the final sweet on Cyril's plate this day.

As he crossed his arms in something close to a pout, Benjamin reflected that he could refuse to eat or to sit at Cullman's table—but then he would just be hungry, thirsty, and neglectful of Miss Oakes. It did not matter that she apparently had decided she was not speaking with him—since she had not said one more word to him since he had kissed her—only that they were presenting the false front to which they had agreed.

She did, however, find plenty to say to Mr. Cullman, admiring his alfresco table, the china from which they ate, and the fine wine that they drank.

Benjamin stifled a sneer, and turned to Miss Mansell. "My horse is running in the next race," he informed her.

"Is it?" Miss Mansell appeared genuinely interested. "What is its name? Is it the favorite?"

"No, not the favorite. A two-year-old. A mare, called Fallen Angel."

"Oh my." Her eyes widened. "A somewhat wicked name, is it not? Have you wagered on her?"

"Of course," he answered, just as the horn blew to announce the race.

"Oh dear! I am too late to place a wager as well." Miss Mansell pouted prettily.

Benjamin shrugged. "Well, perhaps you have saved yourself some coins."

To his surprise, he was mistaken: As Miss Oakes clapped her hands and murmured encouraging, urging cries of "Go, my beauty! Oh, fly, Angel, you have the heart for it!" Fallen Angel came in second, only a neck's length behind the winner.

He'd won eight pounds, Benjamin realized in stunned gratification. On his own horse, the horse whom he had briefly hoped he might keep. And the eight pounds was only the beginning, because there was a purse provided for the first two horses in the race—thirty pounds for the winner, and ten for second place. Eighteen pounds! It was enough, with care, to see Benjamin through until quarter day, even minus the percentage that went to the horse's rider and stabler.

He turned to Miss Oakes, who returned his stunned gaze with a delighted one of her own. "I told you I did not think she would finish in the field!" she crowed, her brown eyes dancing.

"Good guess," he said, still a little numb from the stroke of good fortune. It was difficult to concede Miss Oakes had been exactly right—even after she'd done so well in calling the first three races. She'd told her brothers to wager on the winner in the first race, had missed calling the winner in the second—but only by the length of an equine nose—and named the three who won, placed, or showed in the third race, albeit reversing the last two.

To his surprise, Miss Oakes took no offense at his flat tone. "That's all it ever is, of course, a good guess," she agreed. "But there is a kind of science at work here, too, you must realize. Patterns, and statistics, and calculation of age, experience, training, timing, health of the animal . . ." He must have been staring at her, for her voice faded away and she ducked her head for a long moment.

"Well, she won," she went on in a more subdued manner. "And she will win again, I feel sure." Her enthusiasm could not wane for long, however. "Oh, do say you will send her to Helmman's!"

"Perhaps," he said, even though he'd already half hoped he might somehow manage to pay the entry fee for Helmman's. After all, how could the horse earn anything toward its keep if it did not run?

Now he could afford the fee—not to mention his own rent—and yet he said "perhaps" simply to vex Miss Oakes. He knew he was being contrary, but eating from Cullman's dishes seemed to have put him in a perverse mood.

"Now all the excitement is behind us, I find I would like to stroll for a bit," Miss Mansell suggested, looking directly at Benjamin.

"Oh, er, may I escort you?" Benjamin asked, as manners insisted he must. Miss Mansell accepted with a smile as he wondered how he might stroll and yet still manage to keep Cullman from flirting all the more with Miss Oakes.

To Benjamin's relief, Miss Oakes said she would also like to stroll, and Cullman offered his arm. They ended with a space between the two couples as they strolled, allowing for privacy in conversation, but Benjamin made sure Miss Oakes went before him and was ever in sight.

As they walked, speaking of the crowd and the races already run, they also stopped now and again to chat with other racegoers. It was impossible to miss that Miss Mansell's presence on Benjamin's arm created a noticeable shift. Those who had snubbed Miss Oakes before, now turned to greet Miss Violet Mansell. They might still cast wary glances at Benjamin, but they greeted him with nods or small curtsies, and introductions were made. All to the good, especially in the arena of employment for Benjamin, who could only stand to profit from a widening circle of acquaintances.

Miss Mansell, for one, seemed to approve of him. She placed both hands upon his arm, one draped over the other, the posture necessitating she walk nestled near his side. She did not fit against him in the same unaware but intimate way Miss Oakes did, but that could hardly be counted a fault. In fact, there was not much about Miss Mansell to be faulted.

She was pretty, lovely even, with her blond hair and blue eyes. If her slender figure could not rival Miss Oakes's fuller, curvier shape, it was still not a figure to be overlooked. At least she did not spout nonsense about numerical patterns and race performances, nor carry a large tome about, filled with facts that could only be considered useless to a young woman.

Not useless, Benjamin had to correct himself, *not to Miss*

Oakes, who means to breed and sell horses—howsoever foolish such an endeavor must be reckoned.

When he and Miss Mansell approached the table to which Cullman and Miss Oakes had already returned, it was to find Miss Oakes's brothers gathered around their sister, asking which horse to wager on in the fifth race.

"Really, gentlemen, this will not do," Benjamin said in a low voice. He glanced around, hoping others were not so keenly aware of Miss Oakes's "pastime" as he was—no thanks to her brothers. "Enough of racing for today. I propose we return to the City."

"There are two more races set to be run!" Lewis cried.

"All the same. I will collect the purse Fallen Angel won, and speak with my horse's trainer and jockey, and then I wish to leave."

"Katherine?" Mercer made the inquiry but all three brothers looked to her.

She nodded. "I am content to go home soon." Her manner and her voice both lacked the liveliness she'd shown earlier when she was updating her racing journals.

Her brothers groaned and Lewis kicked at the railing, only to yelp in pain, but all three of them ceased to argue the matter. Benjamin felt his brows lift in surprise, for Miss Oakes was unruly and undisciplined in self-restraint, but he had never realized before that she also had a kind of *presence* to her, call it an assurance, one that obviously held sway over her three older brothers.

Benjamin collected his purse and winnings, spoke with the trainer and the jockey, and paid them their percentage. After a hesitation, he gave the trainer the entry fee and instructed him to run Fallen Angel at Helmman's in Kent, with the same jockey, who happily agreed.

After all, Benjamin was not a fool. Only a fool would ignore the evidence of his eyes and ears. He had heard Miss Oakes name the likely horses who had indeed come across the finish line foremost; he had seen her brothers' rapt attention when she spoke on the horses; he had seen their purses expand, stuffed with the banknotes they had won. He may not think Society would approve of Miss Oakes's skill, but even though he had tried, he could no longer deny it existed.

"You have the oddest look on your face," Mercer said as Benjamin stepped up last into the coach. "As if you're smiling and scowling all at once."

Benjamin was tempted to put out his tongue—gadzooks, but this Oakes clan was having a poor influence on his manners!— but instead he settled for a grunt and for studiously staring out the window, which was to say avoiding Miss Oakes's gaze.

Chapter 12

A week later, Katherine was grabbed by the hand and yanked close by Lord Benjamin. He made the move seem as if it were part of the dance in which they were engaged, but actually it was to pull her close enough to hear his snarled whisper. "Do not dance again with Cullman."

"I dance with whom I please," Katherine hissed back.

"It is too soon for our breakup."

"Who says?"

"Good God, woman, can you not be compliant in just one matter, one that favors *you*?" he replied, his eyes a snapping blue fire.

"It favors you as well," came her quick response just before she straightened for the next movement.

"*You* are the one who needs time in which to have her cottage and lands readied. I need time in which to get it done," he pointed out, still in that hissed whisper, as they passed each other in a move that left them on opposite sides of where they'd started. He had passed her deftly, too, for Katherine suspected it had looked more as if he had tried to plant a kiss on her cheek than it had looked like an excuse for a hotly whispered reminder.

She pursed her lips and finished the dance without exchanging another word with him, vexed because he was right. He had probably long settled his wager that he could be betrothed before dawn; he presumably had no more need of her company. Katherine, on the other hand, needed the length of a month to have any hope of having her land ready before she could claim it upon her birthday. He was right, curse him for it.

At least he had reminded her that she had something she'd been meaning to say to him. "Lord Benjamin," she said as they exchanged the ending bow and curtsy of the dance, "may I talk privately with you for a moment?"

"Oh, *can* you spare a moment away from Cullman's side?"

She wanted to slap him, but that would hardly give the impression they were delighted with one another. "If you can spare one away from Miss Mansell," she retorted.

Lord Benjamin scowled at her. "I hope you are not saying I have been remiss in my duty to you, in my paying polite attention to Miss—"

"I shan't waste much of your time," Katherine interrupted crisply. Whether he did or did not flirt to excess with the woman was not her concern.

Once they had retreated to a corner, she opened her reticule and took out a piece of folded parchment. "That is a confirmation from the solicitor of all that you have had done for my property." She swallowed her annoyance, and gazed directly up at him. "I just wanted to thank you, my lord. Papa would not have done anything I asked of him concerning my property, out of meaning well and out of wanting to keep me in his home, I am afraid. He still sees me as a little girl, and he tries too hard to protect me."

"Not very successfully," Lord Benjamin pointed out as he returned the list to her.

Katherine felt her lips thin, as if to echo the thinning of her patience with this man, but she nodded all the same. "No, I suppose not."

Lord Benjamin gazed down at her, and shook his head on a sigh. "Were I your father, I would not think you old enough to manage a cottage and a venture on horsebreeding either. Your age aside, a woman alone has no protection. And who will buy the horses you hope to breed, Miss Oakes, assuming the land can be made to support them? Who will turn to a . . . an *unusual* female when there are reputable men throughout the land who can supply worthy horses?"

Katherine looked away. "I know it will be difficult. But perhaps I will marry. My husband can represent the business side of things, while I tend to the labor."

Lord Benjamin shook his head again. "Your horses had best all be winners, Miss Oakes, at least at first. You've no room for average horses—just one will kill your dream."

She straightened her shoulders. "At least then I will have had my dream for a short while. That is to be preferred to never even trying to fulfill it, surely?"

Something crossed his features, understanding perhaps, or empathy. In that moment, his pleasant face acquired another quality beyond physical comeliness. It took Katherine a moment to realize it was the look her brothers *used* to have on their faces way back when she had been allowed to accompany them and walk among the horses at the races. Something precious and rare. It was the face of camaraderie, of fellow feeling, even call it friendship.

"Yes, Miss Oakes," Lord Benjamin said, now without amusement or irritation in his tone, but only simple acceptance. "It is to be preferred. I accept your thanks, even though I was only doing as I'd promised I would."

Katherine looked down at the floor, then at the walls and the crowd, anywhere that she might avoid his gaze, for she felt the prickle of tears behind her eyes and she was loath to have them spill forth. All he had said was that he understood she must strive after her dream, and here she was on the verge of weeping. *Peagoose,* she chided herself.

A few blinks dispelled the unshed tears and she allowed herself one deep breath to help restore her poise. "Not everyone does as they promise, you know. I think I half expected you to . . . not comply."

"So when I told you I was a gentleman, you did not believe me."

"No."

He laughed. "I know there is much between us that annoys one another, but I have to say I rather admire your honest answers. I may not like them, but I admire them."

There it was again, that flash of fellowship between them. It was enough to make Katherine's blood race from her head to her toes, warming her all over.

Heads turned their way.

"There, everyone is staring at us, and you are laughing as though pleased with me. I think we have corrected any other impression we may have given tonight."

"But you are nearly scowling. People will think I suggested something untoward."

"People must know you better than I thought."

Lord Benjamin lifted his eyebrows, not quite grinning, and offered her his arm. "Another dance? I must keep up with Mr. Cullman, after all."

His words reminded her of the other man, the one he'd just recently been scolding her not to dance with again. He had no right, of course, to tell her anything about how she must behave . . . but, truth was, she *did* need to be at least a little circumspect. Cyril tended to push her, make her go beyond proper boundaries . . . and it was flattering. His almost constant attention—when he was not at Miss Mansell's side—reminded her she was wanted. Katherine knew she let Cyril take up too much of her time, and knew she had to force herself to linger at Benjamin's side if Cyril were in the room.

She would have to be more firm with Cyril in the future. After all, a week had already gone by, and the next three would not take long. This week, in fact, had flown by. It had not been nearly so dreadful as she'd feared. There were worse—far worse—companions than Lord Benjamin, she had to concede.

She agreed to dance again with her pretend fiancé, somewhat relieved to learn from the tunings of the musicians that it was not to be a waltz. The waltz was a rather shockingly intimate dance, with man facing woman and their clothes brushing together, and Katherine never quite knew whether to gaze into her partner's eyes or not.

Thankfully it was another country dance in which they partook, twining among a set of six other dancers. There was nothing intimate in the dance beyond the touching of hands, and Katherine and Lord Benjamin danced it in wordless accord—but all the same she felt a shadow of relief when it was over and she could give her hand to any other gentleman besides her false fiancé.

She was not quite sure how to explain the tingling that seemed to linger in her hand long after his touch had left hers—nor why that tingling had not assaulted her after Cyril had held her hand during their minuet. But then another gentleman claimed a dance with her, and she found she was enjoying her evening, and decided enjoying herself was ever so much more pleasant than trying to comprehend the incomprehensible.

Chapter 13

Four evenings later, Katherine spied her supposed fiancé where he waited behind a screen, and had to bite back a smile at the sight of him. Not that he looked any more ridiculous than the other three gentlemen also in plumed helms and abbreviated aprons that had been painted to resemble Roman breastplates, worn incongruously over their waistcoats and shirts. They whispered among themselves, obviously anxious about the performance they were about to give.

Their host was Sir Oliver Pearson, whose penchant for the theater had led him to propose an evening of *tableaux vivant,* with the unusual addition that they would be performed by males only and must include song.

"I do not know which are more entertaining," Katherine whispered to Miss Irving, "the good performances or the poor ones."

"Oh, the poor ones, I think!" her chaperone replied at once. "Although I do hope Mr. Softon is aware he was on a different key than everyone else in the Neptune tableau. I should hate to think he thought he was harmonizing!"

Katherine smothered a giggle with a gloveless hand, for after the first tableau—some odd bit about hounds and foxes in which the costumes had made it unclear which was which—Sir Oliver had pronounced the ladies' praise not sufficient, so that Katherine and most of the other ladies had removed their gloves in order to clap more loudly.

Mrs. Glinsbury had gone so far as to cast one of her gloves "in praise" at Sir Oliver's feet when he sang a solo piece about King Henry VIII. Even he was not entirely sure if the gesture was meant as a compliment. "Am I to gag m'self?" he'd asked

Mrs. Glinsbury, only to receive more, and louder, applause, to which he offered an ironic bow.

Now Lord Benjamin and the other three suffering pseudo-Romans marched out from behind the screen. Lord Benjamin cast Katherine a quick glance, filled with tribulation, and raising a ripple of laughter from the observers. He crossed to seat himself at the pianoforte.

Lord Benjamin played while the other three sang. The tune was an old drinking song whose tune everyone knew, but the gentlemen had rewritten the words. They sang all about going to war, and blood, and dying for the glory of Rome, with at least as much verve as tune. They were roundly applauded when they finished with a thumping of their wooden swords against their breastplates, even if the sound was a dull whump against cloth instead of a ringing clang.

Lord Benjamin returned to Katherine's side after he was divested of his costume, his charcoal coat now resumed in obvious relief. He lifted a hand in thanks at the "well done, Lord Benjamin" comments that were thrown his way as he took his seat in the audience.

"You did not sing," Katherine commented over the sounds of the next group of gentlemen—cavaliers, to judge by their motley gathering of oversized hats—assembling.

"You would not care to hear my singing," he said with a rueful grin. "You could say I sang like a toad, except it would be unkind to the toad."

Katherine laughed and put her gloveless hand on his arm, half leaning in toward him, in a small silent scold as one does with a friend who has made one laugh when one ought to be whispering. Lord Benjamin looked down at her hand, went very still for a moment, then casually covered it with his own. He turned at once toward the performance, leaving Katherine to wonder rather breathlessly how she must take back her bare hand, but that she did not really want to move it. *It would look awkward, unnatural, unaffectionate,* she told herself, and left her hand under the warmth that spread from his.

She tried to concentrate on the tableau—yet again an inappropriate term since the gentlemen were staging a singing sword fight filled with swashbuckling and leapings about—but her attention kept focusing on her hand under Lord Benjamin's—and the fact that Cyril was not present at Sir Oliver's affair tonight.

Had Cyril not been invited? The First Beau? Or was this too common an affair for his taste? Could he be ill, or simply occupied elsewhere?

Although she had determined she ought not to depend on it so, Katherine had become used to Cyril's presence, his personality a counterweight to that of Lord Benjamin's. One was so handsome as to be beautiful; the other was handsome, too, but more quietly so.

To be honest with herself, she knew she was confused as to how both could be attractive, yet so many miles apart in their look and demeanor.

She wanted to hate Lord Benjamin for the situation he had placed her in—but just when she thought she would gladly condemn him to eternal flames, he would say something kind, do something thoughtful, or give her a sheepish grin from underneath a mock-Roman helm, and it became difficult to keep hold of her annoyance. Truth was, the man had a certain measure of charm when he was not being blustery, demanding, or contrary.

For instance, she had learned he had a pleasant laugh, almost as charming as Cyril's. Cyril laughed a great deal, which was to Katherine's mind a primary facet of his attractiveness—but she had to admit Lord Benjamin had an infectious laugh of his own. Even his grin was catching, perhaps because it was only offered when something truly struck him as amusing or ironic.

And there was that one thing she could say for Lord Benjamin, over Cyril: Lord Benjamin's kiss was superior. She had given the matter some thought—more than a little, after Lord Benjamin had kissed her a second time, there in the field beside Epsom Downs. As she'd lain in bed of a night, memories had returned, comparisons had been evaluated.

She'd come, rather against her will, to an honest conclusion: One kiss was not like another. Even though logic said they could not be much different—they could. Cyril's mouth was . . . wetter, hungrier, less gentle, and yet somehow demanding. Katherine ought to come away from Cyril's kiss all breathless and shaken . . . yet it was Lord Benjamin's kisses that had made her tremble.

Cyril had kissed her again, just last night, dancing her away

from Lord Benjamin, out of Lady Danielson's soiree for a quick
tryst on their hostess' balcony. But perhaps it was not fair to
look at that quickly exchanged peck, because they'd been
forced to flee the balcony when others of seemingly similar inclination had invaded it as well.

"It is not yet time for me to be seen growing away from Lord
Benjamin," Katherine had whispered to Cyril, turning her head
and slipping her hand free from his so that what would have
been another kiss had gone wide of her cheek, let alone her
mouth.

She frowned, remembering that her mouth had not longed
for more of his last night—but, in all fairness, she had been
concerned at being caught out. Her reluctance had nothing to do
with the quality of Cyril's kisses, or, well, perhaps just the tiniest bit. . . .

Technique, it was all about technique—like learning to ride a
horse. Yes! Cyril was a fine horseman, so there was no reason
to think that marriage and a word or two suggested by her
might not also make of him a fine kisser.

Katherine closed her eyes, then shook her head, forbidding
herself to think about kisses, not here, not with Lord Benjamin
touching her ungloved hand. She opened her eyes and was surprised to see pirates now filled the tableau area set up at one end
of Sir Oliver's ballroom.

"Would you care for something to drink?" Lord Benjamin
asked her, and she suspected it was the second time he had
asked, while her thoughts had been busily tumbling.

"Please. Ratafia would be fine."

He rose to fetch the liqueur, his hand sliding away from hers.
For a moment cool air touched her hand's unprotected skin,
making her wish his hand back, but a moment's further thought
had her pulling on her gloves.

When he did not return at once, she cast a glance about, finding him lingering at the table filled with refreshments. Standing
before him was Miss Mansell, once again dressed in violet, but
this was an evening gown, cut very low over her bosom. Lord
Benjamin smiled at the young woman. He must have offered to
fill her glass, for Miss Mansell handed it to him as she proceeded to chat quietly with him.

Katherine watched Lord Benjamin out of the corner of her

eye, and tried to see him as Miss Mansell might. How would he seem to Katherine if she had met him with nothing between them, no tiresome wagers to cloud her impressions?

He was physically attractive, commanding a second glance by the width of his shoulders, although he was not so striking as Cyril. Lord Benjamin's pale blue eyes made her search for an adequate word to describe them (*"heavenly blue"* came to mind), and his hair was the mixed hues of a sunlit wheat field. It had grown, now tending to wave at his temples and over his ears. He was not the Adonis that Cyril was, but Lord Benjamin was a fine-looking man.

Appearance aside, if Katherine had just met Lord Benjamin with no betrothal or complication between them, he would still bear the tattered reputation he possessed. He would still be the mercurial creature who teased one moment and brooded the next.

But for all of that, Katherine thought she might have taken a liking to Lord Benjamin had she met him under different circumstances, for despite his reputation he struck her as a man of principles. His principles and hers may stand on opposite sides of the same fence, but opposing views did not necessarily foes make.

She wondered, as she had fleetingly before, how it was that he'd come to sell naval supplies to smugglers. It was difficult to imagine Lord Benjamin deliberately committing a criminal act—could it be that he had, somehow, not known his acts were wrong? Katherine shook her head, for if she knew nothing else about Lord Benjamin, she had come to know in this past week that he was far from thick-witted. What he had done, he had done knowingly. She wondered if she would ever dare to ask him the whys and wherefores of the deed that had changed his life.

She glanced at him again, observing as he returned Miss Mansell's full glass to her, seeing the two of them exchange conversation and smiles. Lord Benjamin looked sober in his charcoal ensemble, but that sobriety in his dress suited him as Cyril's plums and bottle-greens would not. Too, it behooved him to dress with a certain decorum, not flash, because she knew he was seeking employment; he must look reliable, not dashing.

She knew he sought work because on the drive home from Lady Danielson's soiree last night, they had fallen to talking, and Lord Benjamin had revealed one of his goals in coming to London was to find suitable work.

Once he had that, she assumed he would seek out the obvious next goal: a wife.

So why pretend to be betrothed to *her*? To elicit sympathy, that prospective employers must think that a soon-to-be-married man must have an income? Katherine thought it might tend to do the reverse, to convince others that Lord Benjamin had other income if he felt he could afford a bride, but she had not felt it her place to say as much to him. Besides, he surely had other reasons, not least of which was the wager he had formed with someone—Cyril? Papa?—that he could be betrothed before cock's crow. Not that it mattered. His reasons were his own, and Katherine need know nothing of them nor have anything to do with them in a little more than a fortnight.

Lord Benjamin returned with her glass of ratafia and with Miss Mansell on his arm. Katherine exchanged "how do you dos" with Miss Mansell, but then was quickly left to her own devices as Miss Mansell and Lord Benjamin sat beside one another and fell into a running discussion of the tableaux already completed.

Katherine turned to the lady on her right, but Miss Pontefroy still had her back firmly turned to Katherine, as she had since she'd sat down, clearly indicating a disinclination to pursue a deeper acquaintance—although Miss Pontefroy had spoken to Katherine last night when she had stood at the side of the First Beau. Without Cyril at her side tonight, however, Katherine was clearly not deemed worthy of the lady's conversation.

Katherine stifled a sigh, and stood. She saw out of the corner of her eye that Lord Benjamin looked up as she rose, hastening to politely stand as well. Still, by the time Katherine had moved a few steps, Miss Mansell had put her hand on his arm and drawn him to sit once more.

Katherine spied a small group of ladies she knew would include her in their discourse, with or without the First Beau at hand. These ladies were less particular of Katherine's own reputation or at least kinder in their tolerance of it, and she felt a little cheered to be able to cross the room and join them.

Benjamin glanced around the room, as he already had several times, finally spying Miss Oakes standing with a group of ladies who were laughingly helping to organize the puttings on and takings off of costumes and props used by the gentlemen performers. He felt his shoulders relax, and wondered why they had been tense, beyond the obvious fact that Sir Albert would strike his head from his shoulders should any harm come to his daughter, Katherine.

Katherine. It was a beautiful name, suitable for a queen, but, too, soft enough to be whispered in the night.

Too bad the woman does not suit the name, he thought, but then felt a little ashamed, for that was not quite true. Katherine Oakes was fetching enough, with an impish sort of comeliness. Her red hair, curling around her face, made the most of her good cheekbones and excellent mouth . . . but it was not of her appearance that he had truly been thinking. It was her temperament, her approach to life, her deportment. Her brothers had done her no favors by allowing her to run free and unfettered. The world was not used to unfettered women. . . . Benjamin frowned at his own thoughts, balking at his own attempts to cast a set of limitations upon the woman.

He did not like limitations, especially ones that derived from nothing more than tradition or one man's concept of how things should be—his father had been one to impose such limitations. Papa had been harsh with his three sons, so harsh that Gideon had nearly ruined himself by trying with every ounce of his soul to go in exactly the opposite direction their father had set.

Only love, in the end, had saved Gideon, and not even the love of his brothers, but of a stranger come among them, Elizabeth. She had brought tolerance and forgiveness and strength to the house where Gideon resided with her now as his bride, and had pushed aside the old limitations that had bound them all in the past. With her had come hope, and love, and new beginnings, not least of which was the child she now carried.

No, limitations were not to Benjamin's liking. Besides, putting a limitation on Katherine would be like imposing an order to "stay" upon the wind.

Only look at her now. She did her reputation no good by helping to turn a coat's sleeve right side out—but Benjamin would not tell her to stop. She would not care one whit if he told her that this was a labor eschewed by the dandy set, that only the "second tier" of ladies were left to sort the props or bits of costuming. There was not a high flyer among the ladies assisting the gentlemen. Miss Granby had a lisp serious enough to make her difficult to understand over the clamor of a ballroom; and Mrs. Watkins was a widow of little beauty and less fortune; Miss Tarkinton was a pleasant conversationalist but otherwise lacked every social grace such as watercoloring, playing an instrument, or even dancing, making her prospects as a wife rather thin; and Miss Peabody, speaking of thin, was so slender she appeared as if a high wind would carry her away.

Not a one of them shone through with enough beauty, style, fortune, or grandness of birth, and so did what they could to promote themselves through offers of service, goodwill, and that less valued but more worthy attribute know as Christian kindness.

Of course, Miss Oakes would not care, for Miss Oakes had not a single thought in her head of promoting herself on the marriage mart. She hoped to marry Mr. Cullman—and even if she did not, she knew she would still be leaving her father's home, even if it was to live in a swamp. *Her* swamp, she would say with a proud glitter in her eyes.

Miss Oakes, Benjamin decided as he put back his shoulders, could have done worse than to affiliate herself with these, the second-best ladies of the *ton*. The cousins who might get invited to Almack's, but who were not expected to marry from its ranks. The women who actually gave of themselves, through the work of their hands, and so were gazed down upon by those who need never lift a finger, nor think to. These ladies would not promote Miss Oakes's standing, but neither would they be casually cruel to her, having each of them known at least a touch of fate's cruelty themselves.

Then there were the women such as Miss Mansell, accepted everywhere, more decorative than their cousins, with richer or better-born parents. It was from the ranks of the Miss Mansells of this world that Benjamin knew he should marry, had long since determined would bring him and his family name the prestige now lacking, if only he could persuade such a paragon to have him.

He looked again to where Miss Oakes helped an army lieutenant shrug into a patchwork coat perhaps meant to approximate a harlequin figure, saw the two of them exchange a comment and a laugh, frowned ever so slightly, and slowly turned back to face Miss Mansell.

Her face visibly brightened at the return of his attention, and Benjamin could not help but feel flattered. Cullman flirted with this lady, when he was not engaged in trifling with Katherine Oakes's affections, and yet she sought out Benjamin's company whenever they met. Benjamin, preferred to the First Beau?

He acknowledged to himself that a case of infatuation might serve him well here, with this lady whose every attribute outstripped his own. He acknowledged that he should be grateful she gave him two moments of her time despite his empty purse and his tattered name, but all the same he had to suppress a sigh, one that he would have been hard-pressed to explain.

Chapter 14

*A*t least attending all these affairs has not cost me one penny, Benjamin reflected as he crossed yet another ballroom in search of yet another glass of refreshment for a lady. For the third time in as many days he fetched lemonade not for his fiancée, but for Miss Mansell. Miss Oakes had been again swept away from his side by her circle of ladies he thought of as "the second cousins," soon after he and she had arrived at yet another ball, the fifth one in the past two weeks. Miss Oakes had become a bit of a favorite among the second-best level of the *ton*. "The Placers," as the horse-mad Miss Oakes herself might say.

He supposed he ought to count himself among the "Placers," as he had yet to achieve an offer of employment.

Perhaps he should not have paid rent at his bachelor apartment, instead moving into the rubble that had once formed the family residence on Seymour Street. He couldn't help but wonder if he might have had an offer of employment by now if he could have given the superior direction that was Seymour Street. The *appearance* of wealth spoke almost as loudly in Town as did the actual existence of it.

In this morning's search for employment, Benjamin had made the rounds of the colleges he could drive his phaeton to in three hours' time. The effort had resulted in only one housekeeper's assertion, "The headmaster's in Brighton, but expected tomorrow. Come back then, at three."

He would come back. Then, presuming failure there, he would go back to the docks, to see if—a week later than his last appearance there—anyone had decided they needed to hire a new man. He would keep looking. He must.

Benjamin handed Miss Mansell her glass of lemonade, and

wondered if she had any notion of how poor he was. Or if she realized his brother's wife was to have a child, so that Benjamin's chance of ever becoming the Marquess of Greyleigh were almost as thin as was his desire to inherit. Benjamin wished his brother, God willing, would live to see a hundred, and his nephew-to-be as well.

He could not guess what Miss Mansell hoped, but three days of fetching lemonade for the pretty young woman had shown him one thing: No matter that Miss Mansell was "perfect" as a bride for him, he did not want to court her. He did not want to ask her to be his bride, not even when he was free of Miss Oakes.

He was not sure why. Miss Mansell was everything he would have looked for in a helpmeet—but *something* was lacking. Attraction? She was pretty enough. Intellectual connection? She was bright enough. *I do not know what is missing,* Benjamin thought. He only knew it was not there.

As the musicians began tuning, the precursor to the first dance, Miss Mansell gave Benjamin a shy smile, clearly hoping he would ask to share it with her.

First dance. Benjamin looked around for his supposed fiancée, for he ought to share it with Miss Oakes—Katherine, yesterday she had bid him call her Katherine.

"You look like a Ben," she'd said as they'd toured past the paintings for sale at the Royal Academy of Arts.

"Ben?" he had echoed. "I have never been called 'Ben' in my life, always Benjamin."

She'd grinned up at him. "You object to 'Ben'? Why?"

"It sounds . . . simple. Countrified. As though I live in the Colonies, or some such savage place."

"I find it a strong, capable name. Although I like 'Benjamin,' too, my lord."

"Come now, you cannot dub me 'Ben' then revert to calling me 'my lord.' I insist, since we have been betrothed over three weeks now, that in informal moments we must use Christian names. You are to call me Benjamin, without the 'Lord' before it, and I shall call you 'Kate.' Or perhaps 'Katie' as your brothers do," he teased.

"Or you could call me Kitty," Miss Oakes had then suggested, not taking umbrage as he'd expected. "Mama used to call me Kitty."

"Do you remember her?" he had asked, surprised, and aware of the shadow of regret that even now passed momentarily over her features.

"Not really. I can tell from her painting that she was pretty, but what I am really remembering is the stories I've been told."

"And she called you Kitty."

Katherine smiled. "Papa always preferred Kate. I am not particular, as you may have noticed, since I allow my brothers to call me The Repository. Perhaps you should nickname me Reppie," she said, then gave a little laugh.

Benjamin had made an exaggerated face. "I will call you Katherine, and you will call me Benjamin, and then neither of us need offend the ears of the other."

"Very well, Benjamin," she'd said on a crooked but surprisingly engaging grin, and then had proceeded to ask him how his most recent meeting with the solicitor had gone, to which he had happily been able to answer that all went well, that the new pond was nearly dug.

In fact, later this morning more news had come to him on that front, and he now recalled that he had forgotten to tell it to her when he'd come to fetch her up for this ball being held at Lord and Lady Alwell's. He would tell her during the first dance.

Except, she was nowhere in sight.

Miss Mansell's foot had begun to tap beneath the hem of her gown, and her smile had taken on a brittle quality. She clearly awaited an invitation to dance.

"Would you excuse me, please?" Benjamin asked, knowing by the shock in Miss Mansell's eyes that this was not the reaction she'd expected. "I must dance with my fiancée for the first dance," he said, to soften the rejection. He did not, however, wait for Miss Mansell to find her voice, instead turning and moving away, searching the crowd for Miss Oakes's red head.

Benjamin made his way around the assembling dancers, until he was finally able to spy her curls. She stood debating some topic within a group of young bucks. *Good for her,* Benjamin thought, then realized with a start that he had actually approved of Miss Oakes being outspoken. But, why not? Among the five or six bucks gathered around her, it could be that one of them would be charmed by Miss Oakes's outspoken nature—it was possible. At least they would not be misled as to her true personality.

He listened as the group debated the merits of foxhunting— Miss Oakes thought it a cruel sport—and became a little exasperated that the first dance had come and gone before Miss Oakes was able to turn to him with more than a mere acknowledging glance.

"I have more news regarding your property at Meyerley Creek," he told her.

That secured her attention. "Do you?"

He nodded. She moved between two men, to Benjamin's side. He offered her his arm, she placed her hand there, and he led her away from the young men to a quieter spot.

"I got a letter this morning. Now that the pond is dug, they have been able to locate the head of the underground spring that fed the bog. Your steward thinks that some simple digging will redirect the flow more directly to the pond, and then even more of the land will dry out. As he thought, the water always had flow. It was not stagnant, and now he is certain that you will have sufficient water for the horses and the fields you plant, without having to use the well they dug up by the cottage."

"That is wonderful news," she said, her eyes shining.

Another set of dancers were assembling. A glance between them and a nod from Katherine was sufficient for Benjamin, who led her into the set.

Unfortunately, the dance took them apart, two long rows that moved in opposite directions until the movements brought them back together a few minutes later.

"The steward wrote that your roof is nearly repaired as well," Benjamin took the chance to explain. "Then you only lack for fresh plastering, and the house will be habitable. You may move in on your birthday if you like."

"Wonderful! I do wonder if Papa will allow me to take my bed there with me," she said, then looked up with a startled expression. "But what a thing to say!" There were the twin spots of color that so easily bloomed on her cheeks. Exertion might bring out the "apples" on her cheeks, and naturally embarrassment, and even delight. Her cheeks, when she had watched Fallen Angel take second place, had bloomed red with pleasure.

She would hate it, he supposed, but he rather liked it. Besides, to concentrate on her blushes was to divert sudden thoughts of her in bed, her curls lying against her pillow. . . . He pulled his mind back to the moment, frowning at the tenor of his thoughts, as unbidden and unexpected as the kiss he'd taken from her at the racecourse . . . and just as tempting.

"Your papa is not pleased that you are determined to live alone, but barring that I cannot imagine he would begrudge you a few belongings," he said, his voice mostly steady. "Perhaps you should make a list, and ask which of them he would grant you."

"An excellent suggestion."

The dance took them apart again.

"Also, have you thought," he said, when next they stood opposite each other, just keeping a frown from his face and wondering why it tried to form there, "if you were to marry, you could ask your papa to make those belongings a wedding gift to you."

"The gentleman I marry will bring some effects with him, I suppose," Katherine put in. She tilted her head a little on one side, thinking as she danced. "The cottage is not large, only four rooms counting the kitchen at the back. I might not want for so much as I think I do. I wonder if my wardrobe is too large for my, er, bedchamber?"

"I meant to go," Benjamin found himself telling her, "to see for myself. To be sure all was well. Now I really ought to go, so that I can measure the rooms for you."

"Oh, you needn't!" she said, looking discomfited.

"No, no, I really should. I consider it"—he dropped his voice and bowed at the dance's end, saying the last only for her ears—"I consider it part of our bargain. You wanted a livable cottage and arable fields. It is my duty to see that you get what I said would be delivered to you."

She curtsied in her turn. "Thank you, my lord."

"My lord? I thought I was 'Benjamin' to you now."

"We are not in private," she pointed out, smiling and for once not blushing.

"Anything but," he agreed. "Have I said already that we are going to the races again?" He schooled himself not to make a face. "With Miss Mansell and Mr. Cullman." Plans had been made last night, before Benjamin had realized he had no true interest in Miss Mansell's company.

"Lovely," Katherine said, her expression unreadable. He had expected excitement, not this neutral acceptance.

"To see Fallen Angel run again," he thought to add.

Her eyes brightened. "Tomorrow? Oh, I *am* glad."

He nodded, just before she turned to laughingly agree with a uniformed marine who touched her elbow that she had indeed promised him the next dance.

Benjamin watched as the marine led Katherine into the next set, and for a moment regretting having no Miss Mansell at hand, now that he stood here alone and unpartnered.

A glance around the room would be enough to provide another dancing partner, even if some of the ladies made a point of avoiding Benjamin's gaze. One Miss Adamson, one of Miss Oakes's new friends, had no such scruples, however. She happily agreed to give Benjamin a dance. She was no beauty, but she had a kind face, and he soon learned she was accomplished at dancing.

Benjamin smiled down at the lady swaying at his side, and thought that there were worse things to be than a "Placer" . . . and perhaps that was why Miss Mansell had not appealed to him, for she, being a "Winner," would never understand how someone might enjoy a position—and the freedoms to be had there—somewhere below the topmost.

After he had restored Katherine to her father's home, Benjamin was still pondering his position in life as the second son when Mr. Finchley, the manager of his apartments, handed him a sealed missive. Benjamin recognized the script at once. He tore open the seal and quickly scanned the page.

"Not happy news, sir?" Mr. Finchley sounded doubtful.

"I am to call upon my brother," Benjamin said numbly. "He is in London, and he wants to meet my fiancée."

Chapter 15

The Marquess and Marchioness of Greyleigh wanted to meet Katherine, and now she stood before the dismantled pile that was the marquess's London residence.

She knew Benjamin—she was slowly getting used to calling him without the honorific "Lord" attached to his name—had not been eager for the meeting. He'd delayed it by two days, by making a rapid trip to Kent and back again, to view her property there, which he had then declared most adequately prepared. He'd promised he would go—but he could have done so *after* bringing Katherine to meet his brother. Not that she blamed him for wanting a delay; she would not mind one herself.

What did the marquess want? Katherine had said Benjamin must go ahead and tell his brother the truth, because it was only three days to her birthday, and they had already agreed that tonight was the night she would publicly cry off from the betrothal.

Benjamin had shaken his head. "First let us see what he wants with us."

The oddity of meeting a man who was not really going to be her brother-in-law, and doing so in the midst of a crumbled pile of bricks that had once been a house, all made Katherine feel unsettled—in large part because Miss Irving was not at her side.

Her chaperone had left for Kent by mail coach early this morning, to tend to her ailing mother. While Katherine had been a little startled by her father's generosity of spirit in letting Miss Irving leave for at least two weeks in the middle of what was, after all, Katherine's first Season, she had kissed her chaperone on the cheek and bid her best wishes for her mama's health. Papa had declared Lord Benjamin capable of keeping Katherine safe—and here Katherine stood, alone with Benjamin, before a ruined house.

At her side, Benjamin shook his head slightly as he gazed at the house's shell. There was no front door, only a wooden frame where a door had once been.

It was not of the house he spoke, however. "How do you mean to cry off?" he asked quietly, still gazing at the rubble but speaking to Katherine.

"I do not know," she said, her eyebrows lifting. "I had not given it much thought."

"Nothing too dramatic, please," Benjamin said, a pained look on his face, which he could not hold so that it turned into a smile. Still, did the smile look a shade rueful? Why would it? It must be her imagination.

"If the crying off is too elaborate an affair," he went on, "my family will assume I am crushed, and will attempt to whisk me back to Severn's Well to ply me with tea and tisanes. Or worse, with hugs and hearty words about the brightness of the future once I've overcome the storm, et cetera. I'd far, far rather remain in London."

"No hysterics, I promise," she said, trying to echo his light mood, even though she did not feel particularly carefree. "A few glares. A few pouts. Perhaps a tear down my cheek. If I can manage to summon a tear, that is."

"Just one tear? I'd always thought I'd be worth a bucketful, to the right lady."

To the right lady. That was the rub, was it not? Katherine was not that right lady. They both knew that. And tonight would be the night she gave her performance, the night she rid herself of this unwanted fiancé.

She could wish their "scene" had been last night, for then she would not be here today at Benjamin's brother's half-demolished house.

"Do you know how he learned about our supposed betrothal?" Katherine asked, also gazing at the house. Its state of ruin seemed an omen, as if to represent that this interview could not go well. What had brought Benjamin's brother all the way from the west of England? And not just his brother, but the marchioness as well.

"He heard no word of it through me, I can assure you."

She shrugged, looking down at the small reticule she carried, just for somewhere else to look other than his face. "These things get about, even so far afield. But I am sorry. It will prove a trifle awkward for you, I have no doubt." She turned her head to then look up into his face, and it was the first time she could ever remember seeing him care-worn. Angry, yes. Aggravated, certainly, but never before given over to worry.

"Perhaps your brother will disapprove of me," she said on a small laugh. "That would actually make everything easier, when all this does not end in marriage."

Benjamin did not seize on the idea of her unsuitability—instead only shaking his head in denial.

It would have been so simple for him to agree, even to play up her faults. He could have called on his brother by himself, could have told the marquess that Katherine Oakes was a forward, intemperate, heedless creature, with whom he'd made an affiliation only to meet a temporary need. He could have told his brother that she was a nuisance of which he would soon be free.

But he had not. He'd brought her here today, a witness to what he would tell his brother. Unless she was mistaken, unless this was some elaborate ruse and the brother already knew . . . but why then bring her at all?

"What do you mean to say?" she asked softly. "Are we to playact that the betrothal is real?" Katherine asked. The words were not bitter, but she thought perhaps they sounded . . . a little sad? She would not enjoy telling lies, not this late into the day . . . but Benjamin knew his brother best, and Katherine knew him not at all, so Benjamin's decision would have to stand. "I will not object if you want to tell him that this was all in order to settle a wager."

He gazed at her blankly for a moment, as if she'd spoken in a foreign language. "That I offered for you because I was forced to?" he said with a scowl.

So it was *his* hand that had been forced—which meant Papa had to have done the forcing, just as Cyril had thought. Katherine had once pondered that theory among others, but it still stung to hear it put that way, to know her presence had been pressed upon someone.

"But I could not do that, Katherine," Benjamin went on calmly. "For your sake no one must know this betrothal was a fabrication. Society would forgive you for changing your mind, but never for conducting a ruse. Until you cry off, we must act just as any couple would. You must meet my brother, as would be expected."

Katherine gazed up at him, and felt something inside her break away, like an icicle falling of its own weight from the eaves of a house, a harbinger of spring. By that one simple act—choosing not to deny her—he'd proven himself at his core to be a gentleman. It mattered not what the gossips said about his military career, or madness in his family. In that moment, for that moment, he was a man of distinction, of integrity, for he had sacrificed his own ease for her sake.

She felt tears forming in her eyes, but she could not let them fall, not when she must put on a good face for this man's brother. She pretended to sneeze, and hid her face, for one long moment, behind her hands.

"God bless you," Benjamin said, and she felt the cloth of a kerchief pressed against one of her hands.

She uncovered her face, murmured "Thank you," as she accepted his kerchief, and decided all at once that if this man had sold supplies to smugglers, he'd done it for reasons that he had counted important at the time. Whatever had caused him to do the act, right or wrong, she was certain he'd had some higher motive in committing the act, something far from greed. It was curious that she could have such conviction when she'd known the man little more than three weeks . . . but the seeds of friendship were not always sown by logic's reckoning.

He put his hand on her elbow, and then they passed through the open doorway, across what had been the front hall, and to a door that led into a part of the house still standing. A butler greeted their knock, showing them in with a courtesy unmarred by the disintegration around him.

"Master Benjamin!" the butler cried when they were issued inside a space that must have once been a drawing room. Warmth was written across the butler's smiling face.

"Caulfield, you old devil. Did you come back from the military to resume caring for this pile of rubble?"

"I did, my lord, at your brother's request."

"It is good to see you. Good to know that once the place is restored, it will be properly tended."

"Thank you, sir. That it will be, with old Caulfield minding the doors."

The butler showed them to a parlor that retained all of its walls except for an upper portion on the outer wall, and which contained two chairs, obviously placed there today. The room was otherwise barren, except for peeling wallpaper and a fireplace bare of any decoration. Before departing, the butler begged their pardon for keeping them waiting in such sad estate while he announced their presence. "But the front parlors are all under repair."

Katherine could not help a giggle at the obvious, which oddly made her feel rather more in control of her emotions. Benjamin stared with open interest down at the floor, which had had most of its tiles chipped up, exposing bare wood and plaster dust beneath. He glanced at Katherine's gown, completely white but for the royal blue flowers embroidered at random around her hem and blue ribbons on her sleeves and just below her bosom.

"I suspect you might have done better to dress in dark colors," he said, himself dressed soberly as usual, in dark gray accented with black—even his cravat and waistcoat were black—only his white lawn shirt relieved the severity of the look.

Katherine gave a rueful smile, wishing she'd worn walking boots. Her slippers *might* recover from a traipse through dust and ruin if scrubbed with the soap the stable lads used on the harnesses, but she was not overly hopeful.

Caulfield soon returned, saying as expected that the marquess was quite pleased to receive his guests. He led the way through a maze of construction and tools, left as they lay for when the workers returned next. Benjamin took Katherine's arm, for they had to step over piles of debris and sawdust and supplies.

The hallway to the rear of the house was completely blocked by a large, rolled carpet. Benjamin leaped over it, then put his hands around Katherine's waist and lifted her in one smooth motion up and over it as well. She murmured her thanks, not quite able to meet his gaze as he released her, for an unexpected thrill chased through her. She fixed her gaze on the butler instead, as if it were vitally important to watch him scramble over the carpet.

"I hope this is not Gideon's idea of a maze," Benjamin said lightly.

"We must be sure to tell him they are usually built out-of-doors," Katherine said.

Benjamin laughed, and Katherine began to tremble, just a little, telling herself it was not Benjamin's laugh that had wrought the sensation, but from wondering if the marquess would be as dour as Benjamin had first seemed.

Seemed. She knew now that Lord Benjamin was a creature of moods, but not all of them were dark or forbidding. He had a lighter side, even, call it a playful side. Hopefully his brother was the same.

The butler opened a parlor door, revealing a room that had suffered the least amount of alteration so far, and announced, "Lord Benjamin, and Miss Oakes."

Katherine saw the marchioness first, a very dark-haired woman in an emerald-green gown that allowed for her pregnancy of six months' time, Katherine guessed. The marchioness had been folding Holland clothes while seated before a cheerily crackling fire, but as soon as Caulfield announced them, she put aside a cloth and stood. She came across the room, arms outstretched to her brother-in-law.

"Benjamin! Such a pleasure to see you again. But look at your hair! I believe I like it longer like this."

He accepted her into his arms for an embrace, and Katherine saw brotherly affection displace the uncertain expression he'd been sporting since he'd taken Katherine up in his phaeton. "Elizabeth, you look very well. But was it wise to travel now?" he asked as he stepped back to survey her length.

"I think we all know I am hardly fragile," she said, and then both smiled at some private jest Katherine must remember to ask Benjamin about later. For now her attention shifted to the approaching other occupant of the room. Her mouth dropped open, and she glanced up quickly at Benjamin, wanting to scold him for not alerting her as to what to expect of the Marquess of Greyleigh—for the marquess had an extraordinary appearance.

The man had white-blond hair, worn long and presently in a queue that trailed well past his shoulders, its pale color giving him a ghostly aspect despite lightly tanned skin. Strangely, the old style did not age him, for he was clearly only a few years older than Benjamin. His face was handsome, similar to Benjamin's, although the latter's was longer of line—but one forgot to notice the marquess's attractive features once one came to gaze into his eyes.

At a quick glance, Katherine thought he must be blind, that the pale gray irises were a reflection of damaged eyes, but then she felt his gaze fix on her unmistakably. She'd never seen such pale gray eyes, like rain, even though before today she would have said that rain has no color. Then she detected the faintest hint of blue ringing their periphery. If Benjamin's eyes were the pale blue at the zenith of the sky, the marquess's were a curious otherworldly uncolor that must mark the edges of heaven.

Katherine forcibly closed her mouth, and swallowed, but she could not keep herself from staring. The marquess stared back, not blinking, folding his hands together behind his back, as Benjamin was wont to do.

"Gideon, Elizabeth, this is Miss Katherine Oakes," Benjamin said. "Katherine, my brother and new sister, the Marquess and Marchioness of Greyleigh."

Katherine made as if to curtsy, but Elizabeth clucked her tongue. "No bowing between those who will be sisters once you are wed to Benjamin!" she chided, gathering Katherine into an embrace and planting a kiss on both her cheeks. "You must call me Elizabeth, please."

"How do you do?" Katherine said, knowing she was showing her fluster.

"Quite well," Elizabeth answered.

Katherine glanced up at Benjamin at the awkwardness of being greeted so warmly when they were only pretending they would one day marry, but she could hardly return warmth with coolness. "Please," she said, stumbling over the words a little, "call me Katherine, or Kate if you like."

The marchioness smiled and stepped back, and then Katherine's hands were taken up by the marquess's. He airily planted a kiss on both her cheeks as well.

"Well met," he said, and smiled down at her. His smile was so familiar, his voice so similar to Benjamin's that Katherine instantly lost half the dread she'd carried into the room with her.

"How do you do, my lord?" she said back to him, nodding a greeting.

"Well enough," came his answer. "Call me Gideon. When we are in the country we are seldom formal with our friends, and never with family, not even in Town," he said as he stepped back, only to step forward again so that he and Benjamin might embrace. They heartily slapped each other on the back, then drew back long enough to take a long moment to gaze into one another's eyes, after which each of them nodded as though satisfied.

Katherine knew that look; she had exchanged it with her own brothers. It was a silent way of letting each other know that life was tolerably well, as much as it was a moment of recommitment to a long, old, cherished bond. She felt a new flutter in her stomach, this one an uncomplicated happy response to seeing the warm affection the two brothers shared.

The marquess made a gesture toward the chairs. "Please be seated. I apologize for the discomfort of my home at present, but we could hardly meet at Benjamin's chambers, and I thought this might be more private than a park or theater or someplace like that."

"Your home will be beautiful," Katherine said, taking a seat on a settee. Benjamin sat beside her . . . as one would expect of a fiancé.

The marquess laughed, and Katherine felt even more of her nervousness drain away. "'Will be' are the correct words. It assuredly is not at the moment, but I thank you for your compliment all the same."

"I am sorry we cannot offer refreshments," Elizabeth said. "The kitchens are being renovated as well."

Polite conversation began, now that it was clear that everyone was well. They spoke of the weather, the war, what Parliament had last voted upon, what living in London was like after living aboard ship—but Benjamin kept turning the conversation away from the subject of marriage. His sister-in-law, Elizabeth, looked on him with a perplexed amusement clear on her face, and finally took matters in her own hands by turning to

Katherine. "When do you marry?" she asked pleasantly, if directly. "Have your banns been posted? Here in London?"

"No banns yet," Benjamin hastened to say, but he was brought up short when Elizabeth gave him a speaking glance.

"Talk to Gideon," she instructed him firmly, "while Katherine and I have a little coze."

"I wish there were time," Benjamin said, standing and consulting the only decoration in the room, a clock mounted above the mantelpiece. "Unfortunately, we have another engagement. I am sorry this was so brief, as I know you mean to leave London for home tomorrow, but since I . . . we did not know you were coming, we had made other plans." He turned to offer Katherine his arm. She rose, gathering up her reticule, knowing she must appear flustered.

"I am so sorry our visit was so brief," she said, only briefly able to hold Elizabeth's startled gaze lest the woman read too much in her own.

"We would not dream of making you late for another affair," the marquess said blandly. "Katherine, it was a pleasure to meet you. I look forward to when next we meet. Benjamin, write to me, and not just about our chess games."

Benjamin inclined his head.

"Please accept my best wishes on the pending birth of your child," Katherine said to Elizabeth.

Elizabeth thanked her and extended similar sentiments of best wishes in the coming days as they escorted their guests to the parlor door, where Caulfield had come upon hearing the bellpull, to escort the guests past the rubble.

Once the door was closed behind them, Benjamin emphatically shook his head when Katherine parted her lips to speak. It was not until they were in his phaeton and driving away that he let his shoulders slump. He said hollowly, "I was not clever enough. Gideon knows something is amiss."

Katherine did not know what to say.

"I thought about telling him, right there and then—but how could I possibly explain that I'd won the betrothal in a card game?" he said, shaking his head. "There is no way to say it that is flattering for you." He shrugged. "Whatever impressions my brother and Elizabeth are left with when this is all behind us, I must take the blame myself, not shift any part of it to you.

I could not let them think you and your papa to be so . . . I do not know the word. Vile, perhaps."

"Oh," Katherine said, but instead of fretting at the thought of how he might favorably phrase their odd bargain, Katherine felt an increasingly familiar warmth growing in her very center, spreading outward to the tips of her fingers and toes. She felt it thrum through her, welcome and thrilling and achingly sweet.

He had done it again. He had protected her, at cost to himself.

She gazed up at him, vitally aware of his leg pressed against hers because of the narrowness of the phaeton's seat, aware of his hands strong and sure on the reins, aware of the agitation he felt but tried to hide from her gaze. Even now, when he had taken steps to preserve her reputation in the eyes of people beloved to him but strangers to her, he also struggled to keep his aggravation turned in, to not transfer any blame or reproof onto her.

"Benjamin," she breathed his name, "thank you."

He glanced down at her, still battling to hide his disgruntlement. "I only did as any gentlemen must."

Katherine sat at his side and struggled not to throw her arms around Benjamin's neck and tell him that, no, he was wrong— that he knew more about being a gentleman than half of London could even pretend to know.

Chapter 16

"Tell me why Elizabeth is not to be considered fragile," she said instead, knowing her cheeks had betrayed her yet again by growing red as she furiously fought down the impulse to embrace Benjamin.

The shift in the conversation served its purpose in providing a lighter mood in which they traveled toward her home. Benjamin told her that the striking Lady Greyleigh had once been a penniless runaway who had been cruelly attacked near their home and left in a ditch to die. In nursing her back to health, it had been proved, in the end, that the soul most in need of nursing had been Gideon's.

As a child, Gideon had defied his father and become his frail and unfortunate mama's protector—a caring role he had been unable to shed even after Mama had passed to her reward. He had thought to build a paradise in the home that had been a hell for him and his brothers for so long, and had opened his home to every vagrant or doxy or maimed soldier in whom he saw the potential of redemption. But he had forgotten how to tend to his own needs under the weight of caring for so many needy others. Elizabeth had been the only one able to move past the protective walls he had built around his heart, her love clearing his vision so that he could see again that he must sustain his own soul, rescuing it before he could rescue others.

"So, having gone through all she has, that is what she meant about not being fragile," Benjamin explained.

"How sad a beginning, but, too, how lovely that it ended so well," Katherine said softly.

"The tale will make for an interesting one when their children want to know how Mama and Papa met," Benjamin noted, his agitated mood giving way to gentle humor.

"Oh dear, yes it will," Katherine said, laughing lightly. Then she thought to reach over and pinch his arm.

"Ow! What was that for?" he cried, half laughing in his turn.

"For not warning me about the marquess's appearance. I quite *gaped* at him."

Benjamin grinned, the old devil dancing once again in his gaze. "Believe me or no, but I truly had not considered it. I am accustomed to how Gideon appears. The villagers in Severn's Well are half convinced he's a ghost or a demon," he explained. "Everyone gapes at him."

"I think he was very gracious, given my poor manners. But what did he mean about writing about chess games?"

"We play chess by post. He does so with Sebastian, our wicked little brother, as well." Benjamin shrugged. "Keeping the games going forces us to write to one another, sharing little bits about our lives." He took on a sheepish look. "I have not written to Gideon, for the game or otherwise, in several weeks."

"Since we met."

"Er, yes. How could I write and *not* mention that I was betrothed?"

"Will there be consequences? Will he cut off your funds or something dastardly such as that?"

"Gideon?" Benjamin blew dismissively through his lips. "I would have to cut off the Prince Regent's head before Gideon would think to use access to my funds as punishment. It was one of the first things he did when Papa passed on, that is, to set up funds for all of us. Papa knew money was yet another way to control us, so he gave and took without any hint of regularity or fairness. But if you wonder why I appear, call it *economical,* it is because even my quarterly sum is not princely. Gideon may be generous and timely in his giving, but he's not a fool. He knows young men with too much money tend to buy trouble, and cheerfully told me as much. Still, I felt quite flush when I also had my income from the navy. Well, if *flush* is the correct word. 'Able to eat' might be more accurate. Just as well you are not truly marrying such a pauper, eh?"

She smiled, neither nodding nor shaking her head, and saw with a ripple of disappointment that her house lay just ahead. She would have liked the conversation to go on. She'd suspected he had little funds, for he was careful where Cyril Cullman was extravagant—in his clothing, his single carriage, and she'd never seen Benjamin in any boots but the pair he wore now. Did he truly want for supper of a night? Although their association was almost at an end, if he ever called on her again she would be sure to call for a tea tray.

When Benjamin came around to help her down from the phaeton, he did not merely offer his hand, but encircled her waist as he had done to help her over the carpet. The same thrill chased through her now as it had then, and she had to make an effort not to lean into his length.

She could not think why he would want to, but to her surprise he followed her into the house and the front parlor, and took a chair across from hers when she sat. She rang at once for tea to be served, after dismissing the thought of asking him to leave, to go about his business until they must meet later for a musical evening. Why must he leave? His company was comfortable, even enjoyable. And this way she could be sure he had something to eat today.

Today—or more correctly, tonight: Tonight would be the scene of their "falling apart," the scene that would make it possible for the *ton* to believe Katherine had lost interest in marrying Lord Benjamin and had cried off.

After tonight, he would be free to go to the home of the Marchioness of Greyleigh's father, where Elizabeth and Gideon meant to pass the night before journeying home tomorrow. Elizabeth had confessed that she and Gideon had come to Town just to meet Benjamin's "bride." They had asked to meet Katherine and Benjamin at the ruined house instead of her father's home, because she and her stepmama were not on entirely convivial terms.

"I had rather we had a more congenial first greeting for you, Katherine, than you might have had at my stepmama's house," Elizabeth had explained, covering a touch of sadness with a smile.

After tonight, Benjamin would be free of Katherine's company, and free to go to this stepmama's home, not needing a friendly welcome. He would be free to tell Gideon and Elizabeth as much of the truth as he wanted them to know—at the very least that Katherine was not going to be Elizabeth's "new sister."

He might even let them believe exactly what Society was meant to believe, that Katherine had found Benjamin wanting among the ranks of marriageables. Katherine guessed he would allow that impression, protecting her reputation yet again, taking all blame or criticism onto his own shoulders.

Papa entered the parlor unexpectedly, drawing the gaze of both occupants of the room. He stopped short. There was a rotund older gentleman trailing him, who nearly collided with Papa in the doorway.

"Lord Benjamin!" Papa cried. "Sir Uriah here was just now looking for you. Seems you're seldom at your chambers. Constantly conveying my daughter here and about, as Sir Uriah himself has said. He would speak with you, my lord."

Benjamin stood, a puzzled frown forming on his face, and crossed to nod as Sir Uriah Sembley was introduced over a bow. "If you wish it, Sir Albert, I would be willing to speak privately with Sir Uriah," Benjamin conceded.

It was not even fifteen minutes later—Katherine had been prepared to wait much longer to learn why Sir Uriah had been seeking Benjamin—when another man was announced.

"Mr. Dahl, to see Sir Albert," said the butler, who only then saw the room did not host Sir Albert. "Er, are you home to callers, Miss Oakes?"

Katherine nodded, even though the name was unfamiliar to her. "Mr. Dahl?" she said, standing to greet the unknown gentleman. Langley departed, murmuring he would seek Sir Albert, leaving the parlor door open as he went.

The stranger had freckles, the kind brought out by exposure to the sun, and was dressed well if not with flash.

"Pardon my manners, but are you the Katherine Oakes who is betrothed to Lord Benjamin Whitbury?" he asked.

"Yes."

She watched with interest as his brow cleared. He strode further into the room and bowed to her. "Lord Benjamin is a fine, fine fellow, as you must know. I wish you every happiness with him! I hope I may count on being invited to the wedding, although I've no right to ask, of course."

"No right . . . ? Mr. Dahl, was it?"

"Oh!" he cried in dawning comprehension. "Yes, I am

Stephen Dahl. Lord Benjamin must never have mentioned me. I cannot say I blame him."

"You knew him in the navy?" Katherine suggested.

Mr. Dahl ducked his head for a moment, then looked up from under his brows, guiltily. "I did know him, ma'am. I was also a midshipman on the same ship as he."

She hated repeating everything he said, so instead this time she merely stared at him in incomprehension.

"Ma'am, I was the midshipman who was selling the naval stores to smugglers." At her continued stare, he added with some fluster, "Lord Benjamin took the blame in my place for smuggling goods. But *I* did the crime. You see, I have four sisters and a widowed mother, Miss Oakes, and I could not lose my position—or so I told myself at the time. I was a fool and, worse, a coward. I allowed Lord Benjamin to accept the blame that was all mine. He never sold nor smuggled anything, miss, and so I've sworn this very day to the Admiralty. I've told all to Sir Uriah—"

"Sir Uriah Sembley!" Katherine finished for him, beginning to grasp what she was being told. Benjamin had not done the deed for which he had lost his rank in the navy? Could it be true? What had he said when she'd demanded to know if he'd done such a wicked thing: "I must have done, to have admitted to it." Not a lie, but also not the whole truth . . . .

Benjamin returned to the parlor just then, excitement coursing over his features. He opened his mouth to speak to Katherine, but came to an abrupt halt as he saw Mr. Dahl. "Stephen!" he cried.

Mr. Dahl hung his head once more, and took a step back, looking as if he expected a blow. "I know I must be the last man you care to see, Lord Benjamin." He looked up then. "But I've come to set things right, at long last."

He scarcely managed to get the last words out before Benjamin had crossed the room to clasp one of Dahl's hands in a hearty grip, his other hand squeezing the man's shoulder in warm greeting.

"It is good to see you, Stephen," Benjamin said.

"That cannot be true," Mr. Dahl said, but he seemed pleased around the guilty edges lingering in his manner.

"How are your sisters, and your mother?"

"Very well, thanks to you." Mr. Dahl's expression crumbled, and for several moments he was choked by emotion.

He managed to clear his throat and start anew. "I did it again, Lord Benjamin. I took unclaimed stores out of the ship. For the money, rot me! And I was almost caught again this time, and . . . and I could not live with myself anymore, my lord. I went to the captain, and I confessed it all. How you covered for me, that first time, because of my sisters and mother, who would have starved without me sending home my pay."

"Now, Stephen," Benjamin said quietly, with a quick glance toward Katherine. "You can tell me all this privately, if you like."

"No, I owe you at least the truth, and anyone else who'll listen." It was Mr. Dahl's turn to glance toward Katherine. "Your betrothed didn't do anything wrong, miss. He took my punishment, saying as he'd taken the stuff and sold it for profit, only he hadn't done anything he oughtn't. That's God's own truth! As I told you already, miss, I was sent here to London to tell the Admiralty too—" He cut himself off short, his eyes misting for a moment before he swallowed down his upset.

"I'm quit of the navy," he went on. "They'll not have me any longer, of course—but I'm grateful they've declined to court-martial me! They'll put it in the news sheets that Lord Benjamin was falsely accused, and the 'proper man' punished. I don't deserve such mercy, my name being protected too, but they said as how that was best all the way 'round."

The former midshipman gave Benjamin a sheepish glance. "They're trying to keep things as quiet as possible. They're afraid Lord Benjamin might care to take the matter to court."

"Not if they clear my name," Benjamin said at once.

Mr. Dahl stopped and swallowed, gathering new words if not his composure. "Only, they cannot give Lord Benjamin his position back like I asked, as he told a lie, even though it was to cover for a friend and all! But what they could do was clear his name and find him another position, you see."

"I do see," Katherine said, only half surprised to learn the truth, for she knew it *was* the truth. A rising glee filled her heart, for in some secret corner of that organ she'd already concluded something like this must have happened. She had claimed Benjamin "honorable" in her mind, and this was simply more proof of that fact. She glanced at Benjamin, whose light eyes glittered with satisfaction. What a burden it must have been for him, to have all the world thinking him a liar and a thief.

"So I've done what I could, and the Admiralty has, too. There's a gentleman—"

"Sir Uriah?"

"Exactly, miss! Sir Uriah said he'd help, by helping Lord Benjamin—"

Benjamin interrupted by lifting his hand. "Let me be the one with that news," he requested.

Mr. Dahl subsided with a nod, and Benjamin approached Katherine, a glow of eagerness in his manner.

"Katherine," he said, an excited strain under his voice, "this is a grand day."

His gratification left no room for her to argue otherwise; she knew her day must evolve into a rather dismal one, for this day she must playact at disliking Benjamin to the point of ending their public association . . . but as to Benjamin's concerns, this had to be a fine day indeed, now his name was to be cleared.

"First, I am already feeling flush because word arrived from the trainer that Fallen Angel won the Helmman earlier this week, and yesterday she won the Tremayne." He half turned to glance at Mr. Dahl. "And now today I have a friend returned to me. A friend who has brought with him redemption—and, better yet, employment! Sir Uriah has offered me a post as acting importation registrar for his line of ships. I start tomorrow. I will oversee everything his corporation imports. Spices, sugar, cotton, Portuguese port, Spanish sherry. I will even occasionally be required to travel abroad. I will be on the sea again, which I have missed more than I thought I would." The devil danced in his gaze once more, this time with delight.

"Oh, Benjamin, I am so pleased for you," Katherine said, letting her pleasure shine from her eyes. She wanted to touch him, to take his hands in hers, but instead she folded her own hands into her skirts.

He laughed. "I know it is but a glorified clerk's position, that many will sniff at my need to earn my way, but at least now I know I can stay in London! I can begin to make plans. Not least of which will be wagering more on Fallen Angel at the very next opportunity!"

Benjamin reached for her arms, sliding his hands down to gather hers in his own. "You were utterly right about that horse. You said she would be a winner," he told her.

He looked down at her hands, then up again, the eager light dimmed a little but still burning there. He spoke softly, so softly that Katherine thought Mr. Dahl probably could not hear, even though the man openly leaned forward with a cocked ear. "I used to . . . well, doubt that you could make a go of your plan to breed horses, to build a stud full of winning horses, but I do not doubt it anymore. You have a gift, Katherine, and I was an idiot to think anything else. It is my hope that one day I can be one of the first buyers to purchase a winner from your stables."

Her heart slipped into her throat for a moment, not from the idea of a sale already made, but that the sale would be to Benjamin, that she would see him again one day. "It may take years to beget a winner." She felt she must offer the caution.

"Or not. Time will tell." He made a small, apologetic motion. "My one regret is that I must keep Fallen Angel near, you understand, if I am to see her run. Now I am employed, I will not have leisure time in which to journey to the country. I wish I could send Fallen Angel's keeping to you, but my business will be here in the City, near the docks of course."

"Of course," she said, letting go of the small hope she had harbored that he would not mind having his horse run mostly in Kent, would come to call upon her there, at Katherine's stable, perhaps often.

"Could we give my friend tea?" he asked quietly.

"Of course," Katherine repeated. She glanced toward Mr. Dahl, and thought that Benjamin was generous to many people, for even though Dahl had returned, had taken the blame at last, had taken steps to aid the man he had wronged, Katherine was not so sure she could have been so forgiving to Mr. Dahl as to call him "friend" so quickly.

Benjamin released her hand and turned back to his former shipmate. "We were just about to enjoy some refreshments, if you would care to—"

"You are very kind, Lord Benjamin, and I thank you, but I cannot stay." The man smiled, his guilty sheepishness finally giving away to a brighter humor. "I've a new position myself! A friend of the family has seen fit to employ me as a runner. I go everywhere in the City, to Guildhall, and Lloyd's, and the Staplers, delivering messages or whatever is needed. 'Tis not the sea, but near as exciting, and half again the pay!"

"I am glad for you," Benjamin said.

"It is more than I deserve," Mr. Dahl said, and for a moment his chin trembled. "Am I right to think you have accepted my most humble apology, Lord Benjamin? I never should have let—"

"I have accepted it, Dahl—and let that be enough of all that," Benjamin said firmly.

Despite her reservations, Katherine smiled at Mr. Dahl's sigh of contentment, and watched as Benjamin slapped him heartily on the back before escorting Mr. Dahl out.

When Benjamin returned, he was smiling. Katherine wanted to tell him it came as little surprise to her that his "disgrace" had been the opposite in truth, that she had come to suspect he was not capable of dishonor . . . but he would not allow it by dint of spreading his hands and spreading his smile into his usual devil's grin.

"I am exonerated!" he declared. "I am employed. I own a winning horse. Life is lavish with her bounty!"

"Now all you need for contentment is to be quit of our betrothal," Katherine said the obvious, but she said it to the intricately inlaid cigarillo box on the small table near her, not quite able to look Benjamin in the eye when she said the words. But her presence in his life *was* the only stumbling block keeping him from all he could want.

"And all *you* need for contentment is that your cottage on Meyerley Creek be declared ready for you," he rejoined.

"Hmmm," Katherine said, a faintly agreeing sound.

Just then Langley entered with a puzzled expression. "Is Mr. Cullman not here?"

"Cullman?" Benjamin repeated.

The butler nodded. "He arrived right after Mr. Dahl. I asked him to wait one moment while I set the footman to finding Sir Albert, but when I turned around, he was gone. I . . . guess he left?"

"But then why come at all in the first place?" Benjamin questioned aloud.

"Well, he is not here," Langley concluded. "And Mr. Dahl has gone as well?"

"He has," Katherine said.

Langley uttered the tiniest of exasperated sighs, gave a pre-occupied bow, and exited.

Katherine glanced at Benjamin. "Perhaps Mr. Cullman saw the household was occupied and did not wish to intrude?" she ventured a guess.

Benjamin waved the question away. "I would far rather talk about your Meyerley place, now I've gone to see it myself," he went on in good humor and unfeigned enthusiasm.

"Do tell," Katherine encouraged him as she indicated they ought to take a seat.

"I have to admit it is well suited to the purpose, with its upper and lower fields, which will let one grow while the other is grazed. As you know, I am unable to do aught with the upper field, of course, but if the lower field is any indication, it will do well. There's hay already showing green, and the pond is well placed for watering the horses easily. The two fields are visible from the cottage atop the hill, which I think would appeal to horse owners, who will then know their investments are being closely observed."

"That is my hope."

"Do you have plans? When you will invest in a breeder pair, or two? Equipment? Training? Hands to do the labor? You have a development scheme in mind?"

"I do. I have it all written down—in one of my journals, of course."

He grinned. "Of course. Show your plans to me."

It was flattering, his attention to the copious notes she had made, the speculations she had thought out on paper, almost as flattering as his declaration that were he the owner, he would do little else different. "You must keep your steward, you realize. Your stablehands will not obey the orders of a woman. You will have to be a little aloof, play the eccentric Grand Dame."

She smiled. "I know. I cannot play the part of feeble female who never leaves her home and hopes that money will spring from wishes, but I think I might manage to seem eccentric and haughty."

"Haughty? You?" he said on a grin.

She took a handful of rolled cigarillos from the box on the nearby table and threw them at him. He ducked, but winced when several bounced off his head.

"Now show me Fallen Angel's entries in your racing notes," he said, never losing his grin. "I want to know how much to risk on the outlandish hope that she will win her third race in a row."

"Remember, you *asked* to see my many notes," she warned, moving to the shelf across the room that housed her racing journals. She really ought to ask him to leave . . . but then again, why? What harm did it do for him to linger here awhile? After tonight they would have no reason to ever again linger in each other's company . . . so she opted to show him what he asked to see, to have him stay, extend their fragile friendship, just a little longer.

Chapter 17

It was not even a quarter hour later before Katherine had three journals open on the floor, surrounded by a profusion of the last few days' news sheets folded open to the pages with the racing results. And it was not long before Benjamin had joined Katherine, who was also sprawled on the floor of the front parlor, the better to read the many entries aloud to one another.

"Fancy's Feast, out of Fancy-Me-Darling and Poet's Feast," Benjamin quoted as Katherine jotted in one of her journals, "took the fifth race, trailed by Gorham, and Maid of Magnus." He looked up. "Do I recall correctly that Gorham took another second, at Ascot several weeks ago?"

Katherine leafed back through her pages. "Mmm . . . Ascot, on the first of May. Yes. Yes, he did. He will be one to watch." She looked up, a zealous light shining in her eyes. "I could wish his owner would want him stabled and trained at Meyerley Creek."

"Ask," Benjamin advised. "The worst the man could say is no."

"I *will* ask," Katherine confirmed, and Benjamin believed her. She might be the eccentric that Society dubbed her to be, but she knew what the world thought of her and never tried to hide behind a façade.

He laid aside the news sheet, and watched as Katherine jotted some entries in her journals. She probably had no idea that the tip of her tongue showed in the corner of her mouth, and he was certain she would have no idea how fetching she looked in her white gown accented with blue. The hem was a little the worse for having swept through the debris in Gideon's town house, but the combination of white and blue worked as a perfect foil to her red curls.

She looked delicate and pretty and feminine—but Benjamin knew her expertise was as certain as that any male might demonstrate. Still, with her tongue held like that, Benjamin had to suppress a chortle, although he never thought to laugh at the lady. His was more the kind of amusement that stemmed from finding that an unadorned box is filled with rare treasure, a kind of elemental delight at the discovery of the unexpected.

But Katherine had always been a case of the "unexpected": when visiting her horse one last time, disguised as a lad; when recording the races with a passion most women dedicated to learning an instrument or their French. She had told Benjamin how to wager, so that he had profited. Unlike every other female of his acquaintance, Katherine wanted a home of her own, marriage or no. Not to mention her outlandish desire to govern her own business! She flaunted or ignored all that most women held most dear, yet never looked back with regret, never tried to hide or change her nature.

And there was the way she kissed . . . she'd been too naïve or too bold or too *Katherine* to pretend she had not enjoyed sharing his kiss. He wished, even now, that he might have another from her. More than one. Truth was, he wanted more than kisses. She would give herself over to lovemaking as wholeheartedly as she did everything else.

The thought of Katherine in love—or at least deciding in her usual straightforward manner that it was time to wed and go to the marriage bed—with all her typical conviction and dedication in place, made Benjamin glad he was sitting on the floor. He doubted his knees, gone watery at the thought, would support him.

He could picture her creamy skin becoming exposed, inch by inch as the tapes of her gown were untied and the garments lowered; could picture her body pressing against his own with that glovelike molding she instinctually offered; could imagine a shared kiss starting out lightly exploring, only to deepen and build a heat of its own. . . .

But it would not be *Benjamin*'s kiss, never with Katherine. She was not destined to end in *his* arms. Katherine half believed she was to wed Cullman, not having been allowed to know how flawed he was. Cullman was too clever, too good at maintaining the façade in front of her.

Truth was, the month that Benjamin had spent protecting Katherine from seduction was almost up. It ought no longer be his concern . . . only, Benjamin did not want to see her ruined, and ruination was Cullman's sole interest in her.

He would have to tell her what Cullman was like. She would probably hate him for it, would reject his conclusions. As far as Katherine knew, this whole false betrothal had begun through Benjamin's devices, not Cullman's. Why *would* she trust the one she thought had lied and manipulated and stolen her—however temporarily—from Cullman's arms?

But he had to try. Perhaps he could at least plant a doubt in her mind, one that could grow into suspicion and eventually save her from marrying the man? He had to try.

Benjamin thought of how her father had asked him not to woo Katherine with words he did not mean—it seemed a laughable precaution now. It was from Cullman that Sir Albert should have secured a promise. Not that Cullman's word could be trusted.

Just as laughable, but sadder—infinitely sadder—was the conviction that grew in Benjamin's chest as he sat and watched Katherine's tongue worry the corner of her mouth: that he ought to have tried to woo her.

He ought to have worked to win her heart. Not to keep her from Cullman. Not to satisfy her papa—but because he loved her.

He knew it now. Ridiculously lolling on her floor, doing nothing more romantic than reading race results aloud to one another, and yet he knew in every hollow of his being that he had fallen in love with her. Katherine Oakes, the hoyden, the outspoken one, the last woman in the world he ever would have thought could invade his heart.

If he could marry her, she'd bring no prestige to his family's name, no great wealth, no rank or privilege beyond what he already was born to—but he would love her, and cherish her, and knew she would fit into his odd family in a way Miss Mansell could never hope to do.

Miss Mansell would have never understood why Gideon filled his home with castoffs and those in need of a second chance. She would have never helped a mere soldier don his costume out of the simple goal of wishing to help, especially if it meant she must stand among those women Society found to be "second best." No matter how favored a pet it had been, Miss Mansell would never flaunt Society's rules in order to spend a few more minutes with a horse.

Was he being unfair? He had never kissed Miss Mansell. Perhaps if he did, she would show a less formal side of her personality. . . .

But, no, Benjamin had seen Gideon's love for Elizabeth. He had been in the room with it, knew what love felt like, knew its joy when shared.

He also knew Miss Mansell meant nothing to him. Nothing about her stirred his heart, or made him long to kiss her by a public racing course, or here in a sunny front parlor filled with journals and news sheets. Miss Mansell would be perfect for him, or at least for expectations he had once had—but his expectations had been exploded by a woman who would slick back her red curls and don lad's clothing, all in order to whisper a private final farewell to a four-legged friend.

He loved Katherine.

He finally saw the difference, the heart-and-soul difference between the two women—the one was all that was proper, and the other anything but . . . and everything he needed.

But now dismay squeezed in, trying to displace the joy that had been slowly filling his heart all day. No sooner had he realized his love, than he had lost it.

His realization had come too late.

Tonight Katherine would stage a scene that would end their sham betrothal, and she would turn her brown eyes toward the man she'd been secretly betrothed to before. She would look to Cullman for love—never to Benjamin, who had shown her only disdain and censure until it was too late.

No! His mind was made up: Tonight Benjamin must tell her what Cullman wanted from her. She would lose two fiancés in one night, and she would hate him for it, Benjamin supposed, but he had to give her a future, a chance to find a fellow worthy of her.

"Katherine," he said, his voice rough with emotion.

She looked up, her auburn eyebrows lifted in inquiry.

"Although we are going to separate tonight," he said, choosing his words with care, "will you promise me that I may come to call tomorrow? I know it is a few days early, but I would like to give you your birthday gift already."

"Of course," she said, looking surprised. "But you do not need to give me a birthday gift!" she assured him. "Goodness, I do not even know when *your* birthday is!"

"March fourteenth," he said, wanting her to know, wanting her to think of him, perhaps, once a year. "I have already acquired your gift, so you must accept it. Say you will. Say you will receive me tomorrow, even if you feel . . . annoyed with me."

"Annoyed? Why would I be annoyed?"

He shrugged, not meeting her gaze. "Perhaps I will offend you during our crying-off performance tonight."

She waved the thought away. "Nonsense, I will know you are pretending. I only pray I will not say anything to offend *you.*"

"You could not," he said, and swallowed, to be able to get out the words. "All the same, you have yet to promise that you will see me tomorrow, and will accept my gift."

She shook her head, still smiling even though her brows drew together in something of a puzzled frown. "Very well," she said, belying the gesture. "I promise. Tomorrow evening? Shall we say seven?"

He nodded, and started to rise, to make his exit, but then he thought how it was hours yet until he needed to go home to change into evening wear. He could stay awhile yet, be near her for a bit longer, enjoy her company while she was not pretending to fight with him, was not in reality angry with him, not yet. He could love her for a few hours more . . . although he knew he would love her for a lot longer than a few hours. He knew he would miss her and curse his own stupid pride for not realizing her worth a lot sooner, when he might have had a chance to win her heart in return.

Katherine was supposed to be looking displeased with Benjamin this night, at the musical evening at the home of Mr. and Mrs. MacFarlane, but who could completely smother a grin? Benjamin played the pianoforte for the oldest MacFarlane daughter, poor creature, and struggled mightily to match a tempo to Miss MacFarlane's singing.

Still, Katherine had to wonder if she would have grinned at all if Benjamin had looked adoringly upon Miss MacFarlane's fine face and even finer dowry. Katherine doubted humor would have been uppermost in her mind.

What would have been uppermost then? Concern, that her friend would make a misalliance? Annoyance, that Benjamin could settle for a milk-and-water miss who could not keep the meter he tried so diligently to provide for her? Miss MacFarlane, unkind as it was to say, did not possess near enough of the attributes that would make a proper wife for Lord Benjamin Whitbury.

At least Miss Mansell had disappeared from sight. Miss Mansell, according to Cyril, had decided Lord Benjamin was "the worst sort of jackanapes," and would henceforth avoid anywhere Lord Benjamin was likely to be found.

"Oh dear, that is too bad," Katherine had said, and knew that Cyril had wondered why she had smiled.

Miss MacFarlane's performance began to pall, and Katherine began to wonder how she was supposed to go about crying off—the details had never been discussed. She'd tried once, on the drive here tonight, but Benjamin had kept turning the conversation to other things.

She supposed she was to choose a moment, make a bit of a scene with him, and then abandon him and "storm off" home. Whose carriage was she to use? Benjamin's phaeton? She was certainly capable of driving it herself—but then how would Benjamin arrive home?

For his part, she pictured Benjamin moping about, declaring by evening's end that perhaps it was all for the best—and after that they would go their own ways. Katherine would reappear in Society in a day or two, would dance and flirt and deny her heart was broken, and the betrothal would be forgotten soon enough, as all nine-day wonders were forgotten.

So Katherine sat alone, not at Benjamin's side. As he finished playing for Miss MacFarlane, it was hardly difficult to look unhappy. She *was* unhappy, unable to think how she and Benjamin might retain a friendship at the end of all this. For that matter, she was not sure he would even wish to have a friendship with her at day's end.

Someone sat down next to her, drawing Katherine's attention. "Oh, Mr. Cullman," she said, using his surname since they were in public. She silently chided herself at her relief that it was not Benjamin, that it was not quite yet time for their public quarrel.

"I fear I will perish of *ennui* if we have to suffer through too many more performances," he said, his mouth turned down at the corners. "Do you know, MacFarlane has not even supplied a room for gaming. Tedious!"

Far from tedious for me, thought Katherine. *I wish tonight were tedious, ordinary. I wish it was not the end of a friendship. . . .* Although "friendship" was not the whole truth—the whole truth was something she could not look at, not now, not with the crying off looming before her yet this night. Aloud she said, "Stroll with me then."

There were a handful of couples standing in an area provided for those who grew restless with sitting. Too late, Katherine realized Benjamin was among them, with Miss MacFarlane on his arm. "Cyril, let us return to—"

"Lord Benjamin, well met!"

"Cullman," Lord Benjamin acknowledged, his voice and his gaze cool. To everyone's surprise, Benjamin reached out and took up Katherine's wrist. He pulled her from Cullman's side, drawing her to his own, and escorted her without a backward glance into an alcove ill-lit by the room's chandeliers.

Katherine glanced back, seeing Cyril staring after them, for once nonplused.

"Sorry. Did I hurt you?" Benjamin asked at once upon turning to face her.

"No. You did startle me, however."

"I . . . just wanted you away from him, from Cullman—"

"It does provide for quite the scene, does it not?" Katherine said, feeling as nonplused as Cyril had looked. "Benjamin, is this our quarrel? Have we started it?"

He gave a peculiar shrug, partly with his shoulders, partly by ducking his head, as if he were only half sure himself. "I suppose it is. Are you prepared?"

"No . . . well." She took a deep breath and let it out quickly, "I suppose so. What should we do?" She looked up at him, wishing she could pretend the opposite, wishing she could hope he'd kiss her, here in this darkened alcove. One last kiss before

she only shared kisses with Cyril. . . . But this was a fool's
wish, to hope for kisses when the purpose at hand was to look
as though they hated one another, or at least as if they could not
agree to marry. She must not think of "if only . . ."

She would think of Cyril, who had always liked her, always
been one of the few who took Katherine as she was. She would
think of the words he'd been whispering in her ears recently,
words of admiration and . . . and something more *amorous*. She
supposed that was the word for the whispered promises of
kisses he'd like to take from her, and the allusions to intimacies
he said he longed to share with no one other than her. He'd been
so audacious as to say he longed to take her to bed . . . but he
had yet to ask her, again, for her hand in marriage.

No doubt he waited for when Katherine was free to accept an
offer. Best that she get to her act of crying off then, she thought
on a sigh.

"What should we do? How are we to begin?" She said it
again, toward his cravat, not wanting to meet his gaze.

"We show our dislike of one another."

She gave a strained laugh. "It sounds simple enough. I can
even think how I might do that . . . but it *feels* loathsome."

"Ignoble," he agreed, and perhaps there was a shadow of
humor in his tone, but she did not think she was wrong that his
voice also showed strain. "To quarrel, so publicly, with a
woman! It does not reflect well on me, you realize. Perhaps we
should put it off?"

"Poor puppy!" she teased, but then she sobered. She glanced
up at him, then quickly back down at his cravat. "Before all else
goes ahead, I really must thank you for getting my cottage and
land ready for me."

He sighed, a curiously sad sound—or did she just hear what
she wished to hear in his voice? "You are welcome. It was our
bargain. But I did want to assure you that your solicitor says the
dissolution of our betrothal will not undo the work already
done."

"Excellent." She glanced out of the alcove, seeing Cyril
glancing at them, poised to cross to her side. She had only to
meet his eyes, or softly call his name. . . . "We are not fighting,"
she pointed out in a low murmur.

Benjamin thought a moment. "Stomp on my foot."

"I will not!"

"Well, I certainly will not stomp on yours."

"Do not make me laugh!" she scolded, almost doing as she threatened, feeling a bit giddy with nerves. "That is entirely the wrong impression to give." Now she really dared not look up at him, for she knew she would start to giggle, or worse, burst into tears. Instead she reached out and smoothed one side of his cravat.

He put his hand over hers, hesitated a long moment, then reached to wrap his fingers around her upper arms. He pulled her close, and she leaned into him, gasping.

"This first," he said, his expression as sober as any she had ever seen on him before, the dancing devil missing from his gaze. "Only then can we part."

He lowered his head and pressed his mouth to hers, kissing her so deeply that he had to move his hands behind her back to support her against his length.

She did not fight him, did not want to, did not care that murmured exclamations rose around them. She only cared that he kissed her, and that he held her close. She kissed him in return, and it was like that first kiss, shared in a horse stall, the one that had vibrated down into her very marrow.

He drew his mouth away, slowly, his lips yet so close she had but to lift her head and she could kiss him again.

"Slap me," he said.

It was not necessary to fake tears—they sprang at once to her eyes. His kiss, that devastating kiss, had only been part of a performance. A portion of her mind screamed that no, no matter what else happened the kiss had been real, had been a parting gift between friends, but another part of her was awash in sudden misery.

It was not difficult to raise her hand and strike his face, she did it almost with pleasure, as if to punish him for making her care for him . . . for making her wonder if she had chosen wrongly in other matters as well. Should she leave the safety and warmth of Papa's home? Was she as mad as everyone would think her to pursue training horses? Should she marry Cyril? Should she marry at all, when she obviously understood men so little?

She put her hands against Benjamin's chest, pushing, struggling to be free of his embrace, unable to bear it a moment longer, unable to tolerate the carefully blank face that stared down at her, nor the accusing mark in the shape of a hand on his face.

"Let me go!" she cried. The words did what her actions had not, for he released her so quickly that he had to grab her arm again to keep her from falling backward.

"Good-bye, Katherine," he said very softly, only then again surrendering his hold on her.

"Benjamin!" The word was wrenched from deep within her, an oath or a prayer or a curse. She did not know what she meant by saying his name. Perhaps it was a farewell.

An arm slipped around her shoulders, and she gave an audible gasp before realizing it was Cyril.

He glared at Benjamin. "What were you about, you fiend? Anyone can see you have distressed Miss Oakes." He turned his stare down to Katherine. "Come, I will take you home, my dear, away from this brute."

"He is not a brute," she protested, which must have seemed an odd thing to say since tears still ran down her cheeks. A crowd had gathered around, all staring or hiding shocked expressions behind their fans.

"Must you brutalize a woman's person as well as her feelings?" Cyril went on to Benjamin.

"Oh, stop, please stop! I just wish to go home," Katherine said, the words nearly a moan.

"Take her home, Cullman," Benjamin growled. "And be at home yourself, tomorrow, for I *will* call upon you. We have something to discuss."

"Of what do you accuse me?" Cyril demanded, puffing up in indignation.

Benjamin, on the other hand, seemed to deflate. He lifted a hand, then let it drop. "Nothing. I accuse you of nothing, not here, not now."

Cyril parted his lips to demand more, but Katherine stepped in front of him, capturing his attention, tears still marking her face. "Take me home. Now, please."

His other arm came up protectively, to cradle her against his side. "As you wish, my dearest. Time enough later to settle matters with this cretin." He threw Benjamin a scathing look, but

Benjamin's face had been again wiped clean of all expression, only the slap mark revealing anything of what had just happened.

Katherine felt another sob rise in her throat, and savagely drove it down. Even if there had been anything left to say, she could not have spoken. She turned to walk away from Benjamin, embraced within Cyril's arms.

Chapter 18

The next evening, a quick glance out the window revealed dusk had arrived. It was nearly seven o'clock, nearly time to call on Katherine for the last time.

Today had been grueling. Benjamin had gone to his first day working for Sir Uriah's shipping concerns, baffled and battered by the list of things he was expected to learn over the next few weeks. Still, by the workday's end, he'd begun to make a kind of sense out of the place and the position, because he knew much of the sea and something of shipping. Society might look askance at his open engagement in commerce, a task beneath his birth—so it was just as well his entrance into Society had been a means to an end, rather than the conclusion itself.

Like Katherine, Benjamin had done what he must to arrive where he wished to be. He had entered London's exclusive Society in order to earn his daily bread, to find himself, to gain a place of purpose in this world. Katherine had endured a stay in London—and a false betrothal to Benjamin—in order to have her cottage, her horses, and her dream. Once not so long ago, he would have said they had nothing in common, but now he saw commonalities that had unexpectedly led to friendship.

A friendship gone, now. Last night had killed the budding affinity between them.

He had spent the past two hours doing everything he could to make all London believe there was no hint of lingering friendship between him and Katherine—not because he wanted to but because he had said he would. A man was only so good as his word, so Benjamin had made a point all day long of being seen at any club or society that would admit him. He had moped, he had pouted, he had made it abundantly clear that "Miss Oakes has cried off." He had told Katherine he would do this service for her, would complete what they had started with a slap last night, so he had done it, albeit with lead weighting his tongue and an ache in his chest.

Benjamin glanced at the clock on his mantel again, and then checked his appearance for the tenth time in his looking glass, dissatisfied with what he saw. Would his buff breeches and blue coat give him a harmless air? He did not want to seem threatening, or prideful, or capable of cruelties. Katherine had cried real tears last night, so he knew he had to have embarrassed her with his kiss. He'd have to keep his features carefully schooled when he was in her presence tonight; he did not want to embarrass her further by any untoward gesture or expression.

At least he had not told her the truth about Cyril Cullman. Last night, as he had stared down into Katherine's face and listened to her asking how they were to enact a quarrel, it had struck him like a stone between the eyes that he could not tell her that she'd been traded away by Cullman. He could not let her know the man had abandoned her with all the "care" the cad would have used to trade away a dented watch fob. Benjamin could not be the instrument that made her feel that used, that neglected, that unloved. *No!* the word had raged through his mind, there had to be another way to skin the cat. If he could not tell her—could he not somehow warn Cullman away from Katherine, for good, forever?

And Benjamin had found that other way. Small things had all fallen together, in that sudden clarity that desperation sometimes brings. Not a half hour since, he had called upon his old friend, Stephen Dahl. Together they had gone to view a painting, a very specific painting that had been commissioned not long ago and that hung in a prominent place in the Royal Academy of Arts. The painting prompted talk of old times, and of the day Benjamin had accepted the blame of theft that ought to have been accepted by Dahl. The painting had Benjamin thinking to himself that he'd been so right to make Katherine promise to see him one last time.

After seeing Katherine tonight, Benjamin would indeed keep his appointment to see Cullman, to see ended Cullman's pursuit of a woman far, far above his worth.

Benjamin scowled at his image, and tugged at his waistcoat and his cravat, trying to correct there what he could not correct for real. *And if I could correct things?* came the whisper in his brain. *If I could undo all the half-truths? If I could really try to woo her . . .*

He was probably a bigger fool than Cullman, for thinking Katherine would want anything of him, the man who meant to deny Cullman a chance to seduce her, let alone marry her.

He slumped into his bedchamber chair, ignoring his own attempts at sartorial splendor, and determined that there was *one* thing he could do for Katherine. He could hang a new epithet on her, could see that the title of "hoyden" was changed to . . . "original." Yes, that would suit. The dark humor in all this being that his name was not so tainted today as it had been yesterday—he might actually soon possess enough social pull to do Katherine that little bit of good. Sir Uriah had told him the Admiralty would be printing tomorrow the public apology in the three largest news sheets in London. "The least they can do, given the black mark to your name, you know," Sir Uriah had said gruffly, obviously embarrassed for the navy's sake.

Not that Katherine had waited upon Mr. Dahl's word or even the Admiralty's to form her own opinion and extend friendship, Benjamin thought. She was an amazing woman. If only he had known it sooner.

Truth was, she must hate him. She had certainly hated his kiss last night—she'd slapped him for it.

But . . . no. That was not quite true. He would swear she had not detested the kiss. In fact, she had kissed him back, had clung to him—at least until he'd told her she must slap him. Only then had she turned stiff in his arms and cried for him to let her go.

Had she perhaps remembered her one-time vow? When first he had kissed her, in the stable a seeming lifetime ago, she had vowed he would not kiss her again until she was "cold, dead, and in a casket."

Last night she had been anything but cold, at first. At first he would have sworn she hated their parting, too—at least before her wrenching tears had made him begin to wonder if it was just *him* she hated.

He did not know, it was so confusing, his thoughts spilled and jumbled over one another, filled with conflicting impressions.

The only thing he was sure of was that he had made Katherine cry and that she would not thank him for it.

He gazed wearily at the clock on the wall, and saw it was time to leave. Time to call on Katherine. The last time. His heart felt out of place, as if the anguish in him had physically weighted the organ, as if it might as well fall into disuse since it would not need to beat properly ever again.

Benjamin tucked the birthday gifts he had for Katherine under his arm, taking up his gloves and hat. *What is painful is best done quickly,* he told himself, but he knew better. He knew this pain would be a long time hurting, if not forever.

Chapter 19

"You are not happy," Papa said to Katherine, spreading his hands wide in exasperation where he stood before her.

She made no response, merely watching as he sighed at the silent stare she gave back to him.

She glanced at the clock again. It was almost seven.

"This is what you wanted," he continued, now letting his hands drop in exasperation to his sides. "So why are you not happy? We have agreed it is best if we put this Season behind you now instead of later. And in a few days you can remove to your cottage in Bexley! Which, I say to you again, is a terrible idea." He shook his finger at her. "I mean to say, moving to *Bexley,* where you have so little chance of meeting a suitable beau!"

"You never used to worry I would meet a suitable beau," Katherine pointed out quietly.

"Because I—" His face purpled. "I neglected you! I kept hoping you would not grow up. There, now I have said it, and it is true. But I will never neglect you again."

"By seeing to it that I am married."

"Yes!" Papa cried in vexation.

"After my birthday, you will have no say if I marry or not."

"I know!" he all but howled.

"Papa, you are going to have a fit of apoplexy. Please calm yourself. Would it help if I said I will probably marry Mr. Cullman?"

Papa glowered, and threw his length down in a chair, to sulk openly. "No! I do not know! Seems to me the man owes you marriage, after all you have gone through with him and Lord Benjamin. But, I tell you straight Katherine, I cannot like the man. It was he—" Papa stopped speaking abruptly.

"He who started the whole false betrothal to Benjamin?" Katherine asked calmly.

Papa's glower deepened. "I never said that. Lord Benjamin would not have said it to you either."

She shook her head, a small smile forming on her lips for just a moment. "No, he did not. But, Papa, I am hardly stupid. Slow to see at times, but not stupid."

"But that is exactly your problem," Papa agreed. "Too clever by half! You almost killed off old Vicar Harntuttle a half dozen times with your piercing questions." Papa shook his head. "I should have had someone like Miss Irving tending to you much sooner, certainly someone with a firmer hand and a stronger heart than Harntuttle's anyway. Might have curbed that tongue of yours a bit to have a sharp-eyed female watching you all along. And now here's a thought, Katie. Miss Irving might be willing to come back from her mama's and be your companion in that cottage in Bexley, you know. I would be willing to pay her wages—"

Katherine shook her head, and Papa changed topics with the resignation of a sailor changing tack in order to catch the wind. "I would not let you go to that cottage at all, except you promised to dine weekly with your Aunt Jane."

Katherine did not deign to reply, because his threat was hollow and they both knew it. Short of locking her in her room, he could not prevent her removal to Bexley after her twenty-first birthday, in just two days.

Still, to appease him, she had agreed to go to her Aunt Jane on Sundays. Papa's only sister had nine children, seven of whom were female, and of those, four were of a marriageable age. Aunt Jane hosted and attended many parties, well ensconced in the busy rituals of seeking mates for her daughters. It was Papa's transparent hope that at these gatherings a mate might be found for *his* daughter as well. He knew Katherine would never agree to return to London for another Season, so he'd had to settle for Katherine's lukewarm agreement to take Sunday luncheon with her aunt, who lived two miles outside Bexley.

For herself, Katherine did not anticipate much in the way of matchmaking attempts, for Aunt Jane had never before had five minutes to give to Katherine, who had committed the great crime of being born with straighter teeth than any of Jane's daughters.

"So, I say to you again, Katie, you are not happy. I would know why, since you have got all you wanted," Papa demanded, springing up from the chair to pace before the fire, which had been lit on the grate a little earlier, now that the rare, warm June sun had nearly set for the day.

"I am happy, Papa," Katherine said, just stifling a sigh. She put aside the book she'd been holding, so distracted by her thoughts that she'd read the same paragraph over and over, all evening.

"I know you think me half mad, but truly, I am very happy to be going back to Bexley. Mr. Partridge, my steward, writes that he has already found a second horse owner who wishes to board his gelding with us the first of next month. Not a racing horse, mind you. A hunter, but a hunter pays as well for a stall as does a racehorse, and I must build my trade by degrees."

"Trade!" Papa echoed in dismay. "You will make an old maid of yourself with your eccentric ways."

Katherine ignored the comment, since she found she really could not care, much, if she ended her days as an old maid. "And there is a three-year-old already scheduled to arrive the day after my birthday. And Mr. Partridge has hired three lads to do the mucking out and the heavy work and I will train them in how to put the horses through their paces. Did I tell you that I mean to have a racing oval in addition to the paddock—"

"Yes, yes, I have heard all your many plans, my love," Papa said morosely.

The clock chimed seven. Katherine wished Benjamin had already come and gone, that the suspense of again seeing him would be over. She had grown a little numb since last night, probably from lack of sleep, but not numb enough that being in the same room with him would be painless.

At least she would not be alone with Benjamin. Papa was here, and Cyril was supposed to call as well. Last night, confused and grieving at the loss of a friendship, she had confessed that she'd promised Benjamin could come to call tonight and bring her an early birthday gift.

She did not want a gift from him; it was bound to be awkward, possibly hurtful. Anything he gave her would only serve to remind her of him, of an exceptional person who had slipped out of her life because she had let him.

"What could that blackguard possibly call a gift? I must be there, Katherine, to be sure nothing inappropriate or offensive is offered to you," Cyril had declared, and had insisted he be present.

She had also said, more talking to herself than him, that it was difficult to imagine living in her cottage by herself. "I have always been surrounded by my brothers, and Papa, of course. It will seem too quiet, I think."

"Perhaps I could brighten your days by coming there to call upon you?" Cyril had suggested. "It is not so far from London. I could see you frequently. I could stay . . . in Bexley."

There was another of his innuendoes, a little too warmly said to be ignored, a little too vague for her to take umbrage with him. Did he fish for an invitation to stay the night at her cottage—or was she a foul creature to even wonder it of him? Really, she must talk with him and let him know he had a certain indirectness that clouded her responses to him.

"You did not like my property when you saw it before," she had reminded him.

"Well, my dove, it *was* undeveloped, and a swamp. I am sure it is more congenial now, with that you tell me of its improvements."

None done thanks to you, Katherine thought, feeling traitorous even as she thought it, for after all Benjamin had only worked to improve her property when she had forced it upon him as a condition of their agreement. She could hardly blame Cyril for not taking action when he'd never been asked to.

"Besides"—Cyril stared ahead, but he let his eyes angle toward her, a look she would have called "coy" had a female done it—"who knows how long you will want to stay in Bexley? Perhaps there will be reason enough to return to London soon. There are things you will miss. The theater. The bon mots. Certain members of the male gender."

Benjamin's eyebrows would have danced if he'd said as much, an acknowledgment that he flattered himself; Cyril's face was unreadable except for a dark light in his eyes—and Katherine was unsure what to make of that.

"Papa will remain in Town until the end of the Season," she said, deliberately misconstruing his innuendo.

"As will I," he said, his voice a low caress.

She'd been glad they had stopped then before her home, glad to leap from the carriage before he could move to assist her, or hold her hand, or kiss her. She was glad to scamper up her front steps without looking back to view his expression, and relieved to push away, at least for one night, these signs that he still wished to marry her.

She still wished to marry him, did she not? He was not quite the man she had once thought him to be, but did that rule him out as a husband, without further consideration? She had always thought she was not a romantic, that she was prepared to marry for convenience and position and where good sense dictated. But even after a night's sleep—well, a night's tossing and turning—she was not sure if she still wished to marry Cyril Cullman.

As if thoughts of him had drawn him near, Cyril was announced by Langley. Katherine felt the color leave her face, and put the reaction down to not having heard his arrival because she was so deeply lost in her thoughts.

Under Cyril's arm was tucked a package wrapped in pretty paper, and with a sigh of dismay Katherine knew she would have to open yet another early birthday gift when she would as soon have opened none from either gentleman.

Cyril offered Papa a small bow, but Papa returned only a nod, making Cyril's brows rise in discernible surprise. He was not called the First Beau for nothing, though, for he turned with aplomb to Katherine. "My dove, how radiant you look today, like dew upon a rose."

Unlike other things Cyril had said in recent days, this compliment was easy to respond to. Katherine knew the pale blue of her gown achieved a good effect against her red hair. She had chosen the dress for tonight because it made her feel perhaps a little bit prettier, a bit bolder.

"Thank you," she said, but wondered why she felt Cyril's compliment was too effusive . . . perhaps even too calculated. No, she did not really wonder why—she knew she compared him again with Benjamin, who never made her wonder if he meant what he said.

In her heart she knew she would be comparing all men against Benjamin for a long time to come.

"Tell me, Cullman, where did you get yourself off to the other day?" Papa said, not challenging, but not in his usual gruffly friendly manner either. "My butler said you had called, and then you were not to be found."

Cyril went stiff, and blinked rapidly several times, perhaps trying to recall. "The other day, you say? Oh . . . yes, I remember now. Not to carry tales out of school, Sir Albert, but your butler abandoned me in the front entry. I could hear that you had other callers, and clearly the household was busily occupied, so I left, thinking to call on a day more convenient for you."

"Just a social call?" Papa asked. "I had thought that perhaps your papa had sent you with a missive or some such, since I occasionally assist the Home Office in small matters, or at least I have done so out of Kent."

"No indeed, sir, I can assure you," Cyril said archly. "My father and I seldom meet. I cannot imagine him seeking to speak with me, let alone having me play courier."

Katherine saw her papa's posture stiffen at the implication that Cyril was above being an errand boy, but perhaps he was. He was, after all, the First Beau. Katherine had seen during her only Season that some men came to Town to find work, and others to find amusement. Cyril was in the latter category, and would no more change his character than a cat would choose not to stalk mice.

The question of marrying him, then, lay squarely with whether or not Katherine could consent to accept his character as it stood.

Perhaps she could. What if Papa found a position for Cyril? He would not need the money, seemingly, but men did not labor merely for wages. Work was good for the soul—the devil making work for idle hands and all. Or would he prefer to work beside her, to build her dream of a thriving stud? A little toil might be good for Cyril, might remind him there was more to life than dancing and bon mots.

She vowed to learn where Cyril's apparent wealth stemmed from, before she would ever consent to marry him, and felt relief at the decision. It was curious that she knew a great deal about Benjamin's money woes, quarterly allowance, and work, but had no inkling concerning the man to whom she had once been secretly betrothed.

Perhaps this journey to London had not been entirely wasted after all. She reached up to finger a lock of her hair that had grown long enough to have formed a ringlet at her nape. Just as she had given up cutting her hair, had given up donning lad's clothing for the very adult fear of being caught out, so she was now giving up what she saw had been a childlike ignorance. Cyril had whispered in her ear that he loved her, and she had let the words fill her head, never questioning his sincerity, nor even stopping to hear what her own heart had to say.

No more. London had done that much for her anyway, making of her a woman grown. A woman who knew to listen to the still, small voice inside that cried out if something were right, or wrong, for her. She would use her head, as she always had, but she would no longer turn a deaf ear to her heart's edicts.

And the first edict her heart now whispered was that she would do Benjamin no harm, not if she could help it, tonight or ever. Once she had sworn to herself that she would "repay him in kind"—would make sure to embarrass him in public as he had her. If last night's slap and her senseless tears had not already done that, she would offer him no more injury. How could she, why would she want to carry out a meaningless vendetta against this man who had repeatedly gone out of his way to avoid embarrassing *her*?

She had said his brother was likely to disapprove of her, from her reputation, and Benjamin had not seized on that thought. She had been grateful for the grace with which he had turned away an opportunity to insult or blame her for the tangle their lives had become. When he had refused to explain to his family that he had won Katherine's hand over, appallingly, a turn of the cards, something in her had changed toward him forever. Cyril might yet become her husband—but she wondered if he could ever be quite the friend Benjamin had proven himself to be.

So tonight was not, after all, for recriminations. She would have plenty of time to call them down on herself later. Tonight she must be glad for a chance to make a different last impression on Benjamin—she looked up almost eagerly when a knock at the door was heard plainly in the parlor, where she had belatedly thought to ask Cyril to sit.

Jeremy Oakes opened the front door in place of the butler. "I wanted to speak with you, briefly," Katherine's eldest brother said to Benjamin by way of explanation. He stepped back, allowing Benjamin to enter the front hall.

Jeremy eyed the packages under Benjamin's arm, then closed the door and stepped close, his mouth near Benjamin's ear. "I wanted you to know that Papa told me and my brothers about the wager you had with Cullman," he said in a very low voice.

"Ah. Is it to be pistols or swords at dawn?"

"Neither. Papa likes you, you know. He does not like Cullman, although he says he could probably find a way to put up with the fellow should he become a son-in-law. He shudders when he says it, however."

"And you?" Benjamin asked, almost smiling despite Jeremy's cool stare.

"I do not dislike you," Jeremy spoke very frankly, eyeing Benjamin up and down. "Might like you, given time."

"And what do you think of Cullman?"

"First Beau, my arse!"

Benjamin just stifled a laugh, and wondered if men could suffer from hysteria. He felt he could both laugh and cast up his supper. He would really rather just go in, present his gifts to Katherine, and leave, but he knew there was no possibility of bypassing her brother if Jeremy had gone to such trouble to speak with him.

"More like 'First Churl,' I say," Jeremy expanded.

Benjamin put his free hand on the other man's shoulder. "My good man, you have no idea how pleased I am to hear this. You will keep Katherine safe from him." It was more a statement than a question.

"Papa pretends not to smell the stink on the man, but I smell it. And yes, I will make sure that Katherine never marries him. Speaking of dueling—too bad it is illegal."

"Too bad," Benjamin said, and the two men grinned ferally at one another.

"Go give her your gifts. Nothing untoward, are they? I wouldn't want to have to smash your face or anything."

Benjamin shook his head. "No, nothing untoward."

"Good. Katie thinks you are all right. She doesn't call 'em all right, but a good many. Her liking you makes your word good enough for me, Lord Benjamin."

Benjamin nodded and turned toward the butler, who waited patiently by the parlor, where he had obviously been told to wait. He wondered fleetingly if the servant could hear his heart singing at the inane but ludicrously wonderful words "Katie thinks you're all right"—but Jeremy touched his arm to halt him again.

"One other thing you might want to know," Katherine's brother offered. "Papa never let Cullman be alone with Katie, not once he realized Kate had, er, the charms of a young woman. Miss Irving was her constant companion, even when Kate thought she'd slipped the woman." He blushed and shrugged. "Katherine . . . well, you have to give her some leash occasionally, you see? Miss Irving thought better a stolen kiss or two than an elopement that may or may not ever be sanctified, if you take my meaning."

"I do. But, Mr. Oakes, a leash? On Katherine? Might as well leash the wind."

Jeremy stared for a moment, then a wide grin spread across his face. "I see you know Katherine well enough."

"Though I fear, too little and too late." Benjamin felt his corresponding smile slip.

"So, what I am saying, is that when Papa said you were to be trusted with Katherine's well-being, and Miss Irving was sent away—"

"Sent away?"

"She didn't want to go, said it wasn't quite decent, but Papa . . . well, as I said, Papa likes you. I think he hoped . . ." Jeremy's voice faded away for a moment, and he sighed as a puzzled scowl settled across his brow. "But that kind of thinking has all come to naught, eh?"

Benjamin clapped the man on the shoulder again and said nothing, because there was nothing to say. Jeremy had to know what had happened last night. Whatever he knew, it was clear he also thought there was no mending this rift between his sister and Benjamin. That awareness bit deep into Benjamin's chest, making his heart grow heavier yet.

He began to cross to the butler, then stopped short as he heard a familiar voice.

God save him, what had been going to be difficult now became horrific, for the voice belonged to Cyril Cullman. The man was within, waiting to be a witness to Benjamin's dismissal forever from Katherine's life.

Chapter 20

Benjamin entered the parlor, nodding to Sir Albert, who nodded in return. Benjamin made a point of turning his back to Cullman; he would ignore the man, and would say what he had to say. If Cullman minded the cut he'd just received, he said nothing.

Benjamin turned to Katherine, and gave her every ounce of his attention.

"Miss Oakes." He wanted to call her Katherine, but they were in mixed company and he would not insult her by being too casual. Would there ever be a day when they could be so informal with each other again?

Why not? said a small, hopeful voice in his head. Was it really too late . . . ?

The doubt on Jeremy's face came back to him, grinding that small, hopeful voice into silence.

Benjamin reached to set his packages on the table at Katherine's left elbow. Letting his hands fall to his sides, he stood before her, searching her features. "I am glad you received me," he told her with every ounce of sincerity he could put into his voice and his manner.

"Of course I will always receive you, Benjamin," she said, and he did not think she was merely being polite. He thought there might be an echo of the old warmth between them yet in her voice. And she had used his Christian name, in company, deliberately. He reached to gather up both her hands in his. She did not pull them away, and he felt his shoulders relax, just a little.

"Open your gifts," he instructed gently. He reluctantly released her hands, in order to sit in a chair near hers. "That one first."

She took up the package he had indicated. It was not prettily wrapped, as was the gift tucked under Cullman's arm, but was merely bound in brown paper and tied with string. For a moment Benjamin wished he had thought to embellish the wrapping, but then it struck him that if Katherine could be swayed to cherish a gift by nothing more than its wrapping, then she was not the Katherine he had come to know these past few crazed but inestimable weeks in her company.

As the string gave way and the paper was peeled back, Katherine's eyes widened ever so slightly, and then she gave an "Oh!" that was half a laugh as well. She lifted the gift from the paper and laughed again, a plainish bound volume in her hands.

"'Tis a new journal," she explained to her papa's puzzled expression. "You know, like the ones in which I record my racing results."

She turned back to Benjamin, blinked rapidly to hold back tears, making his heart plummet for a moment until he realized she was moved, not upset. She laid a hand over one of his where it rested on his knee. "Thank you. You knew I had nearly used up my latest journal."

"We could not have you missing even so much as a day of results," Benjamin said, amazed at the light tone he'd achieved, but then he sobered a little. "Seriously, Katherine"—now he did use her Christian name—"you are profoundly adept in this art of yours. Let no man tell you otherwise, or make you stop. Talent should never be wasted, regardless of gender. If you ever need another journal, or anything at all to achieve your dream, you have but to write to me and I will see it comes to you. You must promise to do that, because that is my second gift to you, and I know you are too gracious to refuse a gift."

"Katherine Oakes, too gracious?" she said, her eyes laughing but her voice uneven, still attempting to hinder the fall of any tears.

"Promise me."

"I promise," she said, her voice barely a whisper.

"Now—" Cullman started to say, reaching for the gift tucked under his arm.

"Now open the journal," Benjamin interrupted him, without even glancing at the other man.

Katherine did as he bid. Under the frontispiece a handwritten sheet of foolscap had been inserted. She took it out, her hand shaking a little, her eyes misting over anew. Blindly she extended the paper toward her father.

He took it and glanced silently at its message. "It is a legal document stating Katherine's cottage on Meyerley Creek is fitted for occupancy, to be assumed by her on her twenty-first birthday." He lowered the document, glancing past it to give Benjamin a long look. "It is to be known henceforth, legally, as 'Katherine Oakes's School and Stable for Excellence in Horse Racing.'"

"You can have the name changed if you do not like it," Benjamin said. "Or if you marry and change your name."

"But this is a foolish gift. This paper means nothing," Cullman said, sounding puzzled. "It cost Lord Benjamin nothing! He wrote it up himself."

"I did indeed. It is, however, duly witnessed by Katherine's solicitor, as you can see." He pointed to the solicitor's signature and seal at the bottom of the sheet of foolscap, then lifted his gaze to meet Katherine's. "Although he is right. It has no real worth, but I thought it would please you."

She did not speak, still blinking back tears, but she nodded.

"I have brought you more than one gift as well," Cullman told Katherine, stepping between her and Benjamin, crowding against the knees of her skirt. Benjamin stood, not wanting her to be pressed between the two of them. Cullman slipped onto the seat in his absence, and handed her his gift, elegantly wrapped in white tissue bound by gold cording tied in elaborate loops.

Katherine took a deep breath, shook her head as though to clear it of cobwebs, and cast Benjamin a look, one elegant glance filled with genuine thanks. Only then did she unwrap Cullman's gift.

Benjamin almost whistled, for he had priced the set of three handsomely bound volumes at Hatchard's himself when first he had gone there upon settling in London, and had scarce dared touch them at the exorbitant price of fifty pounds for the three, let alone buy them. It was a scholarly set of volumes, the first being the poetry of *Beowulf*; the second the allegory of *The Vision of William Concerning Piers the Plowman*; and the third the romantic tale *Sir Gawain and the Green Knight*. They were bound in finest kid leather, the titles impressed into the leather and gilded with real gold.

Katherine stared down at the volumes, unable to fail to see their intrinsic worth. Cullman stuck his thumbs in his vestpockets, positively smug.

She looked up, and set the books aside, on the table. "Mr. Cullman," she said after one failed attempt to speak. "Thank you, they are lovely, but you must realize I cannot accept such an expensive gift."

"What?" he cried, pulling his thumbs from his pockets, shock written across his face.

"They are lovely, but far too valuable."

"You are not betrothed to Katherine," Sir Albert attested. "I could never allow her to accept so dear a gift from a mere beau."

Cullman sat back in the chair, scowling. "*He* gave her a house!" he snapped.

Sir Albert gave Cullman a speaking glance. "It was her house. He only gave it a name."

"I have one final gift for you, Katherine," Benjamin said from where he stood, suspending the argument between the other two men. He indicated the unwrapped package still on the table, while Cullman threw him a dark look.

"But do not open it now," Benjamin said, taking a step back, as though his motion alone could stop her. He glanced at Cullman, then back at Katherine.

Her lips parted in understanding, and she gave the slightest of nods. Benjamin silently let out the breath he hadn't known he was holding. It was a gift best left for when Cullman had gone. *Gone forever,* if Benjamin had anything to say in the matter.

"What is it?" Cullman asked, eyes narrowed.

"It is a . . . a broken betrothal gift, if you like. I did not feel I could spend nearly a month betrothed to someone without commemorating the event in some small way. I am just returning something Katherine lost."

Cullman's interest in the package waned visibly. "Do I detect that you are finally leaving?" he asked rudely.

"Mr. Cullman!" Sir Albert remonstrated, but Benjamin waved his host's outrage away.

"He is right, I am leaving." He took another step back, then reversed his direction and crossed to gather up Katherine's hands once more, where she stood up from her chair. "Goodbye, my dear. Do you know the worst of it?" he asked, almost able to force a laugh. "Telling Gideon and Elizabeth we are not to wed after all. They'll have my head for having raised their hopes that I was to marry."

Katherine smiled, an unsteady little smile that spoke of smothered emotions. Love? Hate? Weariness? "Do you," she said quietly, shyly, making him wince because he'd never seen Katherine shy before, or call it timid, not once. "Do you know you may call, whenever you like, at the School and Stable for Excellence in Horse Racing?"

He managed a smile and a nod, covering the dance of delight inside his chest at the simple knowledge that Katherine did not banish him forever from her life.

She searched his face for a long moment, and he wondered if somehow he could arrange his expression to be exactly what she wished to see there—could everything then somehow be magically changed? She would fall into his arms and declare she had loved him secretly for weeks now. . . .

There was some kind of twisted humor in that thought, that she be secretly in love with the false fiancé, and not with the fiancé whom she had been once affianced to in secret. . . .

But it was not humor she sought now. What did she look for in his face? What did she hope to find there before she spoke? *Show her you love her, fool,* screamed a voice that almost sounded rational in his brain. *Let her see it on your face and damn your pride and damn the witnesses around you and trust her not to crush your heart*—but, no!, it was too late, she had already looked away, looked down, her eyes fixed on his cravat.

"Even should I marry, the offer still stands. You must always feel you may call upon me."

His heart, already too long heavy, fell to his boots, leaving an aching hole in the center of his chest.

Should I marry, she'd said. *Not you,* she might as well have shouted.

He need not worry about his pride ever again, he realized, for it had been shattered. But not soon enough, not nearly soon enough. A moment's hesitation, and he had lost her forever.

What good was calling upon her, in her home, if it was also home to another man, any other man?

He somehow moved toward the door to the parlor—almost forgetting to take leave before he went out of Katherine's life. He turned back toward the three staring faces.

He had one ounce of courage left, however, and knew he had yet to share that one vitally important thing that Katherine should know, must know.

"Katherine," he said, amazed by the clarity of his voice, so at odds with the weakness of his knees, "I will always be yours to command, whatever you should need. You must call upon me in that need, because you have made me a promise that you would." He paused, struggling for words, hurt by her stare, and stupidly hopeful still that she did stare, that she listened to his every word. He hoped she searched yet for the message that would move her, would keep the sandcastle moments from slipping away, lost forever to the waves of time.

"It . . . it is my fondest wish for you that you never feel a need to marry except out of love," he said, not quite able to look her full in the face now. "Never feel you must settle for less because you are somehow less than Society would have you be. Society is wrong. You are . . . extraordinary. Completely extraordinary. The man you marry . . . Do not let it be Cullman," he blurted out, tired of vagueness, wanting to be as clear as possible.

"You have no say in whom she marries—" Cullman began.

"It cannot be Cullman, Katherine," Benjamin interrupted, his tone easily overriding Cullman's. "He does not know what your husband ought to know. He does not know what I know, that you are to be cherished, that you are one of a kind. Because," he said, now turning his stare downward, to the edge of the carpet where it neared the doorway, staring at its fringed edges as if they represented the fraying nature of the rest of his life, "I know how wonderful you are, how easy it would be for a man to cherish you because"—he swallowed, the words difficult to say so publicly, but far worse to leave unsaid—"because I love you."

He turned, half stumbling through the doorway, slamming the parlor door behind him without having meant to. He howled at the approaching butler to let him be, and lunged for the front door as if it would give him sanctuary from his own breaking heart.

"Go after him, Katie!" said her father, with no gruff humor now, only utter and serious calm.

"She will do nothing of the kind!" Cyril declared.

Papa looked at Cyril with daggers, but spoke to his daughter, "Katie, you have to go after—!"

"Katherine," Cullman overrode Papa. "I love you," he said, stepping beside her. "More than that simpleton Lord Benjamin could ever hope to love anyone."

No, he did not, she knew that now. Her hands formed into fists, and she had to choke back an impulse to scream at Cyril, to tell him no, he did not understand anything at all, least of all about love, or sacrifice, or honor.

He had proven he knew nothing about her, nothing at all. He had given her fancy books filled with, yes, knowledge and beauty and words—instead of a plain, blank journal that she could fill with her own words, her own interests, her own heart's desire. He had given her dust, and could not understand why she did not fawn over its supposed golden glitter.

He said he loved her, and her ears at last heard that he was really saying he loved himself too much to lose a contest, even one involving merely *her*. She knew, without knowing the hows or whys of it, that Cyril had been the one who had cast her off in the first place. He'd cast her off to another man—she supposed any man would have done, but it had been her great, good fortune that other man had been as estimable as was Lord Benjamin Whitbury.

When she had been bound to another, Cyril had felt he could tell her he loved her, tying her with those precious words as a fisherman ties bait to his hook—she saw clearly now that, at best, he'd only wished to bed her. He would have ruined her, and smiled while doing it. And when he was done with his sport, he would have merely cut the line, abandoning her. That sideways smile of his, the one she'd never cared for—it ought to be on his face, at this cruelest moment.

She covered her face with her hands, out of humiliation, out of rage at her own blindness. She shuddered, loss rippling through her like fire through dry grasses, leaving ashes and desolation in its wake.

There was *something* good in all this, however: At long last she could make sense of all that had happened. At long last she understood that, somehow, her papa had acted to protect her. She understood that he and Benjamin had been as cruelly caught in a net of Cyril's making—even as she had been, all along.

She lowered her hands, blind no more. More than anything else, grasping the truth made sense of the dichotomy that was Benjamin—he'd claimed to be a rogue, but had never acted the part. The man she'd found him to be was in actually the man he was; since the moment they'd met, Benjamin had never done one ignoble thing. Even "forcing" her to play at a game of betrothals, Benjamin had insisted in order to save her, a stranger, from herself.

Benjamin had conspired with Papa in some manner, she saw that now. They had come up with a temporary betrothal, making the most of a poor situation. Papa had shouted at Katherine that she was to be betrothed temporarily to Benjamin, and she had been hurt and confused as to why he could make such an unreasonable demand of her. But now she saw that he had to have been manipulated by Cyril—he, Benjamin, and her. Lives had been changed, dreams had been dented, and all for the convenience of one man.

In her ignorance, she had believed Cyril's words of love. She had wondered if she might learn to love him in return. She had been so willing to believe . . . .

Benjamin had said he loved her. More words, yes—but these words she believed, as she'd never quite believed Cyril's claims of love. But how could she, after all the falsehoods she'd been told . . . ?

She could believe, because she *knew* she loved *him*.

Benjamin loved her!

Katherine spun to face the last gift he had given her, the one yet unwrapped. He had asked her to open it when both he and Cyril had left.

She turned to face Cyril again. "Get out," she said, looking directly at him, her gaze steady and dry-eyed. "I will never again receive you in my home."

"I beg your pardon?" he said, drawing back as if she had slapped him.

"I said, get out. I never want to see you again," she said with absolute finality, then turned her back to him.

He came to stand near her, and she could feel him trembling with outrage. "You do not want to do this," he warned in a low voice.

"Yes, I do. Please take your books and go."

"Very well," he growled, snatching his expensive gift from the tabletop. Now all that remained there was Benjamin's final gift. "I warn you, I'll not come back," Cyril snarled.

"Good."

He made a strangulated noise deep in his throat. "I never want to see anyone in this cretinous family again! Be assured that come the morning I shall be delighted to blacken your name to anyone who will lend me an ear! You will be run out of London inside a fortnight," he said savagely.

"And glad enough to go, if your ilk fill this city!" Papa thundered in return. "My Katie said for you to leave." He seized Cyril by his coat lapels, and propelled the man from the room.

When the room was empty of anyone but Katherine, the door was closed behind the departing men, perhaps by Langley or one of Katherine's brothers. She had not turned to look, instead waiting for Cyril Cullman to be gone, away from her and the gift she must open before time could begin to move forward for her once more.

The closed door was all she needed as signal for her to reach out and pull the string from the package. She parted the package's paper, her fingers lingering a little where she thought Benjamin's fingers may have touched.

Inside was naught but a few papers: all the papers he'd had and the bill of sale, now signed over to her, on the racing mare, Fallen Angel.

Tears swam in Katherine's eyes, almost making her miss the note she'd found atop the other documents, written in the same penmanship as on the paper that named her cottage.

"My dearest friend," he had written, the salutation alone enough to make her choke out a sob. She put a hand to her mouth, pressing her lips hard against her teeth, willing her tears to abate and let her read.

"I could never enjoy keeping Fallen Angel," he had written, "knowing how much you were missing her. On the other hand, it is the greatest joy to me to know she goes to one who will love and cherish her, win or lose, all her days. Perhaps by having Fallen Angel near, her presence will occasionally cause you to think of me. I pray that this mare may be the genesis of your stables, that she win important races for you, and that her progeny are as fleet of foot as is she.

"This is too grand a gift, I know, for an unmarried man to give to an unmarried woman of his acquaintance, but I hope you can accept it on the grounds that such a gift is not too much between the very best of friends. As I pray ever to be—Benjamin."

Katherine lowered the note, placing it neatly on top of the papers that allowed her to once again own Fallen Angel, and she could not keep the tears from falling then, even as she gave a blubbery moan of joy.

It was a far, far grander gift than any Cyril could have ever bought with money, even if he'd bought her the finest racehorse ever born.

"Go after him, Kate," Papa had said—and go she would. Her tears dried on her cheeks even as she picked up her skirts and dashed across the parlor to the door.

She flew up the stairs, determined to fetch her cloak and go to Benjamin, to be direct and forward, to be as outspoken as everyone said the hoydenish Miss Oakes was. No more searching his eyes for some sign that he loved her. She would ask him if he could love her yet, despite everything, and he would answer, and the rest of her life's contentment rested on what he would say.

She needed no candle on the stairs, and was not entirely sure she needed feet to carry her upward. The gloom did not slow her . . . but voices did, rising from the hall below. One voice she had learned to hate tonight, the other she loved and suspected she had loved for some time, if only she had let herself admit it.

Benjamin was here! He had not left her home. She did not need her cloak and bonnet, not now, and Papa would be glad she had not taken one of the coaches and boldly, even wickedly, gone to Benjamin's bachelor chambers in pursuit of him. She almost giggled, finally thinking to wonder where his chambers resided? Love would have found him—that, and Papa's ledger of directions he used to write out his invitations to his card parties.

How she loved Benjamin's voice, his stance, his humor, his—

"Remove your hands at once!" Cyril snarled.

Alarmed by the harshness now in the voices, she turned at the top of the stairs and bent down, then able to see the two men standing aggressively close. Her brother, Jeremy, was holding Cyril's arms hard behind his back while Mercer looked on in a readied stance and Lewis unbuttoned the man's coat.

Something was wrong, gravely wrong.

Chapter 21

Benjamin stood outside Sir Albert's home, his heart still racing from having told Katherine aloud that he loved her. He lowered his face into his hands. So much for hopes for the future—he had surely just killed any chance that he and Katherine might remain friends. He moaned, and called himself a thousand times a fool.

And all he had left to "enjoy" for the rest of the evening was calling upon Cullman at the man's chambers.

But wait. Benjamin slowly lifted his head. Why not catch the man in the act, instead of confronting him at his chambers? Here, proof might be had.

Benjamin found himself still trembling with awareness of Katherine, and the aching acknowledgment of the love they might have had, even as he knew he had one last thing to do tonight, the very thing that would keep Cullman from having any chance to woo her. He would have preferred that Cullman had left the house, that the man had no final chance to win Katherine over with false words. No matter. He would take care of Cullman. He would catch the man out, leaving him no room in which to wiggle.

He moved through the moonlit garden surrounding Sir Albert's home, looking for a window that was obtainable. His search, unfortunately, gave him time to think.

He'd told Katherine he loved her. That undoubtedly made him a fool. But she had deserved to know that at least one man had truly loved her, even be it a man she could not tolerate. She would know that not everyone was blind to her merits—she might even find it ironic that the one man who ought not to have fallen in love with her, had.

It only took a minute more to find an unlatched window.

Benjamin had no more than slithered through the opening and half fallen to the floor of Sir Albert's bookroom, when Lewis Oakes's voice said, "Do you, Lord Benjamin, have an objection to butlers?"

"He must, to want to avoid using the front door," Mercer agreed, standing in the darkened room beside his brother. The two of them had parted from the shadows to stare down at a sprawling Benjamin.

"Do you always linger in unlit rooms?" Benjamin queried in return.

"When we are trying to eavesdrop on two beaux and a little sister, we do," Lewis assured him, locking his forearm to Benjamin's and hoisting him to his feet.

"I pray that is not a common event." Benjamin tugged his waistcoat down into place, and regarded these two of Katherine's three brothers. "Now I am in, would you care to know what I am about?" he asked.

Within half a minute of beginning to explain himself, Mercer scurried away to fetch Jeremy to join them. The two returned, quietly, in short order, and a confederacy was formed.

The downfall of most culprits, Benjamin had once read in a book on philosophy, was that they felt compelled to take the easy path. Thieves, he'd read, were basically lazy. If not lazy, they would seek honest labor—but labor was equal to effort, the very thing the thief abhorred. For them, far better the easy path of letting others do the labor, then taking the results of it for themselves.

The problem with seeking the easy path, however, was that a trap could be made to look like the best choice.

Benjamin glanced around the room, and would have had no idea there were three other gentleman within if he'd not seen them assume their positions. Two were hidden behind long curtains, and Mercer was lost among the chair legs under a table. Benjamin chose to stand behind a folding screen, where he could have a view of the room through the cracks between its panels. For a moment it struck him they could all be made to look like utter fools if Cullman did not do as Benjamin expected he would . . . but then the culprit entered the room.

Cullman had carried a candle in with him, and under his arm were the three books he'd tried to give Katherine. He set the books and the candle on the desk that stood near Benjamin's screen. He pulled the candle closer to the edge of the desk, and then began to pull open the drawers of Sir Albert's desk, pawing through any papers he found.

Inside of a minute, he held a paper near the candle, then quickly surveyed a handful of like papers, and nodded in satisfaction. He folded the pages he'd selected into thirds, and tucked them inside his well-fitted coat, patting the buttoned garment to be sure the papers would not slip and fall out. He blew out the candle, picked up his expensive books, then stalked to the bookroom door. He cracked the door open and peered both ways down the hall.

Benjamin approached him from behind, and must have made some sound, because Cullman turned at once, fists already raised. A facer took Benjamin in the lower lip, sending him sprawling backward over a chair.

Cullman moved to flee, but a swarm of other bodies overtook him quickly. His books went flying, and his arms were wrenched behind his back at the elbow. After a brief struggle, Katherine's brothers held him securely.

"Drag him out into the light, gentlemen," Benjamin said.

Katherine's brothers complied at once, and Benjamin followed, gingerly sliding his jaw from side to side, satisfied nothing was broken but wincing at the discovery that his lower lip was split and had dribbled blood down his chin and onto his cravat.

Under the glow of the entry hall's lamps, Benjamin pointed to Cullman. "Open his coat and you will find the papers he took from your father's desk."

"Remove your hands at once!" Cullman said, his voice a high-pitched complaint, but Jeremy held his arms even tighter and Lewis unbuttoned the man's coat. The papers fell to the floor.

Mercer bent down to retrieve the pages, reading them as he stood upright again. "I do not understand," he said, his tone perplexed. He glanced into Cullman's face. "Why would you want Papa's lists?"

"What if they were not merely your papa's lists of farming equipment and goods?" Benjamin asked.

Lewis took a page as well, reading aloud for Jeremy's benefit as Jeremy still held Cullman fast by the arms. "'March the twelfth. Chickens, thirty. Eggs laid, twenty-four. Eggs candled/rejected, six,'" he quoted, shaking his head as he looked up at Benjamin. "These are naught but the weekly reports our steward in Bexley submits to Papa."

"Look again," Mercer said, pointing to a different penmanship on the same page. "'Warehouse, Fenchurch Street. Ordnace,'" he read, "'one hundred, rifled long guns. One hundred ten, pistols.' What is this?"

"Cullman knows," Benjamin said, receiving a glare for his trouble. "He meant to take papers that belong to the Admiralty."

"Liar!" Cullman cried out.

"To avoid just this sort of theft and to keep our enemies guessing as to our strength and readiness, the Admiralty does not like for the location of its wares to be generally known. Imagine if the nation's enemies knew of five warehouses they could burn to incapacitate half the fleet with a lack of supplies and weapons! So the Admiralty keeps their records carefully stored elsewhere, in unlikely spots, not least of which is with known patriots who can be trusted to keep the information until it is needed."

"You mean, Papa had an accounting of where some of the Admiralty's assets are located?" Jeremy said round-eyed.

"That is what Cullman meant to steal, yes." Benjamin blotted his lower lip with the back of his finger, and grunted with satisfaction when it came away with no fresh blood. "Mr. Cullman," he explained, "has been the contact between goods smuggled off ships or out of the Admiralty's supposedly secret warehouses, to those who wish to have them. Smugglers. Including, I suspect, the French."

All three of Katherine's brothers cried out, offended at the very idea of smuggling naval goods to the enemy, depriving good English lads of their use.

"You cannot prove that," Cullman said, but his face had gone ashen.

"True," Benjamin agreed. He stood close to Cullman, his own hands folded voluntarily behind his back, watching while Cullman gave a brief but futile struggle to break free of the hold Jeremy had on him.

When Cullman stilled once more, Benjamin went on. "At

present I cannot prove you have been selling to the French, but I *can* prove you have been selling stores and weapons to the highest bidder among English smugglers, and heaven knows where the stores go from there. I have little doubt a connection could be made that the goods you sold ended in French hands.

"That, Mr. Cullman," Benjamin said solemnly, "is a hanging offense. And even if the connection to France cannot be proved, I feel compelled to point out that smuggling, by itself, especially with governmental goods, is also grounds for death by hanging."

Cullman suddenly went limp in Jeremy's hands, all fight dissolving in him. "No," he mouthed in horror. "You cannot do this. You cannot prove anything."

"Stephen Dahl told me everything."

Cullman slumped even further, forcing Jeremy at last to let his arms go, that the man could form a puddle of misery at Benjamin's feet. Jeremy stood at the ready, but it was evident that the fight had fled out of Cullman.

"Dahl swears he will tell a court of law as well. He hopes for the court's mercy, but he says he will risk hanging in the greater hope that death would cleanse his soul of the crimes he and you committed."

"You are making all of this up," Cullman wailed, but his posture of abject misery did little to persuade that he was being maligned.

"At last I understand why you 'befriended' me that night, asking me to come to Sir Albert's card party," Benjamin went on. "You knew that I had taken the blame that should have been Stephen's, that I had saved him from punishment, because without his income his sisters and mama would have starved. You saw in me the perfect gull, because you knew what I had been accused of, the smuggling I had supposedly done. You knew you could use that against me, could threaten to shred any hint of reputation I had left. One way or another, you had targeted me as the man who must take your place in the betrothal. It was no accident that you chose to 'sponsor' me that night."

Cullman rocked his head from side to side, as if to block hearing anything more Benjamin had to say.

"Stephen Dahl did not know your name—I will give you that much credit, Cullman—but after Dahl had described his accomplice, I took him to view the painting of you that hangs in the Academy of Arts, the painting you had made that all might look upon the visage of the First Beau. He knew you at once. He identified you as his coconspirator."

"No," Cullman mewled, his face to the floor. "No!"

"And there are four witnesses here, Cullman. Four who saw you try to steal papers you thought Sir Albert kept safe for the Admiralty. Do you want to know the humor in that, Cullman?"

"No!" Cullman repeated, his hands over his ears.

"He does not keep papers for the Admiralty, not here in London. He has done so in Kent, as you well knew, because you took an opportunity when it fell into your hands, as you yourself told me. Somehow, by accident or design, you discovered in Bexley that Sir Albert had some of the Admiralty's warehousing papers in his care. He told me himself how he had hidden them among his estate papers, how he never suspected they'd been copied. But you did copy them, or memorized them, and then you arranged to steal the munitions from those locations, with Stephen Dahl as your compatriot in crime. That is how you came by the funds you so desperately wanted, the funds that allowed you to leave the countryside for London."

"But, Cullman, you should have known these pages were different. You should have paid attention to the fact you found no papers the first time you went through Sir Albert's desk here in London, the day you 'disappeared' before the butler could announce you. You found nothing then, and you should have realized these papers were a trap I set just now for you. *I* added those words of ordnance to the weekly reports from Sir Albert's steward."

"I knew it was not Papa's hand!" Lewis affirmed.

"But you are greedy, Cullman. You were willing to try your hand at crime a second time, because it was your only source of income since your father cut you off, trying to force you to earn your way as he'd had to do. So you saw what you wanted to see, and we all witnessed you attempting to take the fake papers."

Benjamin shrugged. "These papers were not real, but their attempted theft still shows intent. I think such testimony in a court of law would be very persuasive of guilt, especially coupled with Mr. Dahl's brave testimony. I suppose there are many other witnesses to be had as well. The recipients of the stolen goods you sold, the servants who were ordered to carry them away in the night, the locals who could not help but note the word "Admiralty" and "Navy" stamped into the newly arrived crates and caskets—"

Cullman slowly sat back on his heels, his normally handsome face ravaged by trepidation. "Enough, Whitbury. You would not bother to take the breath to list my sins if you did not want to be sure I was ready to barter."

"Let no man ever call you feeble-witted," Benjamin said with an inclination of his head. The cur had realized there was no point in denial; he was well and truly caught.

"My proposition is a simple one," Benjamin said with deadly clarity. "Remove yourself from England, never to return, and I will not have you pursued or arrested. Understand that, above anything else, you are never to contact Miss Oakes by any fashion or means, nor cause anyone else to contact her in your stead, nor offer her any form or hint of harm. Do these things, and you will live. The moment you do aught else, I will see you prosecuted unto death," Benjamin said, his voice as cutting as steel.

Cullman stood unsteadily, his jaw working. "I'll go," he said, looking as though he wanted to spit poison.

Benjamin looked him directly in the eyes. "You have until noon tomorrow to be on a ship, or at one minute after I will have a bailiff swear out an arrest warrant on you."

"Noon—!" Cullman started to protest, but something in Benjamin's gaze must have blocked his throat with fear or resignation, for he swallowed his objection.

"Take these, or sell them before you leave. I do not want them here," came a voice, and every man turned to see Katherine had come down the stairs and was bending to pick up one of the three volumes that had fallen to the floor.

She crossed the room, picking up the other two. She approached Cyril, dropped the books into his arms, then turned at once from him. She faced Benjamin, her hands now folded before her skirts, her color high.

"I heard everything," she said. She pointed up the stairs. "Every word spoken here in the entry carries directly up there."

Benjamin's brows drew together. "I am sorry for it. I would

have spared your learning the worst about this vermin." He cast a quick, dismissive glance toward Cullman, only to return his gaze at once to Katherine.

"Spare me? Because I had tried to make myself believe I could come to love him?" she asked, some terrible pain making her brown eyes even darker.

"You must not take his duplicity to heart," Benjamin said with concern. "His evilness, it has nothing to do with you. You were but a pawn—"

She lowered her chin to her chest, and the sight of that bowed head, of Katherine beaten down, made him long to withdraw his offer to Cullman, made him itch to mete out justice, here, now, to strangle the man with his own hands.

"Katherine, I hope you can forgive me for interfering in your life as I have this one last time," he said, willing her to understand, to lift her head and not be defeated by one man's evil selfishness. "I know you would have sent this creature packing eventually, but I could not bear to think how he might hurt you until then. I presumed by stepping in, but please believe I did so out of friendship."

He moved closer to her, his finger to her chin, lifting her head slowly. He wanted to gaze into her eyes, wanted to wipe away whatever pain made her bow her head.

To his amazement, when her gaze met his, he saw laughter there. Laughter!

"Oh, Benjamin," she said, and now she was half laughing, half crying. "I promise I am done making you prove you are my friend! I believe you, truly I do." She stepped even closer to him, putting a gentle finger to his split lip. "Was it not enough that you were forced to declare your love like that, in the parlor, in front of Papa? Now you have taken a beating for me as well?"

"A thousand beatings, if you like," he said, a gentle tease as he caught her hand with his own, his heart soaring, for there was such promise in her eyes.

"No, please, no more pain. Just kiss me soon and swear you'll marry me, and then both of us will be able to believe we can love one another."

He caught his breath. "I would . . . I want to, but . . . first, I must tell you how it is I came to be falsely betrothed to you that night. We must have the air clear between us. I never meant to do anything that would harm or upset you. You see, Cullman wanted to play a hand—"

"Shh. I think I already guess most of the truth about that night. It does not matter."

"No?"

"No."

"Then . . . you said something about . . . ?"

"A kiss? Yes. I want you to kiss me, please soon."

He laughed, because too much joy filled him. Had he slept last night, he would have dreamt she'd say words like these. He almost could not believe them now . . . but she stood so close, he could smell her hair and feel the heat of her body matching his own.

"If you like," he said, his voice a little unsteady.

"Kiss me, and make a real troth between us."

So he did, not caring his lip ached where it pressed to hers, for the ache was gone from his chest, and Katherine was in his arms and kissing him.

"Ho now," Jeremy said, his hand on Benjamin's shoulder, a foreign touch that barely penetrated the cloud of happiness that enveloped him. "I think you two are a match, for there is clearly not a speck of common sense between you. I dread to think of the children of this union. But, you must tell us what to do with—"

"Cullman!" Benjamin gasped out the name, remembering only now that the man had yet to be thrown out on his ear. He looked around the hall, not finding the cur. "What—?"

"Already gone," Jeremy said, his eyes laughing. "Ten seconds after you started kissing my sister."

Katherine laughed and blushed. He wrapped his arms around her, tight, barely able to resist kissing her anew.

"Then what—?" he said toward Jeremy.

Jeremy pointed. "We have been wondering what to do with that."

Katherine and Benjamin turned to look through the open front door. A horse stood there in a red warming rug, on which were stitched black letters that read "Katherine Oakes's School and Stable for Excellence in Horse Racing."

"Fallen Angel!" Katherine cried, a startled hand springing to cover her delighted smile.

"Red for your hair," Benjamin explained the rug, making a sheepish gesture. "I was rather hoping the sight of it would make you fall in love with me," he said.

She shook her head. "The horse would not have done it, nor the blanket."

"Then what?" he asked, at long last sure of her—but still leery of her answer. One could never be sure what answer she would give, his Katherine—and he was going to marry her in order to be there every day as she came up with her outlandish, wonderful, never dull replies.

"The fact that you are still going to allow me to have my stable, of course!" she said. "You are, in fact, going to help me make it a success." She looked up at him from under her lashes, seeking confirmation.

"My darling lady," he said, not funning at all, "I would not dare to stand in your way, especially since you are liable to make us rich."

She smiled widely, throwing her arms around his neck. "Liable to make us poor," she said on a laugh. "But how happy I am that you are going to let me at least try."

"You must try everything your heart desires," he told her seriously, sealing his promise with another kiss.

They were married four weeks later, and chose to live in her cottage, built on the hill overlooking her stables in Bexley. Benjamin left his position at the shipping office after discovering Gideon had left a "bridal gift" of ten thousand pounds in his brother's evening coat pocket. With the money was a note, insisting Gideon would not take the funds back, and Benjamin had "best not be a stiff-necked fool, and so use the money to keep your bride content. For she'll not be content in Bexley with you on the London docks."

Even with such a gift to keep their hearth and home together, Katherine had fretted that leaving his employment would mean not being at sea.

"It was never so much the sea itself," he had explained, gazing into her eyes, "but longing for a place to belong."

"Benjamin, you are giving up so much for me—"

He had taken her in his arms and reminded her of their special creed; "'You must try everything your heart desires,' remember? And for me, right now, making your dream a reality is what I desire. It is the place I long for, being at your side."

As if sensing their happiness, fate seemed inclined to make short work of what should have been longer and harder, for Katherine's papa had a bridal gift of his own when he returned a few weeks later to Bexley from London.

"The thing of it is," he said, looking abashed, "well, I never let Katherine or the boys know that Katie's dowry was never meant to be merely that puny strip of land above her own. She's to have all of the acres attached, between Meyerley Creek and Ramshead Creek."

"That must be two hundred acres!" Benjamin cried, stunned.

"Closer to three, and already planted with maize and oats for the racers and other cattle you will be housing, you see," Sir Albert had explained. Then he had grinned and laughed as his daughter threw herself into his arms, and kissed and thanked him effusively. "I did not want any fortune hunters after you," he said, hugging her in return. He gazed over her shoulder, directly at Lord Benjamin. "I wanted my Katie's husband to be a man who loved her for her own sake, not her land. She'd not thrive with just any man to husband, you know."

Fallen Angel continued to run well, and her sister in the stables, the other racing mare, had also proven swift of foot for her owner, who shared the "secret of his success" with many another owner—namely Katherine's stable and training ground. Within a month, the Katherine Whitbury School and Stables of Excellence in Horse Racing had eight new boarders.

"I cannot believe we have enough funds, with fees paid and purses won by Fallen Angel, to be sure we can last through the winter," Katherine declared as she looked up from the books Benjamin kept for their venture. "With near half the bridal gift from Gideon still in the bank!"

"People think it is my business," Benjamin explained, giving her an apologetic shrug. "They do not really comprehend that you oversee it, even with your name on it."

"But the owners who spend any time here soon know to ask *me* what manner of mash their horse ought to have," Katherine had said with happily glowing eyes.

"They have to, since I say to them 'what's mash?' But, Katherine, enough about the business. Come, you have not answered my request."

Now, as Katherine stood and resumed getting ready for bed by running a brush through her increasingly long red curls, Benjamin repeated the phrase that had become a creed for them: "You must try everything your heart desires."

Katherine gave him an arch look. "*My* heart does not desire that I prance about in only my underthings and boots, as you have suggested."

"Liar. I know quite a bit about your desires."

She did not look at him, and tried to hide a smile.

"How about just boots then?" he suggested.

"Benjamin!" She put her hairbrush down with a clatter, even as she tried to sound shocked—but her laughter bubbled up despite herself.

"You know, you used to like to prance about in boots," he reminded her with an innocent gaze.

"Boys' boots. And several layers of boys' clothing, not to mention the fact my breasts were bound, as you recall," she said primly.

He patted the bed next to where he lay, unclothed himself except for breeches. "No binding your breasts," he chided, patting the bed invitingly again.

She crawled up beside him and snuggled against his side, wondering in gratification why she bothered to put a night rail on anyway before coming to join him. His arms wrapped around her at once, one hand already fiddling with one of the night rail's multiple bows.

"No boots?" he said, pretending to sigh.

"No. I no longer need to wear lads' clothing. I am allowed to be me, as I am. Thank you, good sir."

"You are welcome. Although, you could thank me by putting on those boots . . ."

"Very well," she said, and then she laughed at the astonished look on his face, his jaw dropped in surprise. She put her hand on his bare chest, loving to feel his heart as it beat steadily beneath her touch—but now his eyes narrowed.

"You agreed, and too easily," he said suspiciously, even

though he was grinning. "What is the toll I must pay to see you in naught but boots?"

"Well . . . I cannot think why I should be the only one so attired."

His eyes widened again, and she laughed, and any more talk of boots was forgotten anyway as Benjamin proved that he did indeed know a great deal about his wife's desires.